$2^{50}

# SUN IN THE HUNTER'S EYES

# Sun in the Hunter's Eyes

## by MARK DERBY

NEW YORK :: *The Viking Press* :: MCMLVIII

# SUN IN THE HUNTER'S EYES

# ONE

The curtain fell.

By then I was sick with suspense, my throat dry, my fists aching. It was the final curtain. The previous two hadn't loosed off much applause, but that hadn't worried me much. I knew that I'd avoided the inexperienced dramatist's most common fault, an exciting first act followed by two acts of steadily slackening tension. *Time Bomb* lived up to its name and exploded fifteen minutes before the final curtain. To me, seeing it for the first time with the first-night audience (because I'd kept away from rehearsals) it had seemed terrific, better than ever I'd pictured it. What had the others thought of it?

At once I realized that things were bad.

Half the people in the stalls were leaving, without even a single clap for the first curtain call. Around me in the dress circle the same thing was happening. The full cast took only two curtain calls, and then Mary was alone in the centre of the stage.

For the first time, as she did her lovely bow, almost a ballerina's, the house filled with real applause. Even the mutterings and slight rowdiness in the gallery were silenced. I relaxed my fists and clapped gratefully, devotedly, for Mary had found more in the part than I had put in it, and by now I was beginning to fear that it wasn't anything like good enough for her.

The beautiful girl next to me was obviously one of her most devoted fans. I had taken a seat in the front row of the dress circle, alone, and she sat beside me with a scowling escort nearly twice her age who deserved none of his luck. Several times during the evening I'd turned my eyes to her fine profile in the dim light, wondering what she was thinking of the play. It looked as though she was enjoying herself, but of course it could be just Mary who pleased her. Now I saw.

She was smiling ecstatically, the lights in her hair and the brilliants in her ears trembling as she beat her small hands together. She was lovely—rose pink and chestnut brown, and a glorious dark red mouth with sparkling teeth. The fellow with her was on his feet, ready to go, but she wouldn't get up until the curtain went down on Mary and the applause died and two cries of "Author!" one soprano and the other baritone, sounded through the hush.

That did it.

Perhaps only twenty or thirty in the gallery booed spontaneously, but it took only a few seconds for others to join in. I was getting to my feet to let the girl pass me, but I clutched at the rail like a man physically struck down. The sound that I had never heard before in my life filled the theatre now, a great roar of execration, and it was all for me.

I had thought about the way I would respond to the usual cry of "Author!" when it came. Unless the cries and applause were insistent I would do nothing, I'd decided; but if they were loud and prolonged I would stand up and bow my acknowledgment. That was all. Once or twice I'd tried over a very short speech, just a word of thanks to cast and audience, but I'd decided finally that no matter how warm the reception I wouldn't speak.

I straightened up. The beauty at my side was booing too. As she passed me she turned her wonderful fullface to me, smiling and booing at the same time. Her eyes shone. She was having fun.

I followed and pushed past her up the steps. They were hissing now, as well as booing, the whole gallery and a good part of the rest of the house. It was a thousand against one, and I was helpless. I couldn't even run away, only edge and push my way through the slowly moving crowds that blocked the exits.

Without collecting my overcoat from the cloakroom, and ignoring the jam of taxis outside, I plunged my hands in my pockets and strode up St. Martin's Lane like a fugitive. My Uncle Max had arranged a small family supper at Kettners, but they'd know me better than to expect me to turn up now. I walked for more than an hour. It was very cold, and when it started to rain I went to my hotel and sat there in the dark for hours.

I was still in the chair, still in my dinner jacket, when the page knocked at eight and handed in my mail and the half-dozen morning papers I'd ordered. Then it started all over again.

The first headline I found, over a three-inch notice in an obscure corner, declared: "TIME BOMB" IS A DUD. "Ham-handed is the only word for this unhappy misfire," were the last words of the contemptuous notice.

They were all much the same, differing only in the manners, good or bad, characteristic of the different papers. One of them began: "A programme note told us that Mr. Robert Avery has already been free-lance journalist, mountaineer, soldier, schoolmaster and courier. He would be happier this morning, and we should have been happier last night, if he had not attempted to add dramatist to the list. *Time Bomb* was a painful ordeal for all concerned."

"Painful ordeal." Well, he'd enjoyed his boo, if he hadn't enjoyed the play. Another of them wrote something that gave a new turn of the screw to my misery: "It is to be hoped that the unlucky venture will not prove a serious setback to the careers of several promising players." I hadn't even thought of that. The one time I'd met them they'd all been damned nice to me. I was finished with the stage for good and all, but it was their future. Must I carry the responsibility of compromising the names they'd made for themselves in years of struggle?

A yawn reminded me that I was tired at last. Slowly I undressed, bathed, and climbed into bed, with the programme and the newspapers lying around the floor and the curtains still drawn. When I'd slept I'd get out of London in a hurry. Sitting through these hours in the dark I'd fought my way out of a short spell of rage and a longer spell of self-pity. I'd said good-bye to the West End stage, amazed now that I should ever have miscast myself to the extent of imagining there was a place for me there. The West End was no place for me, either; I knew a hundred better.

Oddly enough, as things turned out, it was Malaya I dreamed about when I slept. That was one of the places that pleased me better than London, and if *Time Bomb* had brought in a useful sum in royalties I should soon have made my way East again. I dreamed of Malaya, vaguely—no action, just a landscape and an atmosphere: a short reach of a jungle river with two houses on stilts up the bank and a couple of old boats and a bathing platform moored below . . . thick, indolent sunshine, a heavy gold light balancing the profound green-black jungle shadows . . . great lazy black butterflies and the scent of unseen flowers and a sweet afternoon languor.

What psychiatrists might call a compensation image, I suppose. . . .

2

I woke at six, and Max Browne rang me not long afterwards. "Robert?"

"Yes. Uncle Max?" He wasn't my uncle—he'd only married my Uncle Richard's widow—but my sister and I had called him "Uncle" for years.

"Yes. Robert, can you come round tomorrow? About this time?"

I hesitated.

"I hope you can," he went on quickly, sounding very businesslike in his effort not to sound sympathetic. "It's your Aunt Julia's will again. A matter of possible action that would need the agreement of you all."

I didn't want to see Uncle Max or any of them. "But I'm leaving London in the morning," I said.

"Oh? Where are you off to?"

I had to tell him I wasn't sure.

"Then won't you put it off a day and meet us all at six tomorrow? It won't be just talk. There's a development."

I saw it as a challenge. Could I face them or couldn't I? "Right, Uncle Max," I said. "I'll be there."

"Fine! Good-bye, Robert." And he rang off briskly.

That night I drank too much, a line-of-least-resistance reaction that put me on bad terms with myself when I woke in the morning. A letter came from the theatre, but I didn't open it. Probably to let me know that *Time Bomb* was being withdrawn, because when I passed the theatre that afternoon LAST PERFORMANCE stickers had been pasted diagonally across the bills. The stickers obliterated my name.

Under a heading BOOING IN THEATRES in *The Times*' correspondence columns there was a letter beginning: "Not even a convicted child murderer leaving the Old Bailey is subjected to such an ordeal of public execration as the author of a play which fails to please certain first-night audiences. Without contending that Mr. Robert Avery's play is any better than your critic reports, I suggest that . . ."

I turned to another page, telling myself that the subject didn't interest me any more. That was a lie, of course. But it was an unhealthy subject, I knew that. The only subjects I had time for were where I was going now and what I was going to do next. My bank account was dismally low and my will seemed to have been numbed by shock; between them these two factors kept the decision right up in the air. I was as undecided as ever when I rang Max Browne's bell in Phillimore Gardens at six that evening.

Sara let me in. The last few times I'd met her I'd told myself she was going to be something of a beauty, small and golden-haired and golden-eyed. She didn't say anything, but she went up on her toes in the hall and kissed me, for the first time in her life, and I saw that she was something of a beauty already. I'd been tied in a knot of prickly hypersensitiveness, but her gesture eased the tension and after it I found my entrance into the sitting-room, where the rest were waiting, reasonably easy.

My watch pointed to a minute past six, but half-full ashtrays and half-empty glasses showed that they must have been there some little time.

I said, "Sorry I'm late, Uncle Max. I thought you said six."

Max Browne, stout and over-energetic, bounced out of his chair and took me by the elbow. "Quite right, my boy. You're not late. Dick has only this minute come in and the others were early. Tio Pepe?"

I said thank you and he poured me a glass while I murmured a general reply to the greetings called from four deep chairs and found a seat between my sister Bay and my cousin Lovat Avery. It took a second glance to make sure that he was Lovat, because he and his brother Bernard, sitting beside Sara, were identical twins. But this was Lovat—he was a good deal untidier than his brother, and I'd usually found that a reliable distinction.

The twins were twenty-two and typical Averys, which meant that they were also strikingly like me, because I'm supposed to be typically Avery in looks. That means black Japanese hair, dark-shadowed blue eyes, and the Avery profile, which is pretty Latin to be quite frank. My sister, the only other Avery present, doesn't look like one. She's ash-blond, with a more practical profile and a restless animation that's quite uncharacteristic. Her husband, Dick Sullivan, was on the other side of her—an underling in a Lombard Street banking house, a very good chap.

Max Browne had a small folder of papers in his hand and he was sitting up very straight in a chair that invited recumbence.

"Well, as I said, there's been a development," he began.

But this is where a sketch of the family tree will help to put you in the picture.

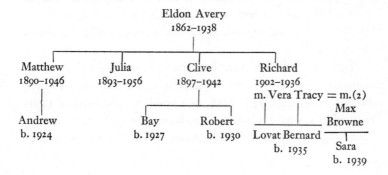

Well, there we are. My grandfather had been a successful surgeon, but none of his sons had taken a medical degree. My Uncle Matthew had been a rubber planter, my father went into the Army, and my Uncle Richard managed hotels. All three had died rather young: my father killed in action in the Western Desert, Uncle Matthew never recovering from three years in Japanese prison camps, and Uncle Richard drowned in a sailing accident outside Tor Bay. Aunt Julia had survived them until four months ago.

Now from the table you'll see that our Aunt Julia was Andrew Avery's aunt as well; but in fact she was much more truly his mother. Matthew's wife had died when her son was only a few months old and Aunt Julia had taken the child and mothered and spoiled him as her own. She devoted her youth to him, you might say, and though she was a good-looking woman she never married until she was over forty, when she became the second wife of a rich neighbour, Clyde Hughley, who was twenty years older. In 1950 he had died, leaving her a fortune, and it was that fortune we had met once again to discuss in Uncle Max's sitting-room.

I said that Aunt Julia spoiled the boy Andrew. There was no doubt about it, and in the way of so many spoiled children he turned into a pretty unsatisfactory adult. In the end even Aunt Julia had had to admit it, and several months before she died she let the rest of us know that she had disinherited him. We—Bay and myself, Lovat and Bernard and Sara—were her new heirs.

Well, we knew we were little more in her sight than an alternative to a cats' home. Aunt Julia had never shown much interest in us, chiefly, I think, as a result of our parents' criticism of the way she spoiled Andrew. We gathered that we hadn't figured at all in her previous will and Uncle Max cautioned us against counting overmuch on ever handling any of old Clyde Hughley's money.

"She can tear up that will any time," he'd warned us. "From what I hear she really has broken off all communication with Andrew and there's been no letter with a Singapore or North Borneo stamp for her in the past six months; so the rift is complete at present. But remember that she cares very little for any of you—except perhaps Sara, who's no Avery, anyway—and if Andrew were to show up in England, or even write again, I think you could say good-bye to every penny."

Sound advice. When Aunt Julia died three months later we soon learned that she'd made a new will on her deathbed. The entire income from the trust she'd turned her fortune into was to go to her nephew Andrew Eldon Avery for life. On his death, or if his death had already taken place, it was to be divided equally between her niece, her three other nephews, and Sara Browne.

She had thought of nothing and nobody through her last weeks but the wild black sheep who had broken her heart, tormented by anxiety for him, haunted by remorse for her "harshness," picturing him still as a lonely little boy whose restless, stormy nature ensured him a rough passage through life and a recurrent need for the help and forgiveness she had been the only one to provide. She had ordered her lawyers to try to get in touch with him, but with no success.

After her death they continued their efforts, but just as unsuccessfully. Uncle Max said that they were a crowd of senile stick-in-the-muds, and we'd decided to appoint an investigator of our own. For a month now a fellow called Smith, an old South-East Asia hand recommended by somebody Uncle Max met at his club, had been making inquiries. With every week and month that went by without news of Andrew's claiming his inheritance, the possibility of his death came nearer to probability, and the corresponding probability grew stronger that the five of us could look forward to a comfortable income for the rest of our lives.

But when?

Uncle Max was going over it again now. "The lawyers tell me there's very little hope as things are of getting a court to grant a legal presumption of Andrew's death for six years. Seven years from the last date on which he was known to be alive is the normal waiting period, and it seems we can't hustle it without strong new evidence."

"It's not always seven years, surely," Dick Sullivan argued.

"No, Dick, not always," Uncle Max agreed. "But it takes strong evidence to reduce it."

Dick slapped his hand across his knee. "For God's sake, Uncle Max, if a waster like Andrew Avery doesn't come forward to claim a quarter of a million—can you ask for evidence stronger than that?"

"Yes, it has to be a lot stronger to be sure of succeeding," Max Browne told him. "The sort of thing that gets the period reduced is this: suppose there were evidence that Andrew was last seen in the middle of a riot, or suppose he'd been a passenger on a ship that sank in mid-ocean and wasn't among the rescued. There wouldn't be actual proof of death, but a legal presumption would fairly easily be obtained without delay. Even if he had been seriously ill when last heard of, that might do the trick, in conjunction with his failure to claim his fortune. But what have we got?"

My brother-in-law stubbed out a half-smoked cigarette. "So we just have to go on hoping for something from Smith."

"No." Uncle Max turned over his papers. "Yesterday I received three letters—one from Smith and two about Smith."

The development. Uncle Max paused and sipped his sherry.

"Smith wrote from Singapore to say that we could expect a report from him within a week—a final report. He was only awaiting an Indonesian visa, he wrote, and expected it within three days. Then it would be merely two or three days more before he could close his investigation and give us the news we've been waiting for."

That sounded encouraging, though the others made no comment and seemed not to be much interested in Smith. Uncle Max laid down his folder and went on, "Now you know that I've been regretting my part in the choice of Smith as our investigator and I'd written in confidence to my partner's brother-in-law, who, I discovered only ten days ago, is a broker in Singapore. Two letters came from him yesterday —one a reply to mine, saying that Smith was a pretty useless sort, a fellow who served a sentence for something very questionable in Sarawak just after the war and a well-known drunk and drifter around Sarawak and Singapore since then. That was his first letter. The second told me that he'd just seen in the morning paper that Smith had been found dead on a road outside Singapore last Sunday."

Back where we started.

Dick Sullivan and I were the only ones who seemed at all startled. The others looked almost as if they'd known it was going to happen anyway. I began to suspect something.

"That is the development," Uncle Max said precisely—the way he addresses his board, I expect. (He is managing director of a small furnishing concern.) "Now we come to the proposed action."

I was aware myself of more expectancy than showed on the faces opposite me. Max Browne ended the pause of a man who has something up his sleeve and went on. "We must start again with another investigator, of course. But having bought one pig in a poke I take it we don't want to buy another, nor do we want more delay. And in fact there is no need for either, because we can approach an admirably qualified investigator here and now."

His eyes swept slowly round the ring of us. "My proposal is that Robert should be our representative, leaving for the East as soon as he is free to go and staying there until he has found Andrew, alive or dead."

The ashtrays that had been half full and the glasses that had been half empty when I arrived at six were explained. Except for Dick Sullivan, the others had been there for some time, being persuaded by Uncle Max to agree to his plan. That was why only Dick and I had shown much reaction to Uncle Max's news, or asked questions.

Bernard said, "It's a great idea."

"It's wonderful!" That was Sara.

Bay said, "Yes, Robert, do go."

Lovat (whom I didn't like much and who didn't like me at all) just grinned, possibly enjoying my confusion. There was a silence before Dick Sullivan, who of course hadn't had his reaction prefabricated and ready, said, "Isn't that a pretty good plan, Robert?"

I drank some sherry. My throat was dry—I suppose it was the sudden excitement, seeing the grey blank into which I had been staring ever since those ugly cries broke out in the gallery filled now with the picture of a future.

Max Browne was very pleased with himself. "No need to decide on the spot, Robert. You can see yourself that you're the obvious man for the job. You'd have been our best choice from the first, but of course there was no question of your being able to give up the time two months ago." He skipped over the unhappy allusion swiftly. "There are so many points in favour. For one thing, you're the only one of us who's ever met Andrew since he was a small boy."

"Steady, Uncle Max," I protested. "He wasn't such a big boy when I stayed those two months with him in Malaya— only sixteen. And I was certainly a small boy at the time, just ten."

"Yes, yes, a small point, I agree. But there are others. You know something of that part of the world."

"Malaya, yes," I admitted. "But Andrew lost his job there in fifty-one and went back to North Borneo. I've never been there." .

"You *liked* the East, anyway," he persisted. "I'm sure I've heard you say you wanted to go back there one day."

I nodded. They were all looking at me as if it was settled, as if two problems had happily been solved at one stroke. But I wasn't able to take it all at once, the skilfully stage-managed proposal, the practical sympathy that avoided any reference to the crash I'd suffered and the empty future I faced.

"You're our best chance, Robert," Sara said quietly.

And Bay put in, "Well, Rob, you're going to be an uncle in seven months' time. A pity if the poor little devil has to wait until he's six before Aunt Julia's money is any use to him!"

That switched the focus from me to her for a minute, and I was able to see things straight and distinguish what was real from what was subjective. They were right, of course: the idea was a perfect solution for my problems. A change of scene, a change of continent, a challenge, an escape from the scene of failure and disgrace—and possibly a fortune at the end of it. What could I do but accept? I saw my hesitation as no better than an insufferable coyness.

Out of his folder Uncle Max had taken a small folded paper which he passed to me—a check. "Pay Robert Avery Esq. £1000," I read.

"Get as far as you can on that, Robert, and let us know if

you need any more. We can draw up a balance sheet later."
He said that hurriedly, shy because of course we all knew
that he was the only one of us with money to spare or venture, because we couldn't hope to pay more than a token share
ourselves. It wasn't as if he were really well off, either.

I looked down at my shoes and folded the check again. I
said, "I'll try it, Uncle Max. It's damned good of you."

Everybody talked at once while I sat there looking at my
shoes and thinking of Malaya and the bright lands close by.
The picture I'd dreamed of the morning after the play's opening rose in my mind, and I thought of the warmth and the
colour and the stimulus of the search.

I thought nothing about risk, because I never foresaw any.

### 3

I opened my investigation a good deal earlier than any of
them could have expected. Next morning, in fact.

When my call to the BBC had been switched through to
the casting desk of the TV Drama Department I asked, "Can
you let me have the address of Miss Nona Nicolas?"

Nothing seemed to register at the other end of the line.

"She's appeared in two or three of your plays recently," I
added.

"Yes, but who is calling?"

I gave my name.

"Is it a professional inquiry?" the cautious voice asked.

"Yes." The lie seemed necessary.

"Then I'll give you her agent's number."

I wrote down the name Jacob Rhein and a Temple Bar
number, which I rang immediately. Without delay I was given
Nona Nicolas's address and phone number, and a moment
later I was ringing that.

"Yes?"

"Can I speak to Miss Nicolas?"

"She's awy." The daily help, it seemed.

"Do you expect her back soon?"

"Couldn't sy."

"Can you give me her number?"

"Fryde not. She's in 'ospital."

"Oh. D'you know if she can see visitors?"

"Oh, yes. There's nothing the matter with 'er."

"Then—?"

"She ain't ill, I mean. It's one of these 'ospitals for people who worry—not a mental 'ome, a plyce where they 'as these breakdowns. Stagford 'ouse, not far from Lewes."

I thanked the lady and rang off.

There hadn't been any point in mentioning Nona Nicolas to Uncle Max or any of the others, because it was just a hunch, this decision to see her again. I'd met her at a party in Hampstead, crowded with lesser theatrical people, shortly before Aunt Julia died, and for someone so quiet and reserved she had stayed in my memory with a curious persistence.

I had been introduced to an alarming woman with a parrot's voice and a genteel accent who'd exclaimed, as soon as she heard my name, "But have you met your beautiful namesake?" (She pronounced it "neemseek," more or less.) And she darted away to grab the elbow of a girl who'd been standing with her back to me. I'd glanced once or twice at this girl's figure and wondered what her face would be like, and now she was dragged up to me, the parrot voice screaming, "Nona, look at this neemseek of yours I've found. Robert Avery, he's called. Don't you think he's quite noteworthy?"

The girl looked at the woman for two seconds as if convinced she was drunk and then turned to smile briefly at me. "How d'you do, Mr. Avery. I'm Nona Nicolas."

The parrot woman registered two exaggerated emotions, the first dismay, the second discretion, and melted away with a vague phrase about finding her husband. Nona Nicolas and I began a fairly commonplace conversation, placing each other, leaning close to hear each other above the battlefield din that fifty people's voices make once a party has got under way. I didn't think her beautiful that day, but she was good to look at—small and quiet, with hair and eyes more vivid, somehow, than the rest of her. Really golden hair and golden eyes with almost black lashes and brows. And her quiet was not completely natural, I felt—a sort of restraint. But, most of all, her reserve impressed me. Though the crowd pressed us almost as close as a pair of dancers, there was a sort of margin of reserve isolating her that I found disconcerting. Nothing of note happened until somebody pushed an elaborately heaped tray between us.

Surprised, the girl exclaimed, "What wonderful kechi makan!"

Now that is the way English mems and their Chinese cooks in Malaya, who rival each other in their abuse of the Malay language, refer to the canapés and miniature oddments handed round to eat with cocktails. So, "You've been in Malaya, then," I said.

She chose a cream-smothered prawn in a pastry nest and said, "I was there, yes. You too?"

"Just for twenty months," I said.

She was eating the prawn while her eyes wandered about the room as if I'd bored her. But I saw the parrot woman screaming away in a corner and I recalled the odd incident of her introduction. I said, "A cousin of mine was in Malaya a few years ago. Andrew Avery. I wonder if you ever came across him."

It was because of her strange reception of that oblique

question that I was going down to Lewes to see her again. Her eyes swept up to meet mine in a short stare of golden innocence that—don't ask me why—struck me instantly as false. "No," she said shortly. "Is he like you?"

"I hope not," I said. "I believe he's rather a black sheep."

She looked away again. "Will you excuse me, Mr. Avery? I came to this party on purpose to meet that man talking to our hostess. He's a TV producer." And she was off before I could answer. Her eyes hadn't once met mine after that one straight stare of denial. The impression I was left with was that for an actress she was a poor liar, though I didn't think much about it because just then somebody I'd come to the party to meet came in.

A month later I'd seen Nona Nicolas in a TV play. A moderately capable performance, I thought, though she hadn't the real sparkle for the part. She had been much better in another play only a couple of weeks ago. As a wife driven towards suicide by a blackmailer she had been strangely memorable, because though the play itself had been pretty unconvincing she had radiated reality and suspense for every moment she was on the screen. Since then, in fact, I'd found myself remembering her with a blend of sympathy and tension, as if she were the character in the play.

Stagford House was an incongruous setting for a neurotics' retreat. A rich and extrovert Victorian family had so obviously built it and led their purposeful lives in it. A pale yellow sun was shining as I walked up the winding drive between monstrous hedges of rhododendron, broken here and there to reveal several people strolling across the snowdrop-and-crocus-decorated lawns, looking every bit as stable and responsible as I did myself. I was still thinking of the place as what used to be called a mental home, so that the decorum and ordinariness of the inmates kept surprising me. I wasn't prepared, either, for the easy self-possession of Nona Nicolas when I met her.

A sort of parlourmaid who looked as if she might have a university degree directed me into a place probably called a sun lounge nowadays, and I saw Nona Nicolas in a corner, sitting at a small table with a cup of coffee and an unopened book. When the parlourmaid announced me she showed little surprise and invited me with a gesture to join her.

"I hope you don't mind my calling," I began—without much assurance, because I suspected that she probably would mind as soon as she learned the object of my visit.

She smiled and said, "Please sit down. Would you like a cup of coffee? Rather good coffee?"

I accepted, and she gave the order. I was strangely baffled by her appearance, because I'd been remembering her on the way down more as the persecuted victim of the TV play than the good-looking girl I'd met for a few minutes at that party in Hampstead. But my main impression of her now was still one of reserve, of vitality held in check by—by what? Shyness? I didn't think so. There was confusion, rather competently masked, but not shyness. A natural eagerness and confidence were betrayed through gaps in a curtain of caution and apprehension—that's how it looked to me.

Her eyes were bright golden and brave—that was the strange mental comment I found myself making. The dark red mouth was not so resolutely controlled. She was pale, I suspected, under her make-up. I liked her dress, a thin woollen one, honey-coloured; and now I remembered her dress at the Hampstead party: that had been perfect too.

Waiting for my coffee, I ventured a comment. "When they said you'd gone into hospital I was afraid you were ill. I'm glad you're only tired."

She didn't acknowledge that. Instead she said, "You haven't told me yet why you've come." She leaned back and crossed her ankles. Her legs were wonderful.

"I'm in a jam," I said, "and I hope perhaps you can help me out."

She said nothing, so I had to start explaining. "There's some money," I said, "a lot of money, and I have to find out whom it belongs to."

"Not to me, you can depend on that," she said with a little laugh.

"No, not to you. Either it belongs to me and four others, or else it belongs to a cousin of mine. Andrew Avery."

Her eyes met mine squarely, the way they had at the party when I'd brought in Andrew's name. "But how d'you imagine I could help you?"

"There was a lady at that party—" I began, but she cut in. "Old Rhoda Munro?"

"I don't know her name. She seemed to think your name was Avery too, and I wondered—"

She cut in again. "But Rhoda Munro is *complètement gaga.* Didn't you know?"

"But why should she imagine your name was Avery?"

"It's no good asking me. She could just as easily have said Gandhi." Her fine eyes held mine aggressively, but my guess was she was lying. My coffee came and she began to drink hers. Her hand was quite steady.

"You could ask her," I suggested.

The answer came smoothly. "I don't know how. She flew to New York last month on her way to Florida, California, or Jamaica for the rest of the winter. She's *gaga,* as I said."

"Did you know Andrew Avery had been left a quarter of a million?" I asked her, and added, "Pounds?"

She blinked and set down her cup. "You asked me before about this Andrew Avery. I told you then I didn't know him. What *is* this?"

"I thought that, your having been in Malaya and that woman telling me you were my namesake, I thought—" I'd tied the sentence into a knot and gave it up.

"I didn't quite get that," she said. She'd meant to sound cold and sharp, but the tone slipped and I began to feel like a bully.

Leaning forward impulsively, I put my two open hands flat on the table in a gesture of candour. "I've got to find Andrew Avery. I'm going to find him or find out what happened to him."

She had turned away, her fingers playing with a gold bracelet round her left wrist. "You mean, his aunt's quarter of a million is going begging because he can't be found to sign a receipt?"

Though I'd mentioned nothing about the money coming from any aunt I didn't point that out to her, because I was growing uneasy. There was a change in her—nothing I can describe, almost as if a different presence had taken her place in the chair opposite me.

I was aware of pity, which is something to which I've always been readily susceptible—I almost said "vulnerable." When I was a year or two old, I've been told, I was an awful nuisance because whenever I heard another small child crying I burst into tears of sympathy myself. I've found it the most disabling of emotions and many a time wished I'd been born with a thicker skin.

I was hating this now. Even the way we were sitting was unfortunate. Her chair was right in a corner, and I was across the small table, facing her, literally cornering her as she shrank slightly from me with her back to the wall. I don't mean that she actually looked pitiful or cornered. She looked cold and a little indignant, or perhaps more like an actress in a cold, indignant scene, an actress who was disturbed by some per- sonal problem as she played the scene.

I leaned back and found myself saying, "I didn't know Andrew Avery either—at least, only for a couple of months when I was a kid."

"Did you like him?" Her question was unexpected. I don't believe she'd expected it herself.

"Yes, I liked him," I told her. "I hated him, too."

"Why? Did he bully you?"

"Sometimes. And sometimes he was so completely the brother I'd never had that I almost worshipped him."

She said, "I expect you exaggerated. I expect you were an imaginative little boy."

"Imaginative?"

"Don't you think all dramatists have to be imaginative little boys first?" she asked.

I looked down at my coffee cup. "I'm no dramatist," I said.

"Not a very good one yet, I suppose," she said. "But it wasn't as bad as they made out."

So she'd read a notice somewhere. "I know now it was bad," I confessed.

"I didn't think it was all that bad," she told me. "The pro- ducer should have got most of the kicks."

"You saw it?" I was blinking at her in amazement.

She nodded. "I saw you, too. I was three rows behind you. When those beasts started booing I tried to speak to you, but you ran away too fast. Then I was glad, because what would have been the good of anything I said?"

I was silent with the small shock of it. We were closer to- gether, somehow, than I'd imagined. After a single five-min- ute encounter I had remembered her distinctly; but she had remembered me too. She had gone to see my play on its first night and she was the first to offer me sympathy in words.

I told her, "I've finished with all that."

Perhaps I was hoping that she'd protest then, try to persuade me to reconsider, to postpone the decision to a less sombre moment. But she only said, "They were beasts. Most of the critics, too."

Then there was a silence for a while. I finished my coffee. The sun had vanished and most of the patients who'd been walking around the crocus-starred lawns under the bare lime branches were returning to the house.

"You've been here only one or two days, then?" I asked her.

"I came yesterday," she told me. "I don't think I'll stay."

"Overwork?"

She turned away. "No. Just one of these fashionable plagues. You know, life not worth living. I expect underwork is at the root of most of them." Her voice trailed off vaguely.

I said, "I saw you in a couple of TV plays. One of them didn't give you a chance, but you were good in the other. As a blackmailed wife—that one."

"It was a trumpery little play," she said negligently. "But just about my level, I suppose."

"You were far better than the play." I said it sincerely, because it was true. "The author hadn't much idea of how a tortured woman felt and acted, but you knew, so the play came alive as long as you were on the screen."

"It was a depressing part," she said, still not looking at me.

I let the silence run for half a minute and then I said, "Are you going to help me?"

She looked at me when she heard that, but didn't answer.

"I'm flying to Singapore on Tuesday, to find out what happened to Andrew Avery. I've got practically no clues to start on. You could help me." By then I was sure of it.

The change in her sharpened. Now she reminded me of the dread-ridden blackmailer's victim of the bad TV play. She said slowly, in a strangely different voice, "Yes, I'll help you. Don't go."

I stared.

She rose from her chair and said it again. "Don't go. That's the best help I can give you. A warning."

I had got up too, and followed her now as she walked towards the entrance hall. "I mean it," she said inside the front door. She was breathing with difficulty, one hand in a tight fist between her breasts. "Don't go."

I couldn't tell her that now she sounded like a ham actress in a bad play. It wasn't true, anyway. She sounded real, never mind how melodramatic the lines were, just as she had in the TV show. She really was afraid—afraid of whom, or for whom, or of what, I couldn't imagine.

"If you tell me what I have to know perhaps I won't need to go," I suggested.

"You think I'm just hysterical, I suppose."

"I think you know it all."

"But you won't listen to me."

"If you talk I'll listen."

A youngish man with grey hair was watching us. In that place you couldn't tell doctors from patients, but I thought he was probably a doctor. He was standing at the foot of the main staircase, which was of heavy and tormented design, and when I met his eyes he turned to the newspaper in his hand.

"You don't believe me." She sighed.

"How can I?" I protested. "You haven't told me anything."

"I can't," she said with whispered intensity. "I can't tell you anything. Only that you mustn't go." Seeing my face, she shut her eyes and shook her head. "Never mind what you're thinking. Just try to believe I want to help."

I said, "I didn't want to distress you, honestly. I can't see why you won't trust me." The fellow with the grey hair was watching us again. His face was freshly tanned. I wondered where he'd found his winter sunshine—the Canaries, Jamaica, Malta, Madeira? "I'm sorry I came," I told her.

Suddenly my hand was caught between hers. I wasn't warm, but her hands were icy. "Good-bye, then," she said. "Remember I tried to help you."

Before I could think how to answer that one she'd turned her back on me and swept up the stairs, her beautiful figure passing out of sight up the wide steps. For a moment I stood there, looking like a fool and feeling like a bully; then there was nothing to do but fetch my hat and coat and leave.

Rain had started to fall, quietly and sadly. A hundred yards from the main gates I'd seen an inn where I could have a drink and wait for the Green Line bus. I had reason for irritation with Nona Nicolas, but irritation wasn't what I was feeling. It was pity again.

It wasn't for nothing she'd come to this place. She was a sick person. Only her body was fit; the rest—mind, heart, and soul—was all to hell. That was my diagnosis, anyway. I wondered whether she had any friends—the real kind.

I'd almost reached the neat, ugly lodge and the main gates when a rush of short footsteps sounded behind me and I turned and saw her running down the drive through the rain, a light, almost ghostly figure against the dark rhododendron hedges. I felt apprehensive and helpless, but then I saw her face and it was pity again, only pity, that I felt.

She came at me blindly, throwing out her arms, her face wet with tears as well as rain. Her cold hands seized the lapels of my overcoat and tugged at them desperately. Her face was out of control, not beautiful any more, and her breathing was agonized.

"Don't go, don't go, don't go!" she gasped. "Don't go!" For a moment her face fell forward and rested against my shoulder and her hair brushed across my mouth. There were tiny raindrops caught in the dark gold of her hair and when I put my arm round her I felt the dankness of her rain-sprin-kled dress overlaying the warmth of her body.

I was hopelessly at sea. Vaguely I recollected that you slapped hysterics in the face, but I knew I couldn't strike her. Besides, this wasn't hysteria—not what I understood by hys-teria, anyway. It was surely the deepest anxiety—reasonable or unreasonable didn't matter—and there was no hope of my being able to relieve it. I didn't consider lying to her, though that might have calmed her, I suppose.

A car came through the gates, and I had to draw her to the side of the drive to let it pass. A distinguished elderly face gazed at us curiously as it swept by. I took off my overcoat and slipped it over her shoulders. It was a heavy coat, and she seemed so frail I almost expected her to collapse under it. Most of the colour and light were draining out of the day.

She said with anguished difficulty, looking down at the wet road, "Don't despise me. I can't help myself. I'm so lonely sometimes. . . ."

I knew it. "Can't I help?" I asked.

She turned away, towards the heavy gates. "You won't help," she said desolately.

You could hear the rain now, the drops beating on the leaves. I began to be scared. There was nothing of the *émo-tionnée* neurotic enjoying herself about this suffering woman leaning so heavily against my arm. I could sense the surf of nightmare that was sucking her under. When pity gets hold of me I start thinking in highly coloured phrases, but that one was fair enough. . . .

Round a bend in the drive behind us came a tall girl in a

waterproof cape, half running and carrying another cape. She came up rather breathlessly and said, "I've brought you a cape, Miss Nicolas. I shouldn't stay out in this."

Nona Nicolas began to tremble violently, but she said nothing and wouldn't look at the girl or take the cape.

"Yes, you should go in," I said.

She held closer to me, her head lowered, her face hidden. "If you will come with me."

With a glance at the girl I turned back, lifting off my overcoat to let the girl throw the cape over her shoulders and adjust the hood over her dark gold head. We walked back· slowly through the rain, my arm round Nona Nicolas, and on the steps up to the front door she looked up with her normal face and said in her normal voice, "I'm sorry about that. I'll be all right now."

I didn't believe that, but she had certainly regained command of herself for the time being. "Try to take it easy," was all I could think of to say.

She stopped just inside the door and looked up at me. "I wish you'd remember what I said," she murmured, and she was gone again, up the wide, dark staircase.

The nurse (I assumed she was a nurse, though she wore a blue twin set and grey pleated skirt instead of a uniform) met my eyes for a moment and then started to follow Nona. On impulse I called after her, "Who is the doctor who's treating Miss Nicolas?"

"Doctor Blake," she told me, and I went into the office where I had announced myself on arrival and asked if I could speak to Dr. Blake.

A minute later I was shown into a small room and found the youngish man with grey hair who'd been watching me and Nona Nicolas in the hall a few minutes earlier, sitting at a desk.

I said, "Doctor Blake, my name's Robert Avery and I'm a friend of Miss Nicolas and concerned about her—her illness. Is there anything you can tell me about it—how likely she is to get better and how soon?"

He didn't reply for a moment. His eyes were pale grey and they and the grey hair gave his tan a deeper look.

"I understand about professional discretion," I added with some uneasiness. "And I'm not claiming to be a close friend of Miss Nicolas. But I am concerned."

"I see." He gave me a long, sombre glance. "Well, there's very little I can tell you in any case. To start with, she arrived here only yesterday morning and I've had only two preliminary conversations with her. And then, I've already formed the opinion that I am not likely to be able to help her much."

He offered me a cigarette. I told him I never smoked.

"In fact," he went on, "if there is anything you feel free to tell me of her history without compromising your friendship I shall be grateful."

I had to shake my head ruefully. "I know her very little," I confessed, "but I know she's lonely and afraid and I'd like to help."

He nodded slowly and began to talk to me rather like a medical witness making things easy for a dense jury. "I see. Well, let me put what little I know in everyday language, Mr. Avery. First of all, there's no doubt about what is wrong with her, but unfortunately that doesn't help me much. Hers is a quite frequent case: unhappy childhood relationships which have undermined her resistance to psychological stress and ordeal in adult life. So this ordeal she is going through now finds her an easy victim. She's brave, she's been putting up a fight; but because of this inescapable vulnerability of hers it's an unequal one and she can hardly hope to win. Not alone."

"And if she doesn't win?"

He blew out a cloud of blue smoke and said through it, "A serious illness. A crisis. Quite possibly one that could permanently damage her reason."

My throat went dry at the ugly picture he'd projected onto my mind. I said, "Can you tell me anything about this—this strain she's under now? What it is?"

He shook his grey head and became less pompous, more talkative and more likeable. "I was hoping you might be able to help me there. It's the whole trouble, you see. She won't say a word about it, won't admit that there is anything causing her anxiety, just swears there's nothing wrong except that she can sleep so little and sleepwalks when she does and suffers from loneliness. She's keeping it all hidden." He puffed out smoke again. "Of course, it's not unusual to meet this initial resistance and often when we've built up confidence the patient overcomes her shame or terror or remorse or whatever the inhibiting emotion is and goes into partnership with us to work a cure. But there are patients who fight to the last to keep the secret that's destroying them, and we're helpless to help them. I'm afraid Miss Nicolas looks like one of them."

I said, "But whatever it is that's giving her such hell—it may let up somehow. I mean"—suddenly I remembered the ending of the TV play I'd seen her in—"just suppose she's being victimized by a blackmailer. Well, the blackmailer may die. Couldn't something of that kind happen?"

"Oh yes, if it were something as straightforward as that this ordeal could pass and she could make an unaided recovery. It's a possibility."

I told him, "I think I may be able to uncover what it is that's causing her this anxiety—from outside investigation, I mean, not your kind of investigation."

"You're a police officer, Mr. Avery?"

"No, no." I wondered for a moment whether I was free to

tell him my suspicion. But he was on her side, too, I told myself, and he'd been unprofessionally frank with me; so I said,
"A cousin of mine disappeared sometime in the past year.
Since the war he's been in different parts of South-East Asia,
and Nona Nicolas was in Malaya part of that time. She de-
nies that she ever knew him, but I'm convinced she did. I'm
going East to find out what happened to him, and she has
been trying to persuade me not to go—no, begging me not
to go. She won't give me any reason. Just now she lost control altogether when she saw I was determined to go. That's
all I know."

"I see." It was his favourite phrase. After a moment he
asked, "What sort of man was your cousin?" He was looking
for clues, and it struck me how closely parallel detective and
psychiatric techniques must be at some stages.

"Well, he was regarded as a bit of a black sheep," I told
him, "though my family's conventional and he certainly
wasn't, so it may have been no more than that. He was spoilt
as a child and got into a few scrapes in later years."

"Did you know him?"

"No. At least, when I was ten I spent two months at his
father's house in Malaya. He was sixteen then."

"Did you find him unconventional then?"

"Yes, I did."

"Looking back now, would you say he approximated to
any well-defined type?"

"I don't know whether a self-appointed outlaw is a well-
defined type, but that was a role he enjoyed playing quite a
bit of the time."

"I see. Of course, most of the troubles suffered by women
come through a man." He was getting pompous again. He'd
said that as if it were a new truth discovered by the latest
methods of psychiatry.

Neither of us could think of anything to say for a moment or two. Rain beat against the leaded window panes, and the view through them was almost monochrome. Then he looked at his watch.

"Well, thank you, Mr. Avery," he said. "It looks as though we're competitors, though I'm afraid my chances of coming to Miss Nicolas's rescue are poorer than yours. So I wish you luck in your journey."

"Then you think her anxiety is mostly illusory?" I asked. "I mean, you don't think I'm likely to discover anything out there bad enough to justify her fears?"

He shook hands with me and said, "I doubt whether anything could be worse for her than the sort of collapse she's threatened with."

They left an ugly echo, those last words of his. Every time I remembered Nona Nicolas in the next few days, and that was often, I heard that echo and I felt the bleak helplessness of pity. I had never imagined such loneliness as I'd seen in her eyes and heard in her voice that afternoon in the grey rain.

## 4

One of the reasons why I went to the Sultan Mustafa Hotel for the few days I meant to spend in Singapore was that there was no knowing how long Uncle Max's thousand pounds might have to last, and the Sultan Mustafa was cheap. The other reason was that I liked the place. I had stayed one of my last weeks in Malaya there, in 1952, when I was almost broke, waiting for my deferred troopship passage home.

It wasn't a very respectable hotel—it wasn't a very respectable neighbourhood, either. The only other European guests had come for single nights in unrespectable mood with unrespectable companions, Chinese taxi-dancers and suchlike. The Asian guests were mostly Chinese, with a few Indians and Indonesians, not all of them on the side of the law. A man had been murdered in the room above mine the month before I stayed there. The owners were Chinese, of course, the manager a Portuguese Eurasian from Timor, the boys a mixed bunch of Malays and Hailams, the hall porter a starvation-thin Shanghai Chinese I didn't like, and the night porter a two-hundred-and-fifty-pound Sikh.

It wasn't a very good hotel, either. The food was good because the cook was Cantonese, but the beds were short, the room lighting fluorescent and ghastly, the neighbourhood incredibly noisy for about twenty hours of the twenty-four; all inner walls stopped nine inches short of the ceiling to increase air circulation and decrease privacy, and informality was carried to considerable lengths: entering a bathroom, for instance, you were likely to find a houseboy washing coffee cups under the bath taps or even, early in the morning, an unexplained old Chinese asleep in the bath.

The gaunt hall porter was still at his desk and gave me his ghastly smile.

"Any mail for me?" I asked him when I'd filled in the visitor's form he handed me.

"No mail," he said with his unreliable smirk.

Five days earlier the following cabled advertisement had appeared in the Singapore newspapers, which were read all over Malaya and North Borneo as well, and also in certain Indonesian papers:

ANDREW ELDON AVERY. Anyone having knowledge of the whereabouts of Andrew Eldon Avery during the past twelve months is asked to write to Robert Avery at the Sultan Mustafa Hotel. Reward for useful information.

"There ought to be some letters for me," I said.

He shook his head with its sparse grey crew-cut. "No letters. Solly."

Bad start.

"But pelaps you telephone this numba," he added slyly. But he said everything slyly; it was his way of speaking.

I took the slip of paper he handed me. It had my name on it and a Singapore phone number. "Who gave you this?" I asked.

"Somebody telephone this message. Two-thlee days ago."

In my cubicle of a room—the price had risen sharply—I switched on the fan and sat on the hard, short bed. It was incredibly bare, the room—nowhere to put anything, no wardrobe or drawers, just three pegs. The only comfort provided, apart from the bed, was a pair of wooden sandals for use in the bathroom. They would have fitted me at the age of thirteen.

Through the window, which was an affair of green-painted wooden louvres, without glass, came a violent torrent of sound: perhaps a hundred Chinese voices clashing in fierce vociferation; the hoarse cries of hawkers and the strange ringing tattoos they produced by banging with a stick on a block of wood; the slap, click, and shuffle of mah-jongg pieces from a neighbouring room; an Indian singer on an imperfectly tuned radio and a Chinese singer on a gramophone; arguments from the restaurant below; the gongs and cymbals of a funeral party down the street—all completely drowning the roar of main-road traffic only a block away.

But I liked it.

A bare brown foot kicked open the door, and a bottle of Tiger beer came in, backed by a dazzling grin. This was Jaafar, whom I remembered from five years back, looking exactly the same, good-natured and indolent, gossipy and amoral, permanently broke and never downhearted. He remembered me too.

We exchanged greetings. It was good to hear Malay spoken again and to speak the half-forgotten phrases once more. As I expected, he needed very little encouragement to tell me all the latest dirt about the Sultan Mustafa, as well as some that was slightly stale. His family had grown from two to four. He had won a small prize in a Federation lottery last year and had been privileged to give evidence in court following his discovery of the stabbed and unconscious body of a Chinese detective in the gents' loo behind the bar some months ago—he'd show me the bloodstains later on. Maureen Swee, one of the taxi-dancers who'd spent frequent nights in the double bedrooms of the Sultan Mustafa back in '52, had become the junior wife of a Chinese millionaire's son. The Sikh night porter's wife had brought scandal on him by drinking, and surviving, a pint of poison. The taxi-dancer with the green eyes, Shirley Chong, had jumped from the window of Room 18 one night after bringing home a hashish-smoking Turkish ship's officer she hadn't been able to handle; she'd broken her ankle and now she was engaged to be married to a trade-union organizer. A cashier had left under suspicion and a rubber estate assistant from Johore had spent six days and nights in Room 30, drunk all the time, and, on leaving, still drunk, had given Jaafar a fifty-dollar tip. Two corporals of the Anti-Vice Squad had raided the place one night, to the inconvenience of everybody, but it was Jaafar's ill luck to have been off duty and at home at the time. The manager's sister and brother-in-law had occupied Room 37 for two months, without signing the register or receiving an account, and the hall porter had been threatened by one of Singapore's three hundred secret societies—at least that was Jaafar's view, based on the hall porter's growing nervousness and his agitation after certain recent phone calls.

I lay on my bed and drank the Tiger. Jaafar leaned against the door, rubbing one naked foot against the other. It was good how swiftly Malay was coming back to me; there wasn't a sentence I didn't get the hang of.

"*Tuan ada kerja sini sekarang?*" he asked when his news was exhausted. Had I got a job in Singapore now?

"*Kerja tidak. Saya chari khabar.*" Not a job, looking for news.

A hoarse, furious shout of "Jaafar!" roused only a flawless grin. It was twice repeated before the boy turned, hooked the door open with his bare toe, and left with indolent grace.

After a shower and a change I went down to the phone at one end of the deserted bar and rang the number on the slip of paper the hall porter had given me. The answer came in English.

"Who is that?"—a strangely intimate voice, a lazy, fat voice, gently insinuating.

I said, "Robert Avery here. I've been given a message to ring your number."

"You inserted an advertisement in the *Straits Times,* Mr. Avery"—an overcorrect accent and diction, the words breathed rather than spoken.

"Yes."

"Then I think we should meet, because I have some news for you." The slow, deep voice seemed very sure of itself.

"Good."

"Then shall I come and see you, Mr. Avery?"

I was snob enough not to favour entertaining strangers at the Sultan Mustafa. "Couldn't I come and see you?" I asked.

"You'll be welcome. When would you like to come? To-morrow morning?"

"Fine."

"At eleven?"

"Fine."

"I shall expect you. Jerampang Road, Number Sixty-one."

"Good." On the point of ringing off, I said quickly, "I don't know your name yet."

The warm, soft voice answered, "My name is Marcos Aragon. I shall expect you at eleven o'clock. Good-bye."

I was left with a blank evening to fill. So far as I could tell, there was not a soul I knew in Singapore. I had a letter of introduction to the brother-in-law of Uncle Max's partner, but little intention of using it. There was an entertaining bar I was going to revisit later on. My Indonesian visa had to be collected from the Consulate-General, but I put that off to the morning.

All the conventional inquiries—of hospitals, cemeteries, police, even the CID—had been made by Smith on Uncle Max's instructions. Not that Andrew had been known to be in Singapore for some time but it was, after all, the hub of a large area and worth a check; but Smith had drawn a series of blanks. Was there any less obvious lead Smith might have overlooked?

Then I reminded myself that within a few hours I might have the whole answer confided to me in Marcos Aragon's furry, fat-lipped whisper. He had given the impression that he knew all I wanted to know. I left the hotel and jostled my way up to the main road, still without any idea of where I was going. A lean, spectacled Punjabi got out of a small yellow-top taxi, and I took his place in it, directing the driver on impulse to the Raffles Hotel. The route took me down to Col-

Iyer Quay and along the front and I noted several changes since I'd left in 1952. Traffic control and discipline had improved out of all knowledge. The taxis all had meters. There was a new waterfront skyscraper, and the white Bank of China building was new to me, though the cab driver said it was four years old. Farther on, the romantically squalid hawkers' market on the Esplanade had been swept away and the area subdued to a formal municipal layout that included a complex of open-air restaurants at any rate a good deal cleaner than their predecessors. The news bills, like the newspapers, made much of the curious local politics, which I was to discover failed to interest many—apart from the local politicians, of course, who were on to a very good thing.

After the choking winter grey of England the colour blaze of equatorial land, sea, and sky was an endless exhilaration. I had no intention of penetrating the shadows of the Raffles, so before we reached the entrance I said, on impulse again, "Koh Han Seng Street." Not that I had any idea where Koh Han Seng Street was, but Smith had lived at Number 6.

It took fifteen minutes to get there, and I was lost after the first five or six. A sad little street it was when we turned up it at last, neither quite in nor quite out of slumdom. Number 6 stood back from the rutted road in a small grove of fruit trees, most of them banana palms with their vast leaves torn to tatters by a recent storm. A myna bird in a large cage hung to a mango branch was saying something over and over again in Malay, something beginning with *Jangan*. I couldn't catch the rest. A double curving flight of stone steps, rather grand, led up to a narrow, mean veranda where a European who hadn't shaved for two or three days was sleeping in crumpled blue pyjamas on a long rattan chair.

He woke as I reached the top step. "Who's that? Who's that? Who's that?" He struggled up, puffing and blinking, and frowning under what I took to be the onset of a hangover. I said to him, "Please don't get up. I wonder if you knew Mr. Smith." I was making it up as I went along, and the dialogue was pretty stilted.

He glared. "Knew Mr. Smith?"

"He lived here, didn't he?"

"Lived here? Of course he lived here." He was waking gradually, a sad wreck of what had probably been a fine-looking man before he'd lost his figure, some of his self-respect, most of his hair, and one or two of his teeth. When I asked again if he'd known Smith he gave me to understand that he and Smith had been inseparable for years.

"Then perhaps you knew he was making some investigations on behalf of my family," I said.

He was wide awake then. "If he'd let that alone he'd've been alive today," he declared with an unfriendly glance from gin-flushed sandy eyes.

The taxi was turning. An angular brown hen had appeared on the veranda, staring insanely about her. I said, "You don't mean that he died as a result of his investigations?" Stilted was the word, but it seemed I couldn't help it. I wished I hadn't come.

"He died as a result of his asthma. But if he'd stayed at home in bed the asthma wouldn't have done him no more harm than usual. He had to rest, see, whenever the asthma got him."

He called it "athsma." His accent was that of a long-exiled Cockney. His hands wouldn't keep still. He and the house were both of a piece. I said, "My name's Robert Avery. My family were hoping, from Smith's last letter, that he'd found some information for us."

"Porter's mine," he said shortly, presumably in response to my self-introduction. "Yes, Smithy'd got whatever it was he'd

been after. Never tasted a drop them last three days. 'No, Jeff,'
he'd say to me, 'a clear head's what I need now. Wait till I've
popped over to Indonesia and got them documents and air-
mailed 'em to London and we can celebrate for a whole
bloody week.' That's what he said. He had hopes of five thousand dollars from your people."

Five thousand Malayan dollars was the sum Uncle Max had
agreed to pay Smith, on top of his retainer, for legally attested
confirmation of Andrew's death or for being put in touch
with Andrew if he should still be living. Not hoping for anything much, I asked, "Did you know what he'd discovered?"

Porter's bare, blunt foot aimed a kick towards the hen,
which squawked in dusty retreat. "You didn't know Smithy.
I did, so I never asked. 'Don't ask me, Jeff,' he said,"—so perhaps he had asked, after all!—"'because it's confidential. The
whole thing's confidential.' That was enough for me. The
Saturday night he sat in that chair, drinking soda water, and
said to me, 'Jeff, I've bust it wide open. Right under my nose
all the time. If only I hadn't been such a scared rabbit and told
a stupid lie the whole thing could've been fixed inside a week.'
That's what he said around sundown on the Saturday. He'd
never slept much the night before, with his asthma giving him
hell once or twice, so I wanted to stop him going out. 'No,
Jeff,' he said, 'I got just a small detail to fix. Be back by ten.'
And by ten he was dead in a monsoon drain off the Bukit
Timah Road."

He turned to spit over the veranda rail.

"The doctor told him his heart wouldn't stand up to action
while the asthma was on him, and he swore by Doctor da Silva
because it was him that found out Smithy's allergies—spices,
specially pepper and cinnamon. Poor old Smithy, a whiff of
pepper or even a sausage that you or I'd never notice was pep-
pery, and he'd be wheezing and choking and tears streaming

from his eyes, poor old bastard. Funny thing, you know, I sat in that room most of the night with him, after they brought the body in, and damn me if I didn't start sneezing and drop a tear or two, as if there was pepper haunting his deathbed. Well, I tell you, it was something unusual for Smithy to forget Doctor da Silva's instructions, but he would go out that night, and evidently he'd been walking up a steepish hill with the asthma on him and fell in the ditch in a heart attack. And if it hadn't been for the job he was doing for your family you can take it from me he'd never have set foot outside this house that night. You can take that from me," he said again and finished.

The myna bird called its Malay slogan again. "What does it say?" I asked Porter.

"*Jangan pergi tidur sampai botol kosong,*" he told me. "Meaning—"

" 'Don't go to bed till the bottle's empty,' " I translated.

He blinked. "So you're an old Malay hand yourself?"

"Couple of months when I was a kid and eighteen more soldiering up in the Federation," I told him.

The bird said it again. "Smithy taught the thing," Porter said. "It can manage a bit of English, too—'Mud in your eye,' and 'Mind the step.' "

"Mud-in-your-eye-mind-the-step," exclaimed the bird in squeaking English.

I said, "We owe Smith some money. How do I—"

"You'd best forget it," Porter said with a shrug. "All Smithy had in the world was a sanctimonious married sister in Southampton, and she'd have nothing to do with him after his slip-up."

"His—?"

"Oh, well, can't do him any harm telling you, now. Ye see, Smithy had the misfortune to collect a six-month sentence over in Sarawak. Year after the war. A matter of surplus military stores, nothing to get shocked about. But his old bitch of a sister sent him a hell of a letter, and he'd never mention her after that. What Smithy and me had we shared. Sometimes I paid the rent for our pair of rooms here, and sometimes he did—whichever of us could manage it easiest, see?"

"But we owe him three hundred dollars," I said uneasily.

"Forget it. He don't want it now."

"Wouldn't he have wanted you to have it?"

"Forget it, I said!" His gin-red eyes flashed ill-temperedly.

The lonely survivor of a long partnership blamed us for his loneliness, but I ventured a second time on the delicate ground. "It's not our money. Smith earned it. If we could ask him who should have it, there's surely not much doubt which way he'd answer." I laid the envelope containing the three hundred dollars beside an empty glass on a rickety bamboo table.

"You take that back!" He looked formidable, glaring and gathering his big hands into fists. I took it back.

For a while I stood thinking and then I asked, "Where does Doctor da Silva live?"

"His bill's been paid," Porter snapped.

But I hadn't been thinking along those lines. Already I'd decided to send Porter the three hundred dollars by post; he probably wouldn't know any address to return it to. "I want to meet him, though," I said.

"Fourth house round the corner," he muttered, throwing a careless hand in the direction of the sinking sun.

I thanked him and said an awkward good-bye. He made a seedy picture, swaying and blinking in his grubby pyjamas, a relic of a man. But he was the survivor of a partnership that had been a better thing, perhaps, than either of the partners, and he wasn't much good at living solo any more. As the taxi carried me out of Koh Han Seng Street and round the corner to Dr. da Silva's, I couldn't escape an unfair sensation of guilt, over and above the familiar helpless nag of pity.

5

"I don't quite understand, Mr. Avery."

Dr. da Silva bent earnestly forward and clasped his bony hands. He was a thin, middle-aged Eurasian, and I'd liked him on sight. What his technical qualifications might be, I had no idea, but conscientiousness and integrity shone unmistakably out of his mild eyes and alert, attentive face.

"Yes, it's a startling suggestion," I admitted. "Or rather, a startling speculation. But let's put it this way. I'm an author, you see." I considered that fair enough, on the strength of a play, three short stories, and perhaps twenty articles published. "And Mr. Smith's death has suggested a plot element to me. I have no medical knowledge, of course, so if you'll allow me to consult you for a suitable fee I shall be greatly obliged. Suppose we have a character called—well, Smith. A sufferer at intervals from asthma. Let us say that he has a violent allergy for pepper, which can bring on a severe asthmatic attack at any time, and let us suppose that he has an enemy, an enemy who wants to move him permanently out of the way without rousing suspicion of foul play. So let us suppose Smith confronted by his enemy during an attack of asthma, and suppose his enemy forces him to inhale a large quantity of black pepper—easily enough done in Smith's already distressed condition. Now, Doctor, could that be the death of him?"

Dr. da Silva smiled, revealing two gold teeth. "It might be all right for a story."

"No, I'm a conscientious author," I said. "Some of my readers must be doctors, and I don't want them sneering at my plot. I gather you don't think it very possible in real life."

He smiled shyly. "Possible, perhaps. But I think not likely unless you have Smith in a state of near-collapse already, and a weakened heart."

"I see. Well, now suppose that, having administered this pepper, and finding Smith still alive, his enemy proceeds to suffocate him."

"Yes?"

"Easily done at that stage, surely?"

"I would think so."

"No need for much violence?"

"Hardly."

"A pad or pillow held over nose and mouth for a couple of minutes, say?"

"Yes."

"There'd be little struggle?"

"I wouldn't expect much."

"So Smith's dead body would show no sign of violence, probably?"

"I suppose not."

"And death would have been due to asphyxia. But wouldn't that leave the body and its organs in much the same state as they would have been if he'd died as a normal consequence of a severe asthmatic attack? I mean, would even a post mortem disclose anything to suggest suspicion?"

"I hardly think so." He said it slowly, cautiously.

"Thank you, Doctor," I said. "That's all I wanted to know. And now, how much do I owe you, please?"

Mildly he said, "You owe me nothing, except some explanation."

I told him, "The explanation is that I'm an author and that I act a good deal on impulse."

"There was no post mortem on Kenbury Smith, by the way," he said then. "His death was a possibility every time he got a bad attack, because he always refused to go into hospital. He knew quite well that any exertion could possibly be fatal —indeed, I told him once that he'd be found dead in a monsoon drain if he didn't stay indoors and in bed at those times. So nothing could have been more likely and straightforward than his death on that hill." He paused and his tone changed. "I think you should be frank with me, Mr. Avery. Because if there is anything more behind these questions of yours than a —a storyteller's curiosity, then it is a very serious matter."

So I had to make up my mind then and there in the shabby room with the creaking overhead fan stirring slow eddies of coolness around us; because this was a man I was not prepared to deceive.

Meeting his mild, alert eyes, I said slowly, "You mean, have I actual grounds for suspicion?" I waited for his nod and then I said, "No, Doctor. None."

## 6

Before I set out for Jerampang Road next morning I went down to the waterfront to collect my visa from the Indonesian Consulate General in the KPM Building. Smith had been going over to Indonesia for "final documents," so I'd be going too.

Though I'd applied for only a single month's tourist visa in London a week earlier, the thing still hadn't come through. Would I call tomorrow? Or would I see Mr. Asinola? Only unfortunately Mr. Asinola wasn't in his office today. Tomorrow, perhaps, or the day after. Oh, but that would be Sunday. Monday, then . . .

I knew better than to make any comment on the efficiency of the organization and said I would call later.

Clumping down the dark stairway again to Finlayson's

Green, I saw, without at first taking any note, the woman climbing up who whirled round suddenly on the steps below me and ran back down to the street. She was almost out of sight before a signal flashed through my consciousness and I blinked after the slim fugitive figure as the high heels tip-tapped headlong down the steps, the thin cream skirt billowing.

By the time I reached the street door I was pretty sure. She was scrambling into a taxi across the road, the wide brim of her straw hat hiding her face, but I was surer still. The taxi was moving before the door slammed. It slammed on her black handbag and flew open again, and I saw something falling into the road. Then the door slammed again and the taxi was out of sight.

When I picked the newspaper and handkerchief out of the gutter I believe I recognized the scent—not one of those expensive, sophisticated French stinks that remind you of cats and tiger lilies; an uncomplicated garden fragrance. And anyway there was the double N embroidered in a corner.

For a moment I stood staring like a fool, shouting for a taxi —playing Sherlock Holmes, I suppose. ("A golden sovereign, my good man, if you keep that cab yonder in view until its occupant alights!") Then, stepping back into the shade, I pushed the handkerchief into my hip pocket and wondered what in God's name Nona Nicolas was doing in Singapore, and what the object of her journey to Indonesia could be— for surely she had been climbing those stairs on the same errand as mine. Possibly Marcos Aragon could tell me. . . .

Jerampang Road turned out to be out at Katong, or just short of Katong—not close to the sea, though. Number 61 was the best-looking house in that end of the road, bigger than its neighbours, more secluded in a smallish but crowded garden. A Tamil gardener with a gleaming, sweaty black skin was cutting grass on a slope fronting the white Spanish-looking house, swinging his long knife through dangerous arcs in the strange scything technique of Tamil *kebons*. A fat Chinese amah nursed a fat baby under a jacquemontia arch, and a good-looking golden Labrador gave me a tolerant glance as I passed him on the neatly paved path. I was received without a word by an old Chinese boy with a pockmarked, distant face, and shown a doorway screened by a beaded curtain.

Passing through the curtain, I found a long, comfortable room with a creeper-shaded window extending for almost the entire length of the two outer walls. A number of toys littered the tile floor, and the man at the far end had to lift a toddler off his knee before he could get up to receive me.

This was Marcos Aragon, then—a heavy, slow-moving man, greeting me with a slow, shy smile that matched his lazy, dreaming voice. His race I couldn't decide on; he could have been Middle Eastern, or Jewish, or even Spanish, as his name suggested. But he was much more an individual than a type, looking rather like a sentimental Orson Welles, somewhere between forty and fifty, probably as generous to himself as to others, a comfort-lover, tolerant and soft-centred and friendly.

And very much a family man. As we were shaking hands a small girl came in, ten or eleven perhaps, and studied me with easy curiosity, while her brother gripped Aragon's blue gabardine trouser leg—both beautiful children, with their father's soft brown eyes.

"Good morning, Mr. Avery," he said, not much above a whisper. "This is my daughter Sophie, and this is *young* Marcos Aragon. Say good morning to Uncle Robert."

The girl smiled charmingly and said, "Good morning, Uncle Robert." The little boy stared. As soon as Aragon showed me a chair and sat down again in his own, his small son climbed back onto his broad knee.

"Well, Mr. Avery, will you have some coffee? I can recommend it, because it is the one I've chosen to drink myself from the various coffees I import from the archipelago. A very smooth *Arabica* from Celebes, selected and roasted by my wife. We know about coffee in this house."

They did. Only once or twice had I tasted any as good. By the time I held the cup in my hand we'd gone through a routine of small talk and young Marcos had been favourably enough impressed by Uncle Robert to have changed his position to my knee. The only point of any interest emerging from these preliminaries was that Aragon had been born in Tangier, which I ought possibly to have guessed, or at least included among my speculations as to his origin. Mixed Spanish and Moorish blood, I suppose.

Then we got down to it.

Lowering his coffee cup, he said, "You wish to know something about Mr. Andrew Avery?"

"Yes, I do."

"Well, there need be no difficulty about that."

"I hope not," I said, hoping.

"What, precisely, though, do you wish to know?" The voice was warm and lazy, a strangely bedroom voice, I found myself reflecting freakishly, intimate and sensuous. He was smiling agreeably, as if our meeting was giving him real pleasure.

"His family have heard nothing of him for about a year," I said. "Naturally we are anxious to know what has happened to him."

"Naturally? Do you mean you are distressed at hearing nothing of him?"

Though it was no business of his, I explained. "Not distressed, really. None of us knew him at all well. But there's a family will awaiting probate and it's necessary to find him now, or find out what's happened to him."

"I understand. Well, it is lucky that I saw your advertisement, because I am most probably your only chance of discovering what you wish to know, just as it happens."

I said I didn't understand that.

"Of course not. But you will not have been offered any useful information by anyone else; I think I can say that with some assurance."

I said he was right there, for the present.

"For the future too—be sure of it, Mr. Avery."

I waited. Young Marcos leaned back against my arm and went to sleep in warm, sighing confidence. The sleeping face was touchingly beautiful, and I recognized that Marcos Aragon was a man to be envied. The girl had served us with the coffee, very gravely, and gone out again.

"I am a businessman, of course," Aragon said then, "so I have taken it for granted that your inquiry was in fact an offer to deal. For information of value your family are prepared to pay, I take it."

"If it is of definite value, yes."

"You can be quite confident of that. Well, Mr. Avery, would you like to make your bid?"

I didn't like that at all. I would never have made a businessman, anyway. Even shopping in the East, where it is still often a mattter of stubborn bargaining, puts me at a glum disadvantage. "I'd rather you quoted your price," I hedged.

"Very good." He folded one heavy knee across the other and smoothed back his glossy hair. "Lady Hughley's fortune was a large one, very large. For the information required to release it, I would not consider ten per cent an unfair price."

My exclamation roused the sleeping boy, who blinked up at me like a small angel and went to sleep again. When at a disadvantage, I find silence a profitable line of least resistance, so I said nothing while I made swift and extensive adjustments to my estimate of Aragon and the course of the interview.

"Sophie!" It was the first time he'd raised his voice much above a whisper. When the child came he nodded significantly towards me, upon which she came over and asked if I would like a second cup of coffee. I could have done with a double brandy, but I accepted her offer.

"And take Marcos," the caressing voice added. "Poor Uncle Robert isn't used to small children. I'm sure he's a bachelor."

"No, don't disturb him," I said. Glad to change the subject for a moment, I added, "You have two fine children, Mr. Aragon. Or three, perhaps?" I'd recalled the baby in the amah's arms under the jacquemontia arch.

"Six," he corrected me proudly. "Where is Angela?" he called after the girl, who was about to plunge back through the bead curtain in search of coffee. Then he rose with a little gasp at the effort and took two framed photographs from a small desk occupying the alcove behind his chair.

"This is our eldest," he said, handing me the first. "David."

I didn't care for the looks of David, a smarmy-looking adolescent photographed in a Hong Kong studio through a red filter to render his complexion a corpselike white.

"And this is Stamford, who will be thirteen next month."

Stamford, named after the founder of Singapore, presumably, had been photographed against a grey landscape under a grey sky, looking cold in the sort of tweed suit with shorts of the Victorian footballer pattern, almost down to the knees, still worn by English preparatory schoolboys. His good-looking face was earnestly resigned.

Aragon mentioned the name of the school with satisfaction, but sighed then because they had not seen Stamford for ten months. Then the bead curtain rustled and Sophie came back slowly with the coffee tray, followed by a small girl a few years younger and just as pretty. Angela was introduced to

Uncle Robert, shook hands shyly, and went to stand by her father, who kissed her fervently.

How had Aragon come to know about Aunt Julia and her money? I said, "You're well briefed on our family affairs."

"Oh yes," was all he said to that.

"You haven't mentioned an actual figure yet," I reminded him. Did he, in fact, have an idea of the extent of the fortune?

"Make it a round one," he said gently. "Twenty-five thousand pounds." He said it dreamily, gazing down at the portraits of his elder sons.

I gave him an impatient stare. "We're wasting each other's time," I said. "My family would never pay a fraction of that, it stands to reason. Did you honestly imagine they might?"

He was replacing the photos on the desk and answered with his back to me. "I suppose I wasn't as well briefed on your family's affairs as I believed. I seem to have overestimated your anxiety to obtain the information."

"Or underestimated our chances of obtaining it elsewhere," I suggested.

"That not, believe me," he said, turning to lift a sombre glance my way. "You may have other leads, I don't know, but for your own sake I hope you won't put much faith in them."

My sleeve was damp with sweat where the sleeping child lay against my arm. His black hair was damp and his face flushed—the fever-look small children have in sleep. I said, "I've been only a day out here and my first lead has just turned out a dud. I have others, yes, and I have plenty of time, and I'm going to do what I came out East to do. For a moment I thought you might provide a short cut. Now I'll have to find the long way round, but I'm going to get there." And I said it again. "I'm going to get there."

I'd decided to treat our interview as abortive and leave no openings. Marcos Aragon wasn't very clever, it seemed, just a devoted family man who'd been dazzled by greed at the idea of meeting a negotiator for the heirs of a large fortune. He knew something. I felt quite sure of that, but his absurd over-estimation of my resources, and perhaps his underestimation of my resolution, had betrayed him into absurdity. I could picture the fond parental wish-fulfilment dreams he must have been indulging in—Oxford for young Stamford, perhaps; a big station wagon for family outings; ponies for the little girls; and possibly pearls for the unseen Mrs. Aragon, or a family trip to Europe . . .

Yet I was reluctantly aware of a formidable simplicity about this man. I'd thought of him as soft-centred, but wasn't I perhaps all wrong there? Was he possibly hard-centred inside his soft, sweet exterior, like a peach? I began to suspect that his calm assurance rested on some concrete advantage he knew he enjoyed over me, and for a moment or two, while his child slept in my arms, I faced the possibility that he had been speaking the literal truth, that he alone knew what had become of Andrew and that if I rejected the help offered at an exorbitant fee I should never find out the answer.

But that was too pessimistic a prospect to be entertained for long. I roused myself to cut Marcos Aragon out of the picture and begin again. When I'd finished my second cup of coffee I asked, "Where do I find a taxi?"

"I will telephone for one," he said and he heaved himself out of his chair, excused himself, and left the room.

For some moments I had been conscious of a large, silver-framed photograph by the garden door, set in another small recess in the wall, like a shrine. The glass caught the light from a window, so that I could see nothing of the portrait beyond a vague feminine head and shoulders. I had been wondering what sort of woman had been Aragon's partner in the establishment of so much domestic felicity, and now I got up on impulse and carried young Marcos across the room.

The portrait was very much what I had expected, the pretty Eurasian girl with big, soft eyes, who had grown comfortably stout in middle age. A good woman, with shrewdness and character as well as the gentleness you noticed first.

And surely that must have been her voice that reached me through the slightly open garden door at that moment, a richly warm voice with the same precise accent as Aragon's own. "We'll ask Daddy when the new uncle's gone," it said.

Then Sophie's breathy small voice: "Uncle Robert's nice. D'you know what he's doing now? Nursing Marcos. Marcos likes him, too. He's gone to sleep on his lap." A pause for a quick breath, and then she asked, "D'you know who Uncle Robert's like? Uncle Andrew. His eyes are the same—terribly blue, but nicer, I think."

I went stiff with the guilty wariness of the eavesdropper.

"I think you should go in and take Marcos from the new uncle," the mother's serene voice suggested, but Sophie came back with a quick refusal.

"No, he likes him. He said so." Then: "Mummy, isn't Uncle Andrew ever coming again?"

Aragon's soft footfall sounded beyond the bead curtain as she spoke, and I was back in my chair when his plump hands appeared and pushed an opening through it with a breast-stroke gesture.

"Well, Mr. Avery"—he sighed, bending over and lifting his son gently out of my arms—"it is sad that you came here for nothing. But when you have exhausted your other leads I shall look forward to seeing you again."

I lost no time in rejecting both presumptions. "Before I have exhausted my other leads I shall know what I've come East to find out," I insisted. "And I shall not be approaching you for help again, Mr. Aragon, under any circumstances."

He only smiled, rocking his little son gently in his arms.

"Look, let us understand each other," I went on. "I can see that you mean what you say, that you will not help me unless your price is paid. Now can't you see that *I* mean what *I* say, that my refusal to negotiate further is final?"

I had nothing to lose in saying that and I didn't expect to gain anything either, except an exit line. He wanted me to bargain, and he'd be ready to drop his price a few notches, though not within sight of anything we could expect Uncle Max to pay. The line made some impression on him, but after an intent silence he made no comment except a short sigh, after which he asked in a social tone, "Are you staying long in Singapore, Mr. Avery?"

"I shall have to stay until my Indonesian visa comes through," I told him, watching for any reaction to that.

His eyebrows reacted, jumping momentarily. "Oh, you're going to Indonesia?"

"So is Andrew Avery's wife," I said, watching closely.

I didn't expect his jaw to drop or his knuckles to turn white; neither would have been in character. But the way his dreamy eyes came wider awake for a second in what looked like a glance of reappraisal gave me satisfaction. I waited for his comment, but he didn't speak for twenty seconds and then only to say, "There's your taxi."

The two small girls were called in from the garden to say good-bye, and Sophie, with her delicious smile, asked, "When are you coming again, Uncle Robert?"

"Uncle Robert's going away for a while, my dear," the father said smoothly. "But he'll be here again before long, I expect."

She asked quickly, "Where are you going, Uncle Robert?"

"To find Uncle Andrew," I said, and turned to give Marcos
Aragon a smiling good-bye.


7

Next day was a blank.

There was nothing for me in the mail, nothing at the Indonesian Consulate, and none of the fifteen hotels I telephoned
had either a Miss Nicolas or a Mrs. Avery occupying a room.
She would be staying with friends somewhere on the island,
I decided—hoping they were good friends.

In fact, I spent a good part of the day thinking about Nona
Nicolas. I wanted to see her again and force some sort of showdown, for my own sake as much as hers. The idea of her
scared of me, running away from me, hiding from me, was
hard to take; so was my curiosity about her. Had she really
been Andrew's wife? Was the secret that drove and tormented
her any more real than most of the terrors and guilts and
nightmares that obsess neurotics? Could there be something
truly frightful about Andrew's death or disappearance, something that made sense of her fear?

That day I found myself looking for her all the time, my
eyes constantly searching the streets, the traffic, the customers
in the bank and the shops and bars. The time came when I
had to ask myself the careful bachelor's questions: Are you
watching out? Are you getting involved?

I had the answers, though. Nona Nicolas was my only lead
now; if I didn't keep her in sight I might miss my one chance
of cracking the mystery. Self-interest dictated a close interest
in her and her movements, if normal curiosity wasn't motive
enough; and elementary decency compelled sympathy with
her distracted loneliness.

Around sunset I returned to the Sultan Mustafa, took a

shower, and lay on my hard, short bed, frowning up at the slowly spinning ceiling fan until I got a headache and the room grew almost dark. Since noon blue-black thunderheads had been advancing through the eastern sky, and now they hung over the sweating island like bomber squadrons massed for an attack, and the air was heavy with suspense, thick and hard to breathe.

When Jaafar brought me my Tiger he set it down and leaned back against the door with a sleepy sigh.

"*Apa khabar*, Jaafar?" I asked him— "How goes it?"

The boy closed his dark eyes and heaved another exhausted sigh. It was the way everybody in Singapore was feeling, waiting for the storm to burst. Not that Jaafar was without words; I knew that well enough. But when he spoke at last it was merely to utter a lifelessly stale announcement. He was going to look for another job, he said.

He was always saying that. All it meant was that he'd fallen out with somebody. I strung him along a little as I drank, and we talked, with long pauses between the exhausted lines of dialogue, until he led up to something of slightly greater interest.

He had been listing the alleged misdemeanours of Bah Feng, his old enemy the hall porter, and dwelling with satisfaction on the fear in which, according to him, Bah Feng went of the individual or organization that was riding him to hell.

"Every time the telephone rings," Jaafar declared, "he begins to shake. I watch him sometimes."

I bet he did, too.

"Last week"—he moved closer and lowered his voice— "last week before you came I saw him listen on the telephone with fear and look all round him and say no. He was speaking English, and many times he said no and he shook his head at the telephone as if the man he fears was there and not telephoning in his house or office. But when he had listened some more he was silent and stopped saying no. And then, after that, he hung his head and said yes. He said yes three times and then he hung up the telephone and looked round him in fear—but he did not see me—and then he took some letters from the rack where the letters of the guests are placed and he called Lee Choy to take his place at the desk for a wink and he went away fast with those letters."

I suggested that the call could have come from somebody who'd booked a room at the Sultan Mustafa but had been invited to stay with a friend instead, so he'd rung the hotel and asked for his mail to be sent round.

Jaafar thought nothing of that. Would Bah Feng go himself on such an errand? "And why then did he shake?" he demanded. "And why was he sweating when he came back, and why did he run into the bar and take a small glass of something he didn't pay for? I saw him. I saw that it was the secret society that had ordered him to steal the letters."

Still I wasn't paying much attention to his tale. The bated heat and airlessness didn't encourage close attention to anything. But then I found myself recalling Bah Feng's sly mask of denial when I'd asked him for mail on my arrival. Not that his face expressed guilelessness at any time.

But then again, during the exhausted silence that followed Jaafar's last words, I reminded myself that mystery and melodrama had thrown their long shadows across me already, so it was not for me to scorn the boy's highly coloured suspicions. And I thought then that if those letters had been mine they could only have been replies to my cabled advertisement asking for news of Andrew, though it was difficult to think of any reason why anybody should want to keep that news from me.

Just the same, it had been kept from me so far. Nona Nicolas had tried hard to stop me from coming East in search of it, and though Marcos Aragon had offered it to me he'd placed a prohibitive price on it. I turned my eyes and met Jaafar's indolent glance.

"We will see," I said suddenly.

While he watched me with muted curiosity I typed an address on an envelope: "Robert Avery Esq., Sultan Mustafa Hotel. BY HAND." Then I folded a sheet of blank paper, put it in the envelope, and sealed the flap.

"We will see, Jaafar," I said. "Put this in your pocket, go out into the street for a minute, and come back with it to Bah Feng, saying a *sais* had stopped a car outside the entrance and handed it to you. Then we will see what he does."

But before he got to the door, with a slow smile of complicity on his face, I called him back, took the note from him, and tore it up. Might as well make a good job of it, I'd decided. I began to type a note:

Dear Robert, Great news for you, but in great haste. My phone's out of order and I'm rushing off to a job up in JB that will keep me till all hours, so will you come along to my office in the morning, any time after nine, and I'll give you all the details about Andrew.

Remembering old Smithy's words to his crony Jeff, I added, "The whole answer was right under our noses all the time! Now I must run. Yrs, Harry."

When I handed over this note, addressed as before, Jaafar went out with something close to alacrity for him. There was a corner by the top of the stairway from which I could see Bah Feng's head bent over a Chinese newspaper. After I'd waited there in my dressing gown for a couple of minutes,

Jaafar came in from the street, admirably casual, and threw the note onto the desk.

The hall porter read the address, but his face, which was like a skull's face, showed no reaction. Nodding briefly to Jaafar, he stuck the note in the mail rack and took up his newspaper again. But the moment Jaafar had strolled through the door into the restaurant he seized the phone and began a conversation, holding it very close to his mouth.

His nerve was bad. When finally he hung up he snatched the note from the rack and pushed it out of sight under the register. His newspaper fell off the desk, but he didn't notice, just sat staring blankly at the wall opposite while his fingers twirled the black beads of his abacus.

When a figure hurried in from the street he turned his head sharply and got off his chair, but sat down again when he saw it was the stout merchant from Jakarta who had the room next to mine, only to jerk up again as a young Chinese followed the merchant through the entrance—a very average Singapore youth, his hair lavishly creamed, his shirt perfectly laundered, his blue cotton slacks sharply pressed and tapering to a waist so slender that twenty inches of slack flopped free past the buckle of his leather belt.

This youngster said nothing to Bah Feng, and Bah Feng said nothing to him, but my note travelled fast from Bah Feng's hand to his, and he went straight out again.

"*Itu-lah!*"

I hadn't realized that Jaafar was at my elbow. His whispered exclamation startled me. He was jubilant, of course, though his typically Malay emotional reserve permitted only one exclamation before his face returned to its handsome impassivity. I gave him a dollar.

"He is bad, as I told you, Tuan," he remarked, adding with

satisfaction, "And now I shall be a *saksi* again." He had evidently enjoyed being a witness, a *saksi*, at the trial of the knifeman accused of stabbing the detective in the bar lavatory, and now he saw himself as a leading player in the trial that would end with a jail sentence, surely, for one of his enemies.

"When the time comes," I said carefully. "Until then, speak of this to nobody."

A fat chance there was of him taking much notice of that. Malays cannot keep secrets. But at least he would withhold the gossip from any of the Chinese, for whom, like all Malays, he had a hearty mistrust.

As I dressed for the evening a distant thunderclap growled through the sky and for five minutes sparse, heavy raindrops sprinkled the city. But the storm-tension hadn't yet reached breaking point, and when I left the hotel the streets were dry and so airless they felt like underground tunnels.

The night's suffocating heat drove me into Compton's, because it was air-conditioned. It was rather smart, too, for Singapore and at least I'd get a decent supper there, for which the artificial coolness and non-humidity would induce an appetite.

In the days when I'd gone around with Zella I'd spent a fair amount of time in Compton's and as soon as I entered the dimly lit chill of the bar I was recognized—first by the little Filipino barman who had invented a cocktail called Tiger Sweat (believed to consist of arak, anisette, and a single drop of iodine), then by a loud-mouthed backslapper I had forgotten with complete success but who hadn't forgotten me; and then, as my eye was appreciating a temptingly bare back that seemed not to mind the chill artificial temperature, the dark head turned over the bare shoulder and Zella was back in my life again.

In the same moment the storm burst—thunder, lightning, and Niagaras of rain all at once.

8

Zella was somebody I'd had a holiday with at the end of my national service in Malaya. When the battalion had sailed home I'd been left in hospital with pneumonia, and before I was discharged I'd talked a good-natured staff officer into fixing me two months' unpaid leave before embarking on a troop-ship home for release. The first month I'd spent in a small Malay village up near the Siamese border; most of the second I'd spent with Zella.

*"Robert!"*

The bare back shivered flatteringly under my hands as I kissed her. She left one arm round my neck while she made a number of not very coherent introductions, clipping her syllables as she always did when she was excited. Her crowd were all dressed for a real party, and I felt inadequate in my Palm Beach suit, so I wasn't sorry when I gathered they were on their way to a dinner at the Raffles given by, or to, a visiting airline chief. We made a date for lunch next day.

But I wasn't at all sure that Zella fitted into my plans I had or expected to have. For one thing, Zella was strictly for play-time. For another, our little holiday in '52 had been perfectly balanced and complete. Everything had been just right, including its duration. At good-bye there'd been a little bitter-sweet, sentimental pain that lasted—for me, anyway—only a few weeks. She'd written one letter and I'd written two, and then our little episode had drifted easily into the past, to be remembered at odd, lonely moments without regret.

But now, after a couple of drinks, I dined alone, frowning

quite a bit over my smoked trout and brochettes, seeing Zella for the first time as a problem. I was short of money, otherwise occupied, didn't know what she expected, and couldn't decide what I wanted myself. She might even be married—I hadn't listened properly to her breathless introductions—though I doubted that. Zella believed that variety was the spice of sex life. . . .

When the waiter called me to the phone I felt a little stab of excitement, realizing somehow that I'd been waiting all the evening for something to happen. But it was only Zella.

"Darling, you don't *have* to lunch with me tomorrow," she began. "No, listen, listen. We learned to understand each other, surely. Didn't we, Robert?"

"Does this mean you don't want to?" I asked her.

A strangled gasp of protest. "Well, of all the crude— Really, Robert, is that all I get for being delicate and— Aren't you ashamed of yourself?"

It had been genuine, then. Zella was fluent only when she was plotting and dissimulating. So I said, "Then let's lunch together, for old times' sake."

"I'd love to, really," she confessed.

I confirmed the RV—Elizabethan Grill at 1:30—and there was a short silence along the line. The phone box had a window, and the downpour's hissing violence echoed through it and once or twice the semi-opacity of the glass turned a dirty yellow as lightning flashed.

"Well, how are you, Robert?" she asked then. "Happy?"

A hell of a question. "Not un-," I told her. "And you?"

"Oh, I don't know. . . ."

I said suddenly, "Did you ever meet my cousin Andrew? Andrew Avery?"

"Was he your cousin?" she asked.

"You knew him, then?"

"A little. Once."

"But not any more?"

"My dear, he's dead, surely."

"Dead? Tell me about it."

"Well, isn't he?"

"I don't know."

"Why should I think he's dead if he isn't?" she demanded.

"Darling, I don't know. I'm asking you."

"Well, surely I heard he was dead."

I asked her for details.

"Oh, Robert, how can I remember?" she came back impatiently, as if I'd been bullying her. "I had this idea he was dead, but perhaps I'm wrong."

"Any idea who'd know for certain?"

"Well, his family, I suppose."

It was no good. All it suggested was that a report of his death may have been going round, somewhere, in the past year and that Zella's rag-bag of a brain had some dim echo of the news on file. Or she could just as easily have confused him with somebody else altogether. I went back to my table and ordered coffee and brandy with a sigh.

I stayed on for more than an hour, reluctant to leave the dry coolness of the place. The storm was long and heavy, even for Singapore. Long after the thunder and lightning faded, the rain came plunging down through the dark sky. But when I left finally, a bit before midnight, it had stopped— at any rate, temporarily. Heavy clouds still hung at what seemed like roof level, and the pressure and tension in the still air had not found release.

Sounds of rushing floodwater came from all directions. Compton's occupied one corner of a crossroads of which three blocks had been built up; but the fourth, an old Chinese burial ground with horseshoe-shaped graves on slopes under frangipani trees, had been preserved from violation by builders. Except for a few cars splashing along the streaming highway, the crossroads was lifeless. After waiting two or three minutes on the chance of spotting an empty taxi, I began walking along the road that passed the dark burial ground. I was reminding myself to order a reinsertion of my advertisement in the local papers, but this time giving a box number for replies to fox Bah Feng, when a shout from across the street made me turn sharply.

An excited Chinese in a soaked shirt and slacks was beckoning me with the gesture Europeans use to shoo away chickens. When I didn't respond at once, he threw out an arm towards the dark cemetery and shouted some agitated Chinese. I went over to him.

Halfway across the road I found myself wading through shallow floodwater. The deep monsoon ditch between the pavement and the cemetery had overflowed, and I saw by a flash of lightning the swollen torrent that plunged down the course of the ditch, sweeping along a tumbling mass of jetsam of all sizes from flower petals to a whole uprooted banana tree and what looked like a hencoop. The Chinese was now pointing upstream and there I saw the scars of a landslide, where part of a small garden and a cemetery-tender's hut had collapsed and been mostly swept away in the flood.

I don't speak more than a dozen words of Chinese, so I asked in English, "What's wrong?" and then in Malay, "*Apa jadi?*"

The short but powerful-looking fellow stood in the floodwater that had drowned the grass verge of the monsoon drain, pointing into the torrent now and saying something I couldn't hear because of a thunderclap. I moved up to him, feeling the water enter my shoes and chill my toes. If he meant that somebody had fallen into that torrent, then there was nothing to be done about it. At ordinary times a stream a few inches deep flowed along the bottom of the deep ditch, to join another at right angles on a corner of the crossroads and dive into a tunnel under the street that came out I don't know where. Now, though, a headlong spate of water, nine or ten feet deep, rushed to meet the other, just as swollen and violent, and choke the underground waterway.

Before I could put another question the man's foot slipped in the mud underlying the floodwater, and he lurched against me. That, I mean, was what I thought had happened. I threw out an arm to steady him, and the next moment I had lost my own footing, I was off my feet, I was sprawling, I was in the water, I was being swept at speed towards the deep under-street conduit that gulped down the floodwaters rushing towards its dark mouth.

I sank and swallowed water. I shot up again and had a glimpse of the Chinese, far upstream of me now, walking away across the road. A wooden box came spinning along the water surface and struck me in the face as I turned. Something had wound itself tightly round my neck. The water was cold. There was mud on my tongue and grit between my teeth.

I'd begun to swim before shock released my brain for thinking. But it wasn't any good. The sides of the ditch were steep, smooth concrete, and there was nothing on the flooded rim I could hope to grab or hold fast to. And there was no time. With the silent swiftness of a jungle beast dragging its prey to its lair the current was dragging me towards the black tunnel mouth.

Light burst round me in a flood the next moment, light from the headlamps of a car descending the slope from the top of the burial ground. It blazed across the water surface that was uneven with little sucking whirlpools and suppurating upcurrents; it picked out the bedraggled plumage of a drowned cock floating alongside me; and it floodlit the mouth of the water tunnel ahead.

What was so horrifying about the tunnel entrance was, first, its unbelievable nearness, and, second, the revelation that it was full. The water had risen so far that instead of the tall Norman arch at the foot of which little Chinese boys played in three or four feet of water there was now nothing but a black crescent only a few inches deep between the water level and the top of the arch.

This shallow crescent came rushing towards me as the headlights swept away to the right. I threw up my hands, and they slapped the cold concrete a foot above the water level, six inches above the top of the arch. Instantly my legs were gulped into the tunnel and I was thrown on my back with my fingers tearing at the concrete before they were sucked into the drowning darkness.

It is true what they say about danger tuning the brain to brilliant clarity and accelerated action. But the memory-storage cells seem not to share this stimulus and drag behind instead, so that recollection of those crystal-clear, spinning moments is usually a blur. What I remember is a blur, anyway. There was the coldness of the water and its devouring speed; the greasy roof of the tunnel as my knuckles and my forehead grazed it; the blind darkness; the smell I can't find a word for; the sharp pain of a torn-off fingernail; the futility of a shout that perished before it found a single echo. . . .

And a brain awhirl with swarming thoughts—of my unknown enemy and of those who might share my danger in his secret campaign: Nona Nicolas with a fear that was devouring her alive; Marcos Aragon in the domestic felicity he believed secure; even Bah Feng, afraid of the telephone.

Blinking dirty water out of my eyes, I stared forward into

the darkness, treading water and using my hands to keep my balance as the fighting currents tried to overturn me. For all I knew, the subterranean waterway could be as little as forty yards long or as much as half a mile. The sea was perhaps seven hundred yards off in a straight line; I might be there before I could seize any initiative.

In fact, I got no more than a dozen yards after that thought flashed through my mind. There was a collision then in the darkness, a shock of tearing, piercing, down-dragging crushing, as if a crocodile had seized me. I had been hurled against a barrier formed of great branches—a whole tree, perhaps—an uprooted barbed-wire fence, timbers from a flood-capsized hut, and the smaller debris the barrier had trapped and held.

Only now that I was stationary did I realize the maniac force of the water. The barrier scarcely checked it, and the violence with which it crushed me to the branches and the tangled wire made it difficult to believe that the waterway was horizontal and not a steeply angled chute.

In the moment of impact I had gone under, and as I freed myself from the tentacles of the barrier some of my clothes had been torn and swept off me and the wire had scored wounds on my shoulders and legs. A twig had jabbed my right eye. To keep my mouth and nostrils above water I had to wedge myself against a heavy board that was itself wedged tightly, and suffer continual bumping of my head against the tunnel roof, because there were no more than eight or nine inches of clearance at that point, owing to the water's rising in a wave at the barrier check.

I was gasping, and gradually I realized that I was moaning too, a self-scaring sound in that unechoing loneliness. As soon as I became aware of it I locked my jaw and set my lips.

That was when the light showed ahead of me—only dim,

the sweep of another car's headlights a long way forward, slowly passing the far mouth of the tunnel. What the dirty, reddish glow revealed was the deathblow to my last stubborn hope. Between me and the tunnel's end was silhouetted a dense forest of branches with debris caught in them. The long, thin crescent of grey-red gloom showed no gap, and I knew it must be like an iceberg, the seen obstruction only a token of the denser greater mass that was submerged. The water checked and swirled, but found its way through. But I couldn't hope to get through, any more than the drowned cockerel that was jammed in the branches right ahead of me.

Behind me, the water was rising.

# TWO

The water was rising.

Inevitably. It was no more than fifteen minutes since the rain had stopped falling, and there would surely be more before long. An exhausted glimmer of lightning came in through each mouth of the waterway, and a few seconds later the echo of a thunderclap murmured along the tunnel roof.

It appeared that almost the entire volume of the landslide fifty yards upstream had choked the tunnel at this point, all building up against the framework of the uprooted tree that had wedged itself in an upright, natural position from floor to roof. Every minute the barrier grew more solid, offering increasing obstruction to the floodwater, of itself tending to raise its level even if the flow were to decrease.

I was going to die—alone and in the dark, squalidly. It was strange how important it became to preserve what shreds of dignity were possible; I suppose it must have been a defence mechanism against panic. After a single dive—or rather, climb —down the barrier on the chance of finding a way through and finding it instead, as I'd expected, denser below the surface, I forced myself to stillness and attempted to control the headlong confusion of my thoughts. Deliberately I thought about the unknown enemy who had sentenced me to death.

It must surely have been the fake letter, reported and handed over by Bah Feng, that had convinced him I was dangerous and must be got rid of. And now he would be trying to trace the writer of the letter—what had I called him? John? George? I couldn't remember. Like Smith, who had also threatened to become my informant, the writer of that note would have to be eliminated.

And what about Marcos Aragon? And Nona Nicolas? He claimed to know it all, and she certainly knew something. Didn't I share my enemy with them?

*Why* was he my enemy?

I had no clue to that. The mere fact that investigation into Andrew's last chapter had involved me in criminal action, that wasn't surprising, even though I hadn't foreseen it. I remembered the boy Andrew, the boy who'd just started to be a man, and though I knew little of crime or criminals it seemed likely enough that somebody who'd seen himself, even then, as a lonely figure, rejecting society, defiantly apart *from* it rather than a part *of* it, could later cast himself as a criminal, at odds and at war with society. It was possible, but I had no evidence to suggest that it had happened. We'd never heard details of the trouble Andrew had got himself into once or twice, but we'd gathered that it was nothing worse than debts and moneylenders, a deliberate exploitation of a rich woman's soft heart.

Yes, Andrew could conceivably have become a criminal, but something much more probable was that he could have been a criminal's victim. A man who alternated between hiding from his creditors and splashing easy money around, who was known to stand next in line for a large inheritance, that sort of man would easily attract criminal companions and hangers-on. But then again, Andrew would have been shrewd, pretty well able to look after himself; even at sixteen he had asserted a proud independence and dominated his father and the servants at Sungei Sunyi—and me, of course.

But suppose Andrew had been murdered—murdered, but not known to have been murdered? Then the murderer would have to protect himself from investigators into Andrew's disappearance, perhaps with other murders.

Wasn't there a flaw in that, though? If he could get rid of Smithy so smartly, counterfeiting a natural death with such skill, and if he could dispose of me now without leaving a scrap of evidence of foul play, then wouldn't his murder of Andrew have been equally expert and safe from exposure?

Well, there could be several answers to that. Andrew's murder might have been unpremeditated and crude, for instance, and there may have been no way of improvising a sound job of covering up. So the secret might lie just beneath the surface—hadn't Smithy said that the answer had been right under his nose all the time?—and the murderer might be forced to stand constantly on guard against exposure. That could be one answer.

But all the time, while these thoughts had occupied one part of my mind, another part was slipping out of control. Now, without warning, it collapsed and plunged me into a frenzy of claustrophobia. I didn't think any more, I only suffered.

I was hideously aware of the monstrous masses that entombed me; the obliterating weight of water piling up behind me; the thin, shrinking layer of air space. My head, wedged against the roof to keep my nostrils above water, felt the crushing weight of the masonry above me, the road and the great buildings and the streaming floodwater. They all pressed unbearably down on my head.

For an hour—longer, I don't know how long—I was reduced to the lowest that was in me. All that was left was a screaming, shaking, mindless pulp, a thing, not even an animal, a mere vehicle for agony. I'm grateful that I can remember so little of it. . . .

The plunge into frenzy had been as swift as a ski-run. The escape from it was as slow and laboured as the climb back to the summit. Reason must have taken hours to re-establish itself while I shivered with a deathly cold and drifted close to the frontier of exhaustion. It took time for me to react when I became aware that the water level was sinking.

When I roused myself to test the extent of the fall I found that my hand was too numb to register anything. I had to detach my aching head from the roof and lower it painfully in a slow bow. Excitement seized me when I found how deep I had to bow before my face met the water. It wasn't much more than waist high.

I said it in a shaking whisper. "I'm not going to die. I'm not going to die."

2

The big Sikh night porter blinked his heavy-lidded eyes, and I could see him deciding that he had another drunk on his hands. His black beard had been trained round a wire hanging from his ears, and his turban was of confectionery pink muslin. He was bigger than ever.

Sometime I was going to ask him why it was that you never saw a Sikh boy or youth who wasn't a stringy weed, but never saw a Sikh over twenty-one who wasn't getting on for a heavyweight; but not tonight. I wondered why his wife had drunk all that poison and listened to myself explaining that I'd fallen down a monsoon drain. I sounded drunk, anyway.

The clock over the restaurant door showed four-fifteen.

I must have smelled the tea, or else I saw the thin coil of steam rising from behind the ledge of his narrow desk. With a greedy lurch I leaned over the desk and saw the breakfast cup, filled to the brim.

"Can I have your tea?" I asked, without shame.

I hadn't yet seen myself in a looking glass. When I did, upstairs, I understood his look better. What was left of my clothes was plastered close to my body with thin, drying slime. My chest, right shoulder, and right leg were naked and marked with red wounds. I was still shivering, and my eyes were fixed in a stare that must have looked closer to lunacy than to drunkenness.

He handed the tea over.

Some of it slopped over and scalded my bare, wire-torn chest, but most of it went down my gullet and worked a miracle somewhere farther down. When I replaced the empty cup in the saucer my hand had stopped shaking. I felt life returning and I felt equal to climbing the stairs.

Stripped in the shower, I saw how my long-soaked skin had shrunk into white ridges and wrinkles, like a half-empty balloon. When I felt clean at last I could scarcely crawl back to my room and the sawn-off bed; but once I'd fallen across it and snapped out the light I found that sleep wouldn't come. Until Jaafar came in with my newspaper and coffee I lay there in a restless fury, determined on a second manhunt. As well as finding the truth about Andrew, I was going to hunt down my enemy and strike back at him.

Jaafar's face never gave away much, but I could see that he must have heard something from the night porter. He looked from my lacerated chest, stained with iodine, to the sodden, smelly rags on the floor.

"Ah!" he said.

I asked him to find some aspirin in my smaller bag. He watched me gulp down three tablets with the coffee, betraying curiosity only by standing erect instead of leaning against the door as he normally did. He was going to let me raise the subject. But when I handed him the empty cup and closed my eyes, he waited only a few moments before remarking, "*Tuan sudah luka.*"

"Yes, I'm wounded, Jaafar," I said. "Is Bah Feng in yet?"

Yes, he said, Bah Feng had just come on duty.

"Tell him to come up here, then," I said.

He went off, and in less than a minute there was a knock on the door. I was out of the bed by then, in shorts and slippers, looking out of the window with my back to the door. The moment Bah Feng was inside I whirled round and got him by the throat and threw him across the bed.

The emaciated, flimsy lightness of his body made it strangely disgusting. I'd been going to sit on his chest and choke the truth out of him; but now I had a sickening suspicion that his frail ribs and lungs might collapse under my weight. He'd gone so limp with terror there was no need for violence, anyway.

I said, "Now you are going to tell me who got those letters you stole from me."

His grey death mask of a face was expressionless; his open, gasping mouth didn't speak. I had relaxed my grip on his stringy throat, loathing the touch of it. "Answer, or you will not get out of this room alive!" I muttered at him, glaring into his small, mud-coloured eyes.

With a weak gesture he shook his grey crew-cut head.

I waited. Jaafar, who had closed the door as Bah Feng came in, must have been regretting his decision as he stood guard outside.

But already disgusted pity had begun to erode my determination. Bah Feng was a poor, poor thing, and it was repulsive to watch him lying there at my mercy and expecting none. His starvation look couldn't have been due to malnutrition, not with the salary he drew, but it could be TB, I told myself suddenly. And he was a man who lived in fear, a fellow victim of my own enemy, it seemed. The compassion that comes so easily to me, blurring my judgment and disarming my resolution, could not resist the misery of the grey, beaten face.

I said, "He will never know you told me. Nothing will happen to you."

Only the weary shake of the grey skull again.

"And you will be free of him." I was glad Jaafar wasn't in the room. He'd have been disgusted by the accent of persuasion—pleading, almost—that had begun to tinge my voice.

Bah Feng said nothing. Five minutes more, and still he'd said nothing. By then I understood. I might have known how it would be. After what I'd seen in 1952, I might have known.

How often in those months I'd gone to Chinese villages or one of the few remaining isolated squatter huts where the Communist terrorists were known to be active and witnessed the futile interrogation of the terrorists' victims. Either they were stubbornly silent, or if they spoke they denied all knowledge of the terrorists' activities, identity, or whereabouts. Once an old man and woman, desolated by the loss of their only son, who'd been tortured to death before their eyes, had declared they had no idea how the thing had happened, swore they'd never seen the killers. And it was always the same.

At first it had enraged me, sickened me. Perhaps you couldn't expect people whose ancestors had for centuries known soldiers and policemen only as oppressors in their own country to recognize that in Malaya they were allies who needed cooperation in wiping out the seedy killers who preyed on them; but for a soldier hunting down those killers that wasn't much consolation. After a while, though, my rage had turned to understanding and pity. I began to see it through their eyes.

The soldiers and policemen came to their poor huts and villages with a great show of weapons and security; yes, but there was no reason to fear them. But when they'd gone again, in the night, the terrorists came back. *They* were the ones with the power, because if *they* were not obeyed they killed. In the end I recognized that if I'd been a poor Chinese villager I should never have lifted a finger or breathed a word of information to help the soldiers or the policemen. The ones poor folk had to cooperate with were the ones who had power and *used* it. A single terrorist with an old Japanese rifle, who was ready to use it and kill, was stronger than a battalion of friendly troops or a thousand policemen who would only question and argue and appeal, or inconvenience and browbeat if they lost patience.

Bah Feng had made the same decision. He knew I wouldn't kill him, but there was somebody else who easily might. He had no real choice.

But I didn't submit at once to the logic of this. First there was an episode I would like to forget. Exhaustion was to blame, I suppose, but should be no excuse. Looking him in the eye, I told him that if he didn't start to talk within thirty seconds I was going to smash his jaw.

"You know you can trust me," I said. "You know you can tell me." And I turned my eyes to the second hand of my watch.

When he saw my fist gathering, he closed his eyes. It was a half-hearted blow, because the resolution was draining out of me. I struck with pity dragging at my elbow, but even so it is a foul memory. His papery body reared up, his grey face contorted for a moment; then he fell back, body slack and face impassive, waiting for the next blow, and the next, for whatever I chose to inflict on him.

Only I believe he knew all along that, like most Europeans, I didn't really mean business, that I hadn't the heart for brutality of, say, the Japanese during the occupation of Malaya, or the new Chinese government. Westerners talked tough, but patient non-cooperation soon exposed the unreality of their threats. There was never any need to take them very seriously.

Well, it worked again. My fury collapsed in shame, and I stared down at him, disgusted with him and myself. There was nothing to be done. I could have called the police, of course, and Bah Feng could have sneered. The police didn't mean business, either. The man whose voice on the phone brought the sweat out on Bah Feng's grey skin—he meant business.

I strode across to the window and said, "Get out!"—glaring down into the street. I didn't hear him go, but when I turned again he had gone. He hadn't spoken one word.

3

Until midday I tried to sleep, but it was no good. I shaved then, showered, and dressed for lunch with Zella. If I'd known her number I'd have phoned her and cried off, but when I'd had the directory in my hand I couldn't for the life of me remember her name.

Graves? Grant? Glyn? No, it wouldn't come. Garth? Gore? Gray? My head was aching. I dropped the directory and went back to bed, where I remembered it as soon as my head was on the pillow. Graham, of course. But I let it go then and closed my eyes again.

Out on the street I remembered suddenly that my life was in danger. It was the same brittle, alert sensation, with an undercurrent of self-mockery, that prickled under my skin when I drove through any notorious ambush area up in the Federation in 1952. And in the same way it rather soon wore off. After all, it was one thing to make an attempt on the life of an unsuspecting victim on a deserted midnight road and quite another to attack an alerted quarry in the crowded mid-day streets of a great city.

I watched the traffic, though.

Watching the traffic, I saw a big but not very new Buick pass me and glimpsed Marcos Aragon sitting beside the smart *sais*. But he didn't see me. A couple of minutes later I saw the blue Buick parked in the space between the Hong Kong and Shanghai Bank and Whiteaways' corner. From the back seat a beautiful smile greeted me as I passed it.

"Hello, Uncle Robert!"

Miss Sophie Aragon and her sister, identically dressed in buttercup yellow with tiny pearl necklaces and small ostrich-leather handbags, showed a flattering pleasure in the meeting. "You said you were going away," Sophie said.

"I am, but not today," I told her.

"And are you really going to see Uncle Andrew?" she asked.

"I hope so."

"Daddy said no. Daddy said you didn't know where Uncle Andrew is. Nobody knows, he said."

I just smiled and let her talk. Aragon wasn't in sight—making a business call, presumably.

"If you do see Uncle Andrew will you tell him I've forgiven him?"

"Yes, I will. But forgiven him what?"

"Oh, he'll know."

The younger one, Angela, said, "He told her she talked too much."

"He was rough," Sophie complained. "He wasn't always the same, you know"—two verdicts I had passed on Andrew myself when I was about her age.

"What did you say, then, to make him rough?" I asked.

"Nothing. I just told him about school that day, how instead of English composition we'd had to stand up at the teacher's desk and talk to the class about something for five minutes. So I talked about him. Well, it was because I liked him."

"And he asked you what you'd said?"

"Yes. And all I'd said was about my Uncle Andrew Avery coming to stay with us when we hadn't expected him, coming in the middle of the night to give us a nice surprise in the morning. And about how tall he was and his nice blue eyes and the way he called me 'Princess Sophie'—he did, you know. And all that. And he frowned and pushed me away and I hit my elbow on Daddy's desk and hurt it and he said, 'You talk too much.' And that night he went away and I left him out of my prayers for a week but then I forgave him. Only he doesn't know I did."

I asked her, "How long ago was that?"

"Oh, a long time." Her lovely eyes went wide and sad. "The week after Marcos's birthday." She sighed. "Perhaps he hasn't forgiven *me*. Perhaps that's why he hasn't come any more. But I didn't do anything."

I asked her when young Marcos's birthday was, and she said the last day of March.

So it was at least eleven months since Andrew had been out to Jerampang Road. And that, of course, was nearly two months after the last letters had passed between him and Aunt Julia. Shortly before he'd left Jerampang Road without saying good-bye to Sophie, all trace of him had been lost.

Because her information was the last I had of him, I thought it over and probed it for significance. But when I could find none I reflected that sudden fits of irrational irritation had been a disconcerting feature of his two-month relationship with me back in 1940. . . . Andrew crouching over his pet green snake or lying naked on the rock above his private pool in the jungle and saying, "Go away, young Robert. I don't want you." . . . And more than once the words that had wounded Sophie; "You talk too much. Shut up, young Robert." . . . That was the sort of treatment that alternated with the spells of intimate, high-spirited friendship that had evoked my uncritical devotion. I knew exactly how Sophie had felt when that sudden frown and shove and snarl had replaced the easy charm and intimacy.

It had never needed any ascertainable provocation to touch off these abrupt mood changes. "I didn't *do* anything," Sophie had said, sighing, echoing my own miserable bewilderment on frequent occasions seventeen years earlier. And surely she hadn't, unless there was something she'd forgotten. If she had spoken for five minutes she must have said more than she'd told me, so I probed a little farther.

"It must have been something else you said."

"Or else she jogged his elbow," Angela put in, bending forward, her white-gloved hands folded on her ostrich bag. "I bet she jogged his elbow. It was in a sling because he broke it when he fell down a ladder in Borneo, a slippery ladder going up to a longhouse, and it hurt and I bet Sophie jogged it. And when he pushed her away she hurt *her* elbow on Daddy's desk, and that," she added, using a grown-up phrase with smug importance, "was a judgment on her." Angela was a little Victorian, very Spanish with her black eyes and old-world miniature elegance and prim voice.

It was amazing how vividly her scrap of childish gossip brought back the most disturbing of all my memories of Andrew—of one of the nights we'd spent together in the jungle, five miles from Sungei Sunyi bungalow, with only the old Malay tracker Ngari as escort. It began by being one of the most intoxicating experiences of my ten years of life, but just when we were going to bed in Andrew's cave something happened. We were throwing some more of the wood we'd gathered onto the fire outside the cave mouth, and I made a clumsy job of rearranging a couple of the half-burned lengths of wood so that one of them twisted in my hand and the burning end fell across Andrew's thigh, searing through the hem of his shorts and the skin beneath.

Before I could gasp out an apology he turned on me with a terrible face, mouthing swear words, his blue eyes blazing in the low-angle firelight. Before I could escape he seized me with his left arm and with his right pulled a flaming brand out of the fire. It was still flaming when he pushed it hard against my thigh.

I screamed in terror, believing he meant to burn me alive. His fury was insane, like nothing I'd ever seen. Ngari had gone to set lines in the river for our breakfast fish, and I thought I would be dead before he could answer my screams.

"That's what you get for hurting *me!*" Andrew whispered through his teeth, holding my thin thigh and the brand together. "And if you tell Ngari or Father or anybody, *ever*, I'll kill you. I'll kill you."

I never did tell anybody. The five-inch scar down my thigh is still entered in my passport in the space reserved for "Special Peculiarities," but for some reason—could it be a never-exorcized fear of Andrew? I wonder—I've never given more than a half-answer when I've been asked about it. "Burnt it on a picnic fire when I was a kid," is the nearest I've ever come to the truth.

Fear even more than pain kept me awake in the cave that night. I hadn't let Ngari see the wound, and I lay crying silently for hours, staring into the red fire as it slowly died outside the cave mouth. In the middle of the night, when I heard Andrew moving about, I went rigid with fear; but he came and lay down beside me and put his arms round me and whispered, "Oh, Robert, I'm sorry, I'm sorry! You're only little and you didn't have a chance."

I was only relieved that he wasn't going to punish me any more. I was clenching my teeth so as not to sob, and so I couldn't say anything. I was too bewildered, anyway, to know what to say.

"In the morning I'll carry you back," he whispered hoarsely, as if he was trying not to cry too. "You can ride on my shoulders, and Ngari will clear a path with his *parang* so that you won't run into any thorns or creepers, Robert. And you can have Hantu Ijau now. I want you to have him. You can always have him."

Hantu Ijau—meaning Green Ghost—was his snake, which he absolutely adored, though I only pretended to like it. As soon as I realized Andrew was really sorry, I began to feel sorry for him. He'd done something cruel and wicked and now he couldn't sleep he was so sorry. Pity made its usual swift conquest of my other emotions, and I was so grateful, anyway, that he was my friend again that I succumbed easily to his demonstrative remorse.

"I'll have Hantu Ijau for three days and three nights," I said. "Then he'll be yours again because he likes you best."

"Does it hurt frightfully?" he asked after a while.

"A bit," I admitted, rigid with the pain, but remembering with uncalled-for remorse that I'd hurt him too. "How about yours, Andrew?"

"Mine's nothing," he said quickly. At sixteen a boy's mental and psychological age vacillates a good deal, I suppose. That midnight Andrew was hardly older than I, frightened by what he'd done in a momentary madness, longing to propitiate his victim and be forgiven. But after a short sigh he became silent—re-emerging from childhood, I think. Only a couple of minutes later he fell easily asleep, one arm still round me, while I lay in agony but grateful for his company and sympathy, already forgetting some of the vicious cruelty of his attack.

It all flashed brilliantly through my mind again, revived by the child Angela's freakish remark about Andrew's broken elbow and Sophie's bruised elbow caused by his impatient push. The whole love-hate and dread-devotion of my weeks as Andrew's companion at Sungei Sunyi seventeen years earlier were brought into close focus again, and I stared over the roof of the car out across the blue roads crowded with ships at anchor and I felt closer to the man I was hunting. . . .

Rousing myself, I asked Sophie, "And that was the last time you saw him?"

"Yes." A little sigh. "He went away in the night with Mr. Lyle."

I asked who Mr. Lyle was, but she shook her head. "We never saw him, Angela and I. He came that night when we'd gone to bed. But I woke up, and there was a car starting, and I heard Daddy say, 'Well, good-bye, Andrew. And good-bye, Mr. Lyle; it's nice to have met you. Look after Mr. Lyle, won't you, Andrew?' And the car went off, and Uncle Andrew hadn't kissed me good-bye or even good night."

I knew all about it, the desolation Andrew could inspire with his displeasure. He made you feel so unworthy. He'd even said to me once, "You're like all the rest. You aren't really my friend, young Robert. I suppose I won't ever find a real friend. You all let me down." Little noodle that I was, that sentimental whine of egomania had evoked nothing but another gush of my ready ten-year-old pity and I'd thought it horribly sad that a fine person like Andrew should never find a friend worthy of him and always be lonely.

It would have been interesting to exchange recollections with Nona Nicolas on the subject.

Then Sophie asked me about the bruise round my eye and the deep wire scratch down my right cheek. I told her I'd run into a fence in the dark, which was true enough. It was a reminder that there was an enemy who couldn't be very far away, and I had a sudden cold sensation of being watched. Hurriedly I said good-bye to the little girls, as if I'd become aware of a dangerous contagion about me and didn't want to expose them to further risk. Already they were threatened, weren't they? for my enemy was apparently the enemy of everyone who sought the truth about Andrew's disappearance, which Marcos Aragon claimed to have discovered already.

As soon as I reached the post-office steps I felt forced to swing round and look about me. There was nothing abnormal to be seen, of course. What had I expected to see? A prowler leaping on my back with upraised stiletto? There were two yellow blurs in the back of the Buick and the smart Boyanese *sais* quickly stubbing out his cigarette and leaving the two other chauffeurs he'd been chatting with; he'd seen Marcos Aragon, in panama hat and Palm Beach suit, coming out of the Bank of China building.

I had the feeling that Sophie had told me something of

value, but it was going round in my head like a bone in a mouthful of fish, for the moment defying isolation and extraction.

4

The wider Zella opened her dramatic eyes, the lower I pitched the key of my narrative. "So then it was just a matter of waiting," I concluded, "until the level fell and the current slackened enough for me to swim against it out of the tunnel. I managed it at the fourth try, and a policeman heard me shouting and brought along a man with a ladder, and I climbed out of the drain around four o'clock. I still haven't slept—do I look like hell?"

"*Dar*ling! But you must feel like the K of D!" Zella uses initials rather a lot.

"I do feel a little like the kiss of death, but I asked what I look like."

"Well, compared with what I'd expect, you look like the L and S of the P."

"That's fine, then. Zella, it's good to see you across a table again."

She smiled her absent-minded smile, with her greeny-grey eyes still brooding a little over the story of my ordeal. It had been good to have somebody to tell it to, and though I'd started with the intention of leaving out the element of foul play, by the time I reached the point where I fell into the drain I kept to the facts. Now, after giving her sole Walewska a few moments' attention, she looked up and said in a lowered voice, "I suppose it's no good asking whether you're in the Secret Service now, because if you were you'd still say you weren't anyway."

"Well, I'm not, Zella," I said.

"That's what I mean." She sighed. She's no birdbrain, really, but she puts on the act now and then. "And this about Andrew Avery, too, and looking over your shoulder all the time. So C-and-D, I mean."

I got that after a blink. "It's not cloak and it's not dagger, my dear, but it's not fun and games, either."

"You're not the type, anyway, so if you are I think it's a great mistake," she declared obscurely. She was wearing a rather prim dress of darkly shaded peacock green, but she didn't look at all prim in it. She's not a prim shape. "Now Andrew Avery *was* rather the C-and-D type, wasn't he?"

"I never met him, except when we were kids," I told her, but that was yet another possible line on his disappearance, I supposed. The two or three espionage agents I'd come across had seemed pretty unbalanced and unaccountable. "Now listen, Zella. I need to find every detail I possibly can about Andrew." And then I told her why.

It was rather gratifying to make yet another profound impression on her. She dropped her fork on hearing the figure of Aunt Julia's estate and became deadly serious.

"But, Robert, I can't tell you anything that'll help. I'm so awfully sorry." She stared tragically across the table and said, "I slapped his face once."

The waiter poured her another glass of Niersteiner. "Why, was he taking too much for granted?" I asked her.

"Oh, no. I saw him being a bastard in the Tanglin Club one night—before I ever met you. There was a young boy there, a new one or a substitute, and first of all he brought Andrew the wrong order and then he brought the right one and spilt half of it over him. It was only a *stengah*, nothing to stain. Well, Andrew took the rest of the glass and threw it over the boy and shouted, 'Now get me another!' So I went across and hauled the best slap I could right across his face."

I could see her doing it, too.

"I got a small round of applause," she said, seeing my grin. "Well, your handsome cousin—he was better-looking than you, Robert, except for the eyes; they were just about identical—he glared at me for a second and then he stood up and said, 'You're quite right. Thank-you!' When the boy came back he smiled and said, '*Jangan marah*,' and said it—well so exactly *right* that the boy grinned and the whole situation cleared. I admired him for that."

But, of course, that was Andrew all over, the familiar flash of charm and generosity that never deserved to get away with the preceding meanness, but usually did. "Was that the only time you met him?" I asked her.

"No, darling, it was the start of a beautiful friendship. He thought so, anyway. I went to a couple of parties with him and came here dancing once or twice."

I didn't care for the idea of Andrew's having preceded me in the list of Zella's friendships. Just a bit resentfully I said, "You never mentioned him to me before."

"But I did," she contradicted. "I asked you once if you were anything to do with Andrew Avery and you said, 'Nothing at all,' with your schoolmaster expression, so I said no more. Anyway, I didn't approve of him either."

"No?"

"He sulked," she said, "and his ego was always getting in the way. Andrew was no good to anybody who hadn't plenty of patience and—well, awe. You had to be awed by him; that's what he wanted, and I'm not much good at awe. So it never came to anything."

That was better. I asked her, "When was this?"

"Nearly a year before I met you. He'd got a job as security officer on an estate up in Johore, but he seemed to take a good deal of time off."

"He left that job under a bit of a cloud, so I heard," I told her. "Aunt Julia had to sign a sizable check."

"I think it was debts with small Chinese shopkeepers. No, not debts. He used to get them to cash checks that bounced. Quite small checks; but that made it dirtier, the small checks and the small shopkeepers."

"D'you know where he went then?"

"North Borneo. Sandakan, I think."

I knew that already. "And that was the last you heard of him?"

"The last I saw of him. I heard a little more of him a long time after from his wife."

"You met his wife?"

"She'd come over from Borneo for a hospital checkup—a little actress who'd toured with a company in Korea and Hong Kong and the Federation. I heard they got married a fortnight after they met."

"Was she so good at awe, then?"

"No, I believe it was a real love story," Zella said. "She was a nice little thing, I thought—desperately in love, though this was three or four years after the marriage, only just over a year ago. She told me that Andrew led a very quiet life nowadays. His former friends would hardly know him, she thought. I think she might have been rather easily fooled."

"Would Andrew have been any good for her, though?" I respected Zella's judgment and wanted to know what she thought.

"Oh, I think so. She'd been a bit of a waif, I should say, and if he really loved her I expect it was wonderful."

"Surely what Andrew needed was somebody to stand up to him," I argued.

"But Robert, you aren't thinking of Andrew and what he needed. You're thinking of the girl." She smiled indulgently.

"The same old Robert, always looking for someone to agonize over!"

"You said 'a nice little thing.' That sounds pretty vulnerable."

She watched the blue flames flickering over her *rognons flambés*. "But isn't that sort of happiness awfully brittle, anyway?"

"What sort of happiness, Zella?"

"The love-story sort. That's what she had. Perhaps they both had it."

"You don't know how it ended?"

"No, but I can guess."

What she guessed was obvious, and I knew enough to realize that her guess had been proved right enough. I changed the subject. "What would you know about a fellow called Marcos Aragon?"

She frowned. "Aragon? You don't suppose I have dealings with *him!*"

"What sort of dealings?"

"And don't you, either."

"What sort of dealings?"

"Only one sort that matters, though he seems to import and export a little."

"Zella, *what* sort?"

"The twenty-five-per-cent sort, of course."

"You mean he's a moneylender?"

"What else, darling!"

I thought about that a bit. Well, Andrew had been no stranger to moneylenders, from what we'd heard.

"I had the idea he was a respectable coffee merchant."

"He *is* a respectable coffee merchant. A respectable family man, too, with a wife and eleven children out at Katong. But a very busy bloodsucker as well, darling."

"Did Andrew know him?"

"That wouldn't surprise me at all."

I said, "It's six children, not eleven. Are you sure you got the rest right?"

"You know him, do you?"

"He claims to know what's happened to Andrew."

"But isn't telling?"

"It would cost too much."

"I expect he does know. I believe he hasn't many clients, but he keeps them. He sticks around, like all bloodsuckers that know their business."

"His children are charming," I said. "The younger ones, anyway."

"He's charming himself, they say." Silence then, until she asked me where I was staying. I told her and she exclaimed, "Not that house of ill fame that was your HQ when I first met you!"

"The same," I admitted.

"But Robert, why on earth?"

"What did you expect me to do? Take a suite in this place?"

She said lightly, "There's a perfectly good bed and bath at my place."

That wasn't so easy. I drank the rest of my wine to postpone the answer a little. This wasn't playtime. Zella was as exciting as ever, and I knew her better than to be nervous of getting involved any deeper or longer than I felt inclined for; but this wasn't playtime.

"And a foam mattress," she added demurely, and we both laughed. I claim the credit for the discovery that on the hottest tropical nights a latex foam mattress, set on the bathroom floor under a gently sprinkling shower, makes for comfort if not for luxury. Actually my most vivid memory-picture of Zella across the years had been of her flooded eyes and drop-let-spangled hair and little sparkling runnels along all the concavities of her body.

She'd made it more difficult.

"Zella, I'm off to Jakarta tomorrow, I hope. Besides," I added, "after last night I'm obviously not very healthy to know."

That was honest enough. I felt the contagion about me again, the moment of apprehension that had put an end to my conversation with the little Aragon girls. I had no right to go to Zella's flat, because I was a wanted man; somebody wanted my blood, and I could have no hand in turning Zella's place into a possible rendezvous for murder. There was more than one reason why the temptation of the offer had to be resisted, but that was the chief of them.

"Well, come and stay when you've settled your business," she suggested, taking my answer easily.

As I said before, Zella was strictly for playtime. You couldn't cast her for melodrama. In the presence of any serious purpose or responsibility she'd be only a distraction and in a situation of risk or danger a definite hindrance. She knew it, too. I said, "Good, when I'm free again we'll have a little holiday, eh?"

That would be fun, she agreed, choosing a slice of pineapple for dessert. I decided on a slice of Gruyère and told her Nona Avery was in Singapore but I couldn't find out where she was staying.

"Do you know what I think?" she said in answer to that. "I think Andrew Avery's in Singapore too."

I gave her a blink and a stare. She often talked wildly and waywardly for effect, but she understood now that my business was serious; she couldn't have said it idly.

She went on, "There's more than one way of disappearing. You believe that he's been put out of the way, that somebody murdered him and when the murderer saw your ad in the *Straits Times* he tried to put you out of the way as well, to stop you finding out what had happened to Andrew. But people can disappear on purpose. If the police are after them, or even creditors, they sometimes go underground. Andrew could have gone underground. If he had, and you came out here hunting for him, he'd—"

"Try to murder me?" I cut in sceptically.

"Well, suppose that's why he went underground? Suppose he'd murdered somebody already? Wouldn't it be worth another murder to stop it coming out?"

"And the fellow who shoved me into the drain was Andrew disguised as a Chinese?"

She came back with, "Oh, Robert, as if you couldn't hire a killer in Singapore for a hundred dollars! You never imagined that Chinese was the one who wants you out of the way, now did you?"

We were silent as the waiter served us with the fruit and cheese. His sober, conventional presence showed up the melodramatic colour of the conversation he had interrupted. When he'd gone I said, "There are plenty of ways of explaining Andrew's disappearance. He may have committed suicide; he may be in Mexico City; he may be hiding because he's got one of those horrible tropical diseases like leprosy or elephantiasis; he may be in prison; he may be in a madhouse— even seventeen years ago, up at Sungei Sunyi, he had some pretty unbalanced moments; he may have gone native somewhere with a dusky bride, or two dusky brides. No need to drag in murder as the explanation."

I expected a swift comeback from Zella, because if any of those was the explanation why should my letters be stolen and my life endangered when I tried to dig up the facts? But instead she asked, "Was it at Sungei Sunyi you stayed with Andrew when you were boys?"

"Yes. It's a rubber estate up in Perak, fifteen miles from—"

"I know. The manager's staying in this hotel. Sam Chester. I expect you met him back in fifty-one."

I told her I had once met the manager of Sungei Sunyi in fifty-one, but his name hadn't been Chester.

"Of course not. Sam was somewhere in Pahang then. He's only been six months at Sungei Sunyi." She put down her fork with sudden animation. "Let's see if they're having lunch. We could have coffee with them. Sam's such fun, and Winnie's a scream."

I got it. Sam Chester was such fun, and I hadn't been fun. I'd bored her with my melodrama, and she was clutching at a possible way out.

Well, the lunch hadn't been so much fun for me, either. I knew I hadn't amused Zella, that I'd been a disappointment. I was ready enough to fall in with her suggestion. When I'd paid the bill we went along to the hotel dining room, and as soon as we were through the door Zella called a greeting and a heavy man with an auburn beard slapped two great hands on his table and lumbered to his feet.

"Nicely timed, Zella!" his deep voice boomed out. "Hadn't the nerve to order a brandy with Winnie looking her usual daggers across the table. Now let her try to stop me!"

Zella laughed, her spirits rising fast, and introduced me to the Chesters. Hearing my name, Sam Chester frowned and boomed, "Avery? Now where was I hearing that name just the other day?"

"My Uncle Matthew planted some of the trees you're tapping up at Sungei Sunyi," I told him. "He was manager there from thirty-six until the Japs came."

"Ah! Must've seen it in the books," he said. I'd never heard a deeper voice. It seemed to vibrate along the ground under your feet, the way pedal notes on an organ do. His light blue eyes were guileless, and there was a sturdy, wholesome look about him, reminding me of the sea-captain hero of a boy's adventure book.

Zella had sat down beside his wife, kissing her first. The two women made a sharply contrasted pair. Like her husband, Winnie Chester was in her fifties, and, unlike Zella, she was not greatly interested in her appearance. She made most of her clothes herself, Zella told me afterwards, and must certainly have made her costume for that day, a salmon-pink dress with a gigantic pattern, giving her the look of a refugee who had been fitted out with the first garment that came to hand from a relief shipment of cast-off clothing. Roominess was its chief merit. Both material and pattern suggested upholstery rather than a covering for the human form.

You couldn't help noticing the dress first, but her face, when you got round to it, made you forget the dress. I suppose all that it's necessary to say is that Winnie Chester was a good woman and you could tell it at a glance. Her calm face had the pink, scrubbed look of so many elderly nuns. Through her glasses her blue eyes were bright with humour and sharp with a shrewd knowledge of the world, but candid and generous.

Zella had a healthily balanced crowd of friends, so it didn't surprise me to find her on affectionate terms with this unsophisticated pair. She was telling them now, "You ought to invite Robert up to Sungei Sunyi. He was there before, when he was a boy."

I was invited on the spot. "Drive back with us the end of the week," Chester suggested, and his wife beamed a welcome. "We don't get so many visitors up there," she said.

"Singapore folk think it takes a hero to venture up our valley."

"Two incidents in the past fourteen months," Chester boasted. "One feller killed in an ambush, and a security guard wounded, that's all. Both before our time. Yet Zella's sure she'd get ambushed, shot up, raped, and—"

"Sam!"

"I was telling him what Zella thinks, dear, not what I think," the big planter boomed defensively, but his wife's glance insisted on a change of subject. She didn't join us in a Rémy Martin afterwards, and Chester turned to me with a confidential air. "If you're coming to stay with us you'd better know that my wife's a little unbalanced on certain subjects. It comes from her being a deserter from the Salvation Army and making up her mind she saved my life when I was dying of alcoholism. All that means is that the first time she ever saw me I was tight."

"In the gutter in Scotland Road, Liverpool," his wife put in calmly.

Their patter seemed to me a weak kind of a joke, but I listened on with a grin. Afterwards I learned from Zella that there'd been very little exaggeration in their story as they told it.

On his last leave, two years earlier, Sam Chester had walked out of a Liverpool hospital, without being discharged, on the same day he'd undergone a minor operation on his elbow. Within half an hour, just as the pubs were opening, he'd met the first engineer of the cargo boat on which he'd sailed home from Singapore, and they celebrated the meeting with a whisky Alice—several whisky Alices, in fact. Five hours after his operation the anaesthetic was still hanging about Chester's system, and it went into ready partnership with the whisky Alices, boosting their kick considerably. Nobody would ever know how Chester got separated from the first engineer, whose Greenock accent had become a barrier to communication anyway, after the third whisky Alice, or how he found his way into Scotland Road. He was observed there, out like a light in the gutter, by Adjutant Winnie Henderson and Ensign Lillian Appleyard on patrol down what some-body—who cannot have been familiar with the West End of London—had called the wickedest street in England.

Though it was usually drunks who provoked the occasions when these two officers went into action, a drunk resting in the gutter and inconveniencing nobody was not properly a target for their intervention. The sort of operation at which Adjutant Henderson excelled was the management of a fight-ing drunk whose wife had yelled for help. There was nobody in the North of England smarter than Winnie Henderson at throwing a two-hundred-pound drunk flat on a bed and truss-ing him to it with the clothesline, secured by three knots fit to dazzle any Boy Scout examiner. But the big, handsome sea-faring man, as she thought, unconscious in the gutter, with a damp wind riffling his fine beard, roused a curiously sharp concern in the adjutant's breast, and, after passing him, she went back and looked again.

It was for the police, not her, to remove him, but, perhaps to Ensign Appleyard's surprise, she called up a taxi, for which she paid herself, and directed it not to the police station but to the Salvation Army shelter, where Sam Chester woke, thir-teen hours later, to see a woman in a hallelujah bonnet and glasses bending over him—so that each had seen the other for the first time in what neither could possibly think of as ro-mantic circumstances. But it was love at first sight, for all that.

When he was ready to leave she asked for half a crown for taxi fare and a contribution to Army funds. He gave her ten pounds. She then begged him to mobilize more resolution

against the temptation of alcohol and tried to hide her disbe-
lief when he told her he got drunk, on an average, three times
a year. Then he told her about his operation the previous day,
and when she asked whether it wasn't still painful he answered
yes, it was damned painful, and then blushed as he apologized.
She prevailed on him to return to the hospital, where it was
found that his fall into the Scotland Road gutter had undone
the work of the operation, necessitating another one, this time
more elaborate.

Learning that he had no friends in Liverpool, she came to
see him during visitors' hour next day, and there could have
been significance in the fact that she wore mufti. Chester had
already, in the slow, dreamy emergence from the anaesthetic,
found himself thinking of her as a woman—to reprove himself sharply later, since he had the idea that Sally Army lasses
were, like nuns, vowed to chastity and lifelong service. He
learned better three days later when, waiting for the London
train, he strolled along to a pub for a slow pint. He'd got the
saloon bar door open when a soft but firm hand was laid on
his arm and he turned to meet soft but firm blue eyes directed
deep into his own through sparkling spectacles under the
arch of a hallelujah bonnet.

"I'm just going to have a cup of coffee, Mr. Chester," she
said. "Come with me."

He went, a little sheepish and mum. Over their coffee in
the station canteen she kept up a flow of conversation, mostly
military shop-talk, to which he paid only vague attention until
he caught the name Colonel Mrs. Holloway.

"What's that?" he cut in then. "D'you mean you have married colonels in your outfit? Married *women* officers?"

As soon as she put him right he showed a good deal more
animation and worked round to an inquiry as to whether the
Army's officers were ever allowed to resign their commissions.

His train left twenty minutes after that, but he wasn't on it. They were married the following month, and on the boat out to Malaya he taught her to fox trot. How far Winnie really believed that in marrying him she was saving him from the moral and physical disintegration of alcoholism, that she was more or less concentrating her career of rescue upon a single sinner, nobody knew. Nobody could doubt that they were happy.

"Well, Mr. Avery, will you come?" Winnie was asking. "Which was your old room? You could have it again."

I told her, "The one with two west-looking windows and a little ru tree outside." I was finding myself quite strongly drawn back to that lonely valley.

"It's not such a little tree now," she said. "Come and see."

I was strongly tempted. All through my eighteen months' soldiering in the Federation I'd hankered after a return to Sungei Sunyi, but when I met the manager at the Ipoh Club one night I'd found him a dour old drunk who hadn't shown any sign of extending the invitation I'd hoped for.

"Well, if you feel like coming back with us," she said, "just give us a ring tomorrow night."

"And don't let Zella put you off," Chester cut in. "Far more murder and sudden death here in Singapore than anywhere around our place."

Zella's eyes met mine.

I remembered something. "Before I forget," I said to Zella, with a glance of apology to the Chesters, "would you know anything about a man called Lyle?"

"Lyle." No, it was evident that the name of the man who'd been at Marcos Aragon's house with Andrew a year ago meant nothing to her. "No, I've never heard that name out here."

"But I have," Chester said slowly, frowning, his fingers tugging at his beard. "Not so long ago, either. Winnie, what was it we heard about a feller called Lyle? Or was it somebody we met?"

But Winnie hadn't the faintest recollection. "When you drink that stuff, Bob," she said, eyeing the balloon glass in his hand, "there's no saying what you'll fancy. I'm sure I've never heard of anybody called Lyle—except the brigadier in Newcastle, of course."

I felt pretty sure that it wouldn't have been a senior officer of the Salvation Army who'd paid that midnight visit to Aragon. Chester was fixing his wife with a mild, expostulatory gaze. "I tell you, Winnie, I've come across that name in the past couple of months, I'll swear it." He turned to me. "Who is he, this feller?"

"Somebody I need a talk with badly," I told him. "His name's almost the only thing I know about him."

Through the fog-belt of mystery surrounding Andrew, this slender lead came like a faint blink of light. Chester was living in one of Andrew's childhood homes, and Chester had heard something of a man called Lyle. It was a sadly weak signal, but in that dark, suffocating fog it offered at least an illusion that I wasn't totally lost, and it was then that the intuition first came to me, like a whisper, that the answers to my questions could best be sought at Sungei Sunyi.

5

Bah Feng and I faced each other uneasily across his desk. I said nothing as I held out my hand for my key, angry and ashamed of myself. Without a word he handed over the key and with it a small slip of paper. I unfolded it at once.

Message from General Hospital for Mr. Avery. Received
1:40. Miss Nicolas asking for you in Ward D2.

My watch showed three-thirty. Fifteen minutes later I
pushed open the Shanghai doors of the private Ward D2 as
soon as a murmur answered my knock. Nona Nicolas, looking
as if she were dying, didn't smile as she saw me. She stared at
me for a long moment, and I fancied she was wishing after all
that I hadn't come.

I didn't know what to say. For a while we looked at each
other in silence. There was no make-up on her pale face, and
her hair was dank, as if she'd just come in from a swim. I had
remembered her as beautiful; seeing her now, like this, was a
shock.

I said, "I was out when your message came."

She looked up at me in a deep, troubled silence.

"I didn't want to ask the sister what was wrong," I said
then. "What is it?"

She spoke at last. "I had an accident."

Abruptly then, her eyes turned to the Shanghai door.
Under it, in the corridor outside, I could see a pair of male
feet in tan brogues, and the bottoms of dark grey flannels.
Her terror was almost a separate presence, laying a cold hand
on me.

I went to the door and opened it. Outside a well-dressed
Chinese stood looking up the corridor. As he turned to meet
my curious eyes a stout and flustered Chinese woman carrying a bunch of clove carnations appeared round the corner he
had been watching. She exclaimed in English, "I lost myself.
Do not leave me alone in this place. So many collidors."

Back at the bedside I said to Nona Nicolas, "Just a Chinese
couple visiting a patient." And I added, "Thank you for asking me to come."

She avoided my eyes and said, "I got into a panic. The friend I'm staying with is going to have a baby next month. I didn't want her to come because I'd upset her. There was nobody but you to send for."

I asked how she'd known where to find me.

"At the Indonesian Consulate your name is next to mine in Mr. Asinola's book. I saw it, with 'Sultan Mustafa Hotel' written underneath."

"I'm glad you realized you could trust me. I was afraid you didn't."

"I don't know . . ." She had shut up again like a shell, as if I'd said something to revive her mistrust. Her hands were outside the sheet, folded together beneath her chin but alive with little restless stirrings. On an impulse I sat on the bed, took her hands, and held them in my own right hand.

"Now, listen," I said. "You sent for me, and here I am. Tell me what it's about. What sort of accident?"

Her eyes were lovely still. They seemed to be asking a question and yearning for an answer, but I couldn't read her signal. I saw her breasts move under the sheet as she took a deep breath, and then she started to tell me in short, exhausted sentences.

"I've been staying at Kuala Pecha, up on the Johore Straits. My friend's house isn't right on the sea, but her neighbours have a beach along the end of their garden, and I've been bathing from there. I sleep very badly and I'm always awake before sunrise. The last three mornings I've been in swimming while the sun rose—it's lovely then. Only this morning there was a speedboat roaring about, one of those things that spin along the surface with their noses in the air and sounding like a factory. It spoiled everything, so I decided after I'd been in for three or four minutes to give up the swim. As soon as I turned back towards the shore it—it came for me."

Her hands were cold and damp, and all the time they tensed and untensed as if her body were racked with pain. She swallowed hard, like someone confessing a crime, and went on. "There was a man in the boat, very sunburnt, wearing black sunglasses. The thing came straight at me, and I threw up my hand to warn him, but he came on. The sun was only just up, and he was heading right into it. I thought at first he must be blinded by it, but he was wearing those dark glasses. I was slow. I didn't believe it possible until it was almost on me, and even then I was paralysed for a second or two before I dived. Then I was too late."

"You mean, you were hit."

"My shoulder—"

"But surely," I cut in, "surely if one of those things hit anything your size at full speed it would break up. Just a graze, you mean?"

She had closed her eyes, as if I'd been shouting at her. "The boat didn't hit me. The man had a sort of long club, like an oar. I suppose he aimed at my head, but it just caught the point of my shoulder. I went under and swallowed a lot of water. When I got hold of myself and started swimming for the beach again I heard the boat coming back, roaring. . . ."

I said, "Take it easy," because under the sheet her whole body had begun to shake.

But when she spoke again her voice had risen sharply, as if she were on the point of bursting into tears, or even hysterics. "And then I thought I was going to be killed and I dived, but too soon and I hadn't taken a deep enough breath. I had to come up after a few seconds, I had to, and I knew I should come up right in front of the boat. But when I surfaced the boat had swung out to sea, and I saw Harry and

Christina on the beach. I'd told them how good a sunrise swim was, and they'd got up early to join me, and the man in the speedboat had seen them and sheared off."

I looked down at her, and the helplessness of her went to my heart—I can't think of any other way of saying it. There may have been a little truth in Zella's taunt that I'm always looking for somebody to agonize over; I don't know. But Nona Nicolas that day was a creature to move a Khrushchev or a Hitler to pity.

I made a mistake then. I said, "Listen, we're in this together. You nearly died this morning. I nearly died last night. We share an enemy, you see. So why don't we fight back together and start by sharing information? It may be our one chance."

She only turned away.

"I know you were Andrew's wife," I told her. "That's no secret any longer."

She was staring under the Shanghai door again. The wheels of a rattling trolley of medicines rolled along the corridor, followed by the white-shoed feet of an orderly. A long half-suppressed groan sounded from the second-class ward along the corridor. The locker by her bed was almost bare—not a flower, not a book, only a newspaper folded to show a headline; LOVERS' SUICIDE PACT: DEATH SLEEP IN LOCKED ROOM.

I didn't know whether she'd taken in what I'd just told her. "Last night somebody tried to murder *me*," I said. And I added, watching her face, "I believe you know who."

"No!" Her eyes flew open on the swift, sobbing denial.

"I don't mean the man in the boat; I mean the man who hired him."

"I don't know."

"But you suspect."

"*No!*"

"I can't help believing you do. You're *afraid* you know."

"No, no!" She had begun to cry, her face plain and hopeless and agonized.

"Nona, don't," I pleaded, desperately moved. "For God's sake, let me help you."

But she shook her head weakly and turned away from me as if I'd betrayed her. I saw a dusky flush, like a stain, below her ear—the edge of the contusion from the blow that had failed to murder her.

There is an instinctive gesture for a man who finds himself helpless to allay a woman's distress. I bent and kissed her. All I could think of to say was, "Tell me where to look for him, this man you're afraid of. Do you really not know?"

Like a child, she sobbed, "No, I really don't, but you won't believe me."

"Is his name Lyle?" I asked, because the name had just flashed through my mind.

In the middle of a sob she went silent, and under the sheet her body stiffened into rigidity—just for a second, just long enough for me to be sure the name had meaning for her. Then she was sobbing again, her head turning helplessly from side to side on the pillow.

The sort of toughness it would have taken to press the inquiry in face of her breakdown is something I haven't got. It would have been like pouring acid into a wound. So I stroked her fever-damp hair and said, "Listen, it's going to be all right. These things don't last forever. Nothing does."

Never mind how trite they were, the words brought her back from her lonely distance, at least, and she began to talk again.

"You don't understand how it is," she said painfully. "Afterwards I wondered why I had tried so hard to escape that boat."

Because I always think in pictures, a picture flashed on my mind's screen then of her body floating dead in the straits, the head broken, the lovely eyes shut. I went cold in the hot little ward and closed my own eyes, as if they had really seen it.

She said it again. "You don't understand how it is—clinging for days and weeks to a cliff edge, feeling the wind sucking you down. It's a dream, I know that; I know that the rest of you don't see what I see or fear what I fear, but that makes no difference. The dream goes on. It's like suffocating because you've forgotten how to breathe and nobody can help you to remember. Slowly, minute by minute and week by week, you suffocate."

"I know," I whispered. "I know." Of course I didn't, except in the sense that I realized she was trying to describe the dark path of what we used to call a nervous breakdown— I believe "acute anxiety state" is the up-to-date jargon for it. As I understand it, the condition amounts to a sort of forgetting how to live. Well, I had the heart and imagination to flinch from the pain and shudder at the danger she spoke of.

She went on, "You've seen those old pictures of dying people and their souls flying like angels away from their bodies. I feel like that, as if my soul, everything that's really me, is being torn out of my body. What I am is being stolen away all the time, till now I'm scarcely me any more, just something to suffer and be afraid and lonely."

Lost for words, I fumbled and said, "Diseases have to be incurable before we have a right to despair. The dream you're in can be cured; people are being set free from dreams as dreadful as yours all the time."

"Only by having their minds stripped and bled white," she said. I knew what she meant—the psychiatrist's probing into secrets she could never surrender. "That sort of doctor cuts off your head to cure a headache."

I thought it better to change the subject. "What did the police say?"

"There was a speedboat stolen yesterday," she said. "From one of the officers at the naval base."

"No idea who the fellow was?"

She shook her head and then told me, "I didn't tell the detective anything about—I let him think it was an accident. I didn't tell Harry or Christina, either. Only you."

When she saw in my eyes the suspicion that flashed through my mind she cried out in protest, "No, not what you're thinking! I've no more idea than you who can have set him onto me. Only—well, for an hour or two I almost went mad inside myself and I really wasn't sure *what* had happened. I was afraid they wouldn't believe me, and then I might not have been able to believe myself any more."

But she had known that I would believe her. That was something.

A long silence began then. Though I didn't realize it, a reaction from the ordeal of the night and the sleepless hours since it had passed had set in, bearing down on me like the roof of the water tunnel. Despair began to seep through me. I felt, helplessly, a fool. I was like a man who stopped his car on a main road through the Malayan jungle and struggled for a few yards into the crowded, living darkness that pressed up to the very roadside. All I knew was the way back. Forward there was only the certainty of losing myself. What was the good of hoping I could ever find a way through this?

And what was happening with me and this girl? My hand held her hands, and I was smoothing the damp hair from her white brow. If anybody looked in they'd think we were that way about each other.

The reflection startled me. A disturbing suspicion followed it closely, a suspicion I had to force myself to face squarely.

Well, that I had been moved by the nearness of suffering merely meant that I was not inhuman. That I was aware of the beauty of her eyes merely meant that I was human. I'd kissed her, yes; but when real help wasn't possible all you could offer was a gesture.

No, there was nothing in that. A big butterfly faltered past the window, dark against the blazing blue sky. I was thinking ahead, to the moment when I should leave the hospital and she would be alone again, listening for a murderer's footsteps, watching the space under the Shanghai door for his feet to halt and the door to inch open.

Would it be any good asking the police for a guard? Surely not. It was so obvious that she was mentally confused, and then she'd withheld the truth from the detective who'd interviewed her that morning. And would she confirm the story if I told it to the police now, anyway? I was ready to do guard duty myself, though I longed for sleep, but I could picture what the hospital authorities' reaction to that proposition would be.

She was staring into the grimness of my face, reading my thoughts, perhaps. I tried a smile, but it can't have been much of a success because she drew one of her hands away with a sudden little moan and held it over her eyes.

"For God's sake help me, Robert!" she whispered. "Tell me what to do."

A sensation of crisis shocked me out of my fatigue. The desperation of not knowing what to do, of being utterly without answer or resource, filled me with a crazy urge for violent action. I spoke her name helplessly, and in a moment I was kissing her cold lips and feeling her hands clasp behind my neck.

I suppose I didn't react at once to the alarm that seized her a moment or two after that. Until I opened my eyes I didn't see how her own were turned towards the door, wide with fear. And the door was swinging gently, as if it had just been softly released.

It took two or three seconds to free myself from her tightly clinging hands and get round the bed to the door. The corridor was empty, except for a pretty Chinese nurse carrying a large green poison bottle. I dashed down it towards the exit, but when I rounded the corner there was only another long corridor with several men patients in pyjamas in sight. Back again and past Ward D2 in the opposite direction. Round that corner I found myself on a balcony with women patients on long chairs and day-beds being visited by a tall European sister. Nobody else.

Uneasy at the thought of her left alone, I went back again. At the door, knocking gently, were a stout Indian doctor and a smallish, baldish man I liked the look of. We all went in together, and after some confusion Nona introduced me and the fellow with the high, bald brow to each other. He was Harry O'Neill, her friend's neighbour, who had taken her out of the sea, wounded and shock-shattered, that morning at sunrise.

He said to her, "Now Christina and I didn't like the idea of your staying alone in here, so I've persuaded Doctor Rajaratnam to sign your order of release on condition that we'll put you to bed and make you rest. Come home with me now. Mrs. Kerr isn't too well today, so you'll be better in with us." I remembered that Nona's friend was going to have a baby in a week or two; that must be the explanation of that last statement.

I was conscious of relief and release. O'Neill, with a house and a wife, could guarantee her the comfort and security she needed, though I realized almost at once that guarantee was a strong word to use with that other word, security. While a nurse helped Nona to dress, I had a word with him at the end of the corridor.

"You don't know me," I began, "and after you've listened to what I'm going to say you may suspect that I'm not all there. It's got to be said, though."

His thoughtful grey eyes studied my face as I spoke, and I realized how I must look to him, grey with exhaustion and anxiety, the barbed-wire cuts scoring my cheek and one eye blinking out of a big blue bruise—looking as unbalanced as what I was going to say would sound, in fact. But that couldn't be helped.

But when I'd told him all of it that was good for him to know, he merely nodded. "Well, I can't put a twenty-four-hour guard on her," he said, "but she'll have an upper-floor bedroom because our place isn't a bungalow, and we've got a good noisy dog."

I liked the sound of that dog. "And tomorrow or next day I hope I'll have a move fixed up for her," I told him.

He said uncertainly then, "Er—we don't know Nona very well, of course. You're her fiancé, I take it."

I almost exclaimed, "Good God, no!" Before I got it out he saw my face and said, "Sorry, I'm not in the picture. Well, never you mind; my wife'll take good care of her. We could see she wasn't awfully well, even before that scare this morning. Quite honestly, I don't know what to make of what you've told me. It doesn't—" But Nona came out of the ward then, pale and with her arm in a sling. We both went forward to help her, but it was my arm she clung to.

O'Neill was just right, acting as if there were no undercurrents to the situation. As I helped her into his car, a Ford convertible, he was saying to her, "Christina'll have a cup of tea ready for you. Just one short call to make in town, and we'll be on our way. Should catch the sunset over the straits."

It was a load off my mind. She smiled, her first smile that day, as the car moved off. Her left hand rose, and she waved to me with her fingers and smiled, a pale little actress giving a gallant performance as a woman with few cares in the world. She deserved to get through this, I thought.

I stood watching the tan and cream Ford out of sight, almost getting run down by the black MG that started with a whoosh of acceleration behind me. When it caught up with the Ford it slowed and followed it, keeping close.

I hadn't seen the driver's face.

6

I yawned like a chasm as I took my key from Bah Feng's bony hand, standing a couple of seconds longer at his desk before the climb up to the second floor. Just as I was moving away a postman came in and threw a pile of letters on the porter's desk.

Before Bah Feng's hand could reach them, I had scooped them up.

"Any for me, I wonder?" I shot a glance at his rigid face as I said that. There were three.

Up in my room I opened the one with the Indonesian stamp first. It was from a friend of Bay's in our embassy at Jakarta, telling me that the Indonesian police authorities declared they had no record of an Englishman named Andrew Eldon Avery. The second had a Singapore stamp and contained a letter that ended in a rococo signature in pale blue ink.

Dear Mr. Avery,

Although you have rejected my services I am offering you a useful piece of information gratis.

It is that already your investigating methods have engaged the attention of a certain deeply interested party. I am afraid you may find the warning theatrical, but I be-

lieve it to be a fact that as a consequence of this your life
is threatened.

I do not ask you to believe me if you decide that this
information is as unacceptable as my assurance that without my help you stand no chance of discovering what has
happened to your cousin. What I do ask is that you will
destroy this note when you have read it and also, if you
should be incautious enough to negotiate with any other
party who may claim to be able to help you then you
will have the goodness not to mention my name.

Yours sincerely,<br>
Marcos Aragon.

If I hadn't been so dog-tired I might have laughed. Old
Auntie Aragon, sitting so smugly on the information I hadn't
found my own way to yet, dropping stale warnings of a danger I'd collided with head-on already! Was *he* as effectively on
guard as he imagined, with his requests for the letter to be
burned and his name not mentioned? If I hadn't happened to
be standing downstairs as the postman arrived, his letter would
already be on its way to the man Bah Feng feared and served,
the man Aragon called "a certain deeply interested party."

There was a Penang stamp on the third letter. The inex-
pertly typed sheet carried the printed heading, "MOHAMMED
KHAN, General Merchant, 15 Alor Star Street, Penang." The
first line was promising.

Dear Sir,

Your advertisement in the *Straits Times* I have seen and
hoping you will come to my assistance. Is owing me $125
Mr. Andrew Avery. Three cheques I cash for him, one
okay but two not any good unfortunately. I am very
happy to hear from you. Till now not successful to find
Mr. Andrew Avery's family. Two letters I sent to Mr.
Lail but not getting any reply unfortunately. Your

brother's cheques one $100 and one $25 can be seen here for your inspection.

Awaiting your kind reply and settlement of same in order to clear family name and Englishman's word of Honour.

Yours faithfully, Sir,<br>Mohammed Khan.

I stared a long time at the letter after I'd read it. Certainly Mohammed Khan would get his $125. There was a sick disgust at the revelation of Andrew's dirty little thefts from small shopkeepers who hadn't liked to refuse someone who looked so sound and seemed so friendly. How many more were there, I wondered, of these humble Asians whose trust had been cynically exploited by a man whose greed was more important to him than decency?

But the letter's arresting line was the reference to "Mr. Lail." That was the way most Asians would spell "Lyle" phonetically, so it was Lyle again. Mohammed Khan had known something which persuaded him that there was a likelihood, or at least a chance, that Lyle would help in some way to get one of Andrew's debts settled—if only to the extent of putting him in touch with Andrew's family.

I tried to decide whether this Pakistani merchant wrote of Andrew as no longer living or merely untraced. I reread the letter. The weak English blurred the meaning here and there. I came to the only useful conclusion—that I would have to meet Mohammed Khan very soon, and not only to pay a debt.

His letter reminded me that I had still forgotten to order the reinsertion of my advertisement in the local papers. If I didn't telephone now, before I slept, it was going to be forgotten again. The two chief Singapore dailies lay on the chair by my bed, their headlines—LOVERS DIE TOGETHER IN SUICIDE PACT and THREATENED LOVERS' DEATH SLEEP—reminding me that there were others who couldn't see a way ahead. I thought of Nona Nicolas and hoped to God she wasn't having to fight the temptation to take that way out.

With the papers' phone numbers noted on the back of Aragon's envelope, I went wearily down the stairs and along to the black hole where the telephone lurked beside the side door giving onto a narrow, smelly alleyway. I had started to dial the first number when everything ceased, all sensation was cut off and there was only an empty blackness.

I didn't even feel the blow. . . .

7

When sensation came leaking back into my brain and body I found myself trying to remember the remaining digits of the number I had been dialling. There was a deep ache in my head and every part of me was damp with the sweat of a terrible heat, except my throat and tongue, which were parched as if a blowlamp had been played on them.

My eyes couldn't bear to open. There was a worse than hangover heaviness holding down their lids. When finally they opened, I found myself fixed by the stare of three unblinking eyes, two of them long and brown and strangely unreflecting, and the third perfectly round, the metal eye of a revolver muzzle.

The moment lasted a long time. I thought first of Nona Nicolas, remembering with relief that she was miles away in a friendly house, guarded by a noisy dog. By then I'd begun to study the brown, still Eurasian face to which the long, metallic eyes belonged, and I made out one of the reasons for the eyes' dangerous look. They were set in circles of pale flesh that contrasted sharply with the deep tan of cheeks and forehead, a sign that dark sunglasses or goggles always hid them out of doors and a reminder of the man who had tried to murder Nona Nicolas that morning.

He had rolled his tight, thin singlet up to his armpits as the Chinese do to cool their torsos, and his powerful, deeply tanned trunk glistened with sweat. The small room was like a furnace, though the closed glass window was so black with night that it reflected me lying on the wide double bed under the sick light of a naked bulb. I decided that this must be the top room of a house, immediately beneath a roof that had fried under twelve hours of unbroken tropical sunshine. With a swimming head I turned to look at the watch on my wrist. Past seven-thirty. So I'd been out for almost two hours.

It was a squalid little room, the walls streaked green with damp, a closed door behind the man with the gun and another smaller one opposite, open and leading into a dark bathroom, judging by the regular water drip that sounded in there, a torment to my parched throat. A pictorial calendar hung crookedly on the wall, with scarlet Chinese lettering and a photograph of a Chinese pin-up model who looked underrehearsed. It still showed the month of January. There was no fan and no furniture apart from the bed, the chair the man with the gun sat astride, and a small bamboo table.

From the table he had lifted a large mug. He drank from it greedily, noisily, his eyes never once blinking, and I raised my hands unconsciously in a gesture of entreaty. At that he took a second mug, a big aluminium one, from the table and handed it to me. With new strength I struggled up and propped myself against the bed-head, took the mug in both hands, and drank with my eyes closed. There must have been close to a pint of the stuff, but I drank it at one go, realizing as I finished that it had been the vilest coffee I'd ever tasted, and cold at that. But for the relief it brought to my tortured throat and mouth I sighed in gratitude as I handed back the mug.

The fellow with the gun took it in his left hand and looked into it before he set it back on the table. And for the first time his long eyes blinked. They blinked twice in their pale circles of untanned skin, and with returning alertness I saw that and thought about it. I thought and then I acted.

Moving one leg off the bed, I pointed towards the bathroom.

"I'll have to go in there," I said.

"If you like," he answered. "There's no window."

He didn't get off his chair as I staggered across the room and through the low doorway. No, there was no window in there, but that wasn't the escape I'd been thinking of. There was just the lavatory pan and a standing tiled tank of water under a dripping tap with a big brass dipper hanging on a nail above it. He didn't follow me in, and I was out of range of his long eyes as soon as I'd turned through the door.

After ten or twelve seconds I pulled the chain. The moment the clamour of the emptying cistern began, I bent over the pan and pushed my forefinger down my throat. Since schooldays I've been able to induce instant and profuse vomiting by that simple means. By the time the cistern ceased its uproar most if not all of the coffee had gone down the drain. After swiftly filling the dipper with water, I buried my lips in it and gulped down half a pint. What poison might be left in me would get heavily diluted that way, which might help.

Back on the bed I stared at the gunman, who was admiring the rich development of the muscle pad covering his stomach, playing the fingertips of his left hand up and down the tightly stretched brown skin. Unless I'd miscalculated, I'd just won myself an important advantage. If that disgusting coffee really had been doctored, either to drug me or to kill me, then I was a jump ahead of the fellow with the gun and the stomach muscles, because I didn't believe there could be much of the stuff left in my system now. What I had to try to account for, if the drug had been intended merely to put me under for a while, was the motive in keeping me alive, so far.

For removal elsewhere? Then what for? Questioning? But what could anybody want to extort from me that could make this melodramatic performance worth while? It was pretty certain that I knew nothing anybody could wish to get out of me by force. Then was I mistakenly believed to know something, and if so what? A few minutes' hard thinking with an aching head got me nowhere. Why not ask? I thought then.

"I don't get the idea of this," I said.

The long eyes, dark and without reflection, moved indolently over my face. "It is not necessary," the guard said.

Few believe any longer the theory about people of mixed blood inheriting only the baser qualities of their two races. The simpletons who cling to it could be enlightened by even a brief acquaintance with the Eurasian community in Singapore and its record. But of course, like other communities, it is disgraced by a minority of no-goods, and this was one of them.

"What comes next?" I asked, keeping it light and conversational.

He showed me a fine row of teeth in a bored sneer.

I was exhausted still. Even normal reverie went on only with a grinding effort. My clothes were drenched in sweat. I hadn't slept for nearly forty hours.

"Are you wise," I asked him then, "hanging around Singapore after this morning? D'you think the police are going to find it so tough laying their hands on a Eurasian with a deep tan, and white circles round his eyes from always wearing dark sun-goggles? A young Eurasian," I added, with a glance at the fingertips that caressed the thick swell of muscle above the right nipple, "with conspicuously fine physical development."

He listened to that. The fingertips trailed down the columns of stomach muscle and fell onto his knee. The show of indifference slipped.

"Of course," I went on, trying to sting him, "you aren't free to get out of town. You have to stay and take the chance, covering up for your boss. You couldn't be more expendable. If only you'd wake up you could . . . you could . . ."

My voice trailed away dreamily. I had forgotten what I'd been going to say. And my eyes had half closed.

But I saw him blink. The second time.

I roused myself to work out the significance of that mark of closer attention. The time I took to interpret it suggested the answer. He had noted the weary abandonment of an uncompleted sentence. It was the first sign of what he was waiting for.

I was supposed to lose consciousness as my system absorbed the drugged coffee. It was time for the performance to start.

Only it had already started. There was no need to put on a show of growing lassitude; already my mouth was wide in a deep, unconscious yawn. The frown of puzzlement as I closed my mouth with a snap was exactly in keeping, of course. I *was* drowsy, anyway. After two days and a night without sleep, even apart from the ordeal that had taken up the best part of that one night, there was nothing surprising in that— except that I was in a situation of danger and suspense that ought to have stimulated brain and nerve to intense excitement, never mind how long I'd been without sleep.

Clearly I hadn't got rid of as much of that coffee as I'd thought; or else the dose of the drug had been so gross that even a mouthful of the coffee was enough to put me under almost immediately, in my exhausted condition. For fifteen minutes I'd believed I had a secret initiative in hand, but now I could feel it slipping away from me and defeat closing round me like a net.

The sudden, heaving effort I made to rouse myself set a complicated rhythm of small movements across the youngster's breast muscles and down his massive right arm, raising the revolver till its muzzle stared at my panting chest. I had propped myself against the headboard again, and the mists of languor were dispersing.

I said, "I hope you've heard a figure put to what your boss stands to collect if this job comes off. But I suppose you'll settle for two or three thousand, when with the responsibility you're carrying you're a fool to take less than ten per cent— say sixty thousand dollars."

It was more with a view to keeping myself talking than making trouble between him and the boss I so desperately wanted to meet that I threw out the poisoned suggestion. I didn't suppose this lout would get more than two or three hundred for his night's work.

For several minutes I tried to convince myself that there was nothing unnatural about the fatigue that beat in waves across my brain and body. I was bloody tired and had good reason to be—was it any more than that? But finally I had to admit that, yes, there was more to it than that.

The young animal astride the chair slapped his shoulder and annihilated a mosquito that had been siphoning off a little of his rich blood. There hadn't been a moment in that room when he couldn't have finished me with almost as little trouble. Without the gun, without his right arm, he could have dealt with any bid for freedom I could have attempted. The mosquito had at least taken a bite out of that self-consciously shapely torso; I couldn't even have matched that.

Now I was sinking, sinking. The waves of fatigue were gongs, beating through my body like a tide in the blood. I was forgetting, I was fighting to hold on to memory and consciousness, but I was forgetting, memory was being torn to tatters and stripped away; the bed was spinning and my blood had accelerated, shooting through my veins to choke my heart.

Almost as soon as I began to wonder whether I was dying I became sure of it, but by then I was so weary that I reacted with only a remote pang of self-pity. After that I was no more than a ghost blown through blackness by the waves of sound from the great gongs.

# THREE

The return from nothingness was the slow, slow awareness of the moon. The setting moon appeared in the top left corner of the window and sank diagonally to the lower right corner. My eyes were open all the time, and it took me all those minutes to recover, bit by bit, the consciousness their dirty drug had stripped away from me. By the time the overripe orange moon rested in the lower corner of the window pane I was ready to take in my situation as well as my newly restored self.

I was still on the stale-smelling double bed in the hot, airless room. But most of my clothes had been removed, and there was something else. . . . Shock slowed down my perceptions again, and I swung back into dream for a while, but before the moon had left the window I knew it was no dream that I wasn't alone on the bed.

There was a warm, utterly still body close to mine. There was hair against my chin, a faint perfume. A woman. Nona.

When I moved I found that my right arm was under her. She was in my arms. The convulsive effort I had to make in order to sit up turned her over on her back but did not rouse her. She lay absolutely still in the hot moonlight. Most of her clothes had been taken off, too.

I stared round the room. The chair was heaped untidily with our clothes. The table had been moved to the bedside, and on it I saw a woman's handbag, my own passport, keys, and wallet, some loose money, two small empty bottles, and a folded newspaper. The newspaper explained it all; before I bent over its moonlit headlines I knew which one would be lying uppermost.

Well, it was a smart enough little scheme. X had wanted to get rid of me and he'd wanted to get rid of Nona. Two simple but clumsy attempts had failed separately, so he'd been faced with the necessity for a new, quick plan that would rouse no suspicion of foul play, two murders the police would never recognize as murders.

That day X must have been in top form. From two scraps of observation he'd constructed a simple, compact plan. Either he or his jackal had seen me kissing Nona through the Shang-hai door of Ward D2 that afternoon; and, like most other lit-erate Singaporeans, he had read the report, or at least its head-lines, of the naval officer's wife and her planter lover who had met for the last time in the top room of a seedy Chinese board-ing house, swallowed a whole bottle of sleeping tablets, and died in each other's arms.

X knew, of course, what every coroner knows, that suicides are to some extent epidemic. A much publicized suicide, or any novel form of suicide, will frequently produce a small crop of subsequent self-killings, often directly imitatory, inspired by the news reports in despairing minds tormented by similar dilemmas. So when Nona and I were found dead in each other's arms with the newspaper folded that way and empty sleeping-medicine bottles by the bed, the verdict would have been automatic. Two murders that it would never occur to anybody to suspect were murders.

I was feeling clumsily for Nona's heartbeat. When I found it I was shocked at its heavy, labouring slowness. She seemed scarcely to be breathing at all, but all the same my spirits were rising giddily. I had recovered the initiative. I'd absorbed only enough of the drug to sink me in—I looked at my watch— seven hours' sleep, and now I'd wakened almost fresh and on my toes, not a victim but an eager avenger. I persuaded myself that when death from these drugs was anywhere near, the breathing was loud and stertorous; my brain insisted that Nona was only drugged into deep sleep, that somehow she too had found a way of rejecting most of the overdose.

Apart from a fierce headache and desperate thirst, I was myself again. Moving softly, I went to the bathroom to drink and came back to put on my clothes and shoes. Then I opened the window.

Not so bad. We were only on the second floor above a street that was a narrow dead end. A dog nosing around an ash can —no other sign of life. I wondered how many would be on guard. There was plainly no need for more than one; no need for one at all, any more, from their point of view. There might be nobody and nothing barring our way out.

First things first. I put my money, passport, and wallet into my pockets and started to dress Nona. It was an awful job. I didn't know how, anyway, and her inert weight made everything more awkward still. I didn't attempt to put on her stockings, only the shoes and the pleated beige dress and finally the sling for her arm.

If her sleep had been normal, or even the unnatural sleep induced by a prescribed dose of sleeping medicine, she would have started up in pain at the first movement of her injured shoulder; but she betrayed not the smallest reaction. That was frightening. When she was dressed after a fashion, I left her and collected the dipper from the bathroom, a heavy brass affair with a black wooden handle, the shape of a saucepan. With that in my right hand I deliberately tapped it against the concrete side of the water tank.

When there was no reaction from outside I walked with a deliberate step across the room, making a noticeable noise, despite my crepe soles. The room had begun to breathe the cool night air through its window. A mosquito whined past my ear. And, quite unmistakably, there were soft sounds outside the door.

I waited, ready for the door to creep ajar. When it was thrown violently open, shock lost me a second of initiative. My blow with the bottom of the dipper should have struck the fellow's Adam's apple and put out his lights, but it caught him on the chin and merely shook him momentarily. He came out of his shock as fast as I came out of mine, and we started level then. I went straight into a clinch with him, scared of his gun, but the blow with the dipper must have loosened his grip on it and he'd still been fumbling when I seized him, because I heard the thing fall and skid across the floor.

Despite his superior physique and training, I was bursting with confidence. A hard stamp on his instep doubled him up and brought his chin down onto the cutting edge of the back of my hand. I think he must have been a little muscle-bound—his mind as well as his showy body. He ought never to have lost a fight to me, but that's what he did in less than three minutes. I had to take one blow from his knee that sent a red flame through my body and flooded my eyes with tears and made me unready for the shaking right to the jaw that followed; but then he had to take a heavy fall with me on top of him and a couple of dirty tricks that put him out like a light.

Winded and streaming with sweat, I staggered to my feet.

My head was spinning so sickly I went almost blind and had to sit on the bed, head doubled between my knees, for a moment or two. The physical-culture pin-up sprawled untidily across the threshold, blowing bloody bubbles.

I got up then, stepped over him, and made my way down the dark stairs. I fancied there was a whiff of opium smoke in the fug that hung about the place. From beyond a door on the landing below came a long, shuddering snore; otherwise all was quiet. The street door I found locked, but the key was in the lock and I got out easily enough.

The little dead end was empty. It was a short double row of shophouses, open-fronted by day, now with their ground floors masked by old wooden shutters. The signs were in Chinese script, mostly red or on a red background, because for the Chinese red is the colour of good fortune. At the corner where the narrow road joined the main street there was a lamp. I didn't recognize the street, which was empty except for two men on bicycles farther down whose voices echoed strangely in the silent street that was so clamorous by day. The only other sound was the clacking of mah-jongg bricks from an all-night session behind a lighted window on the opposite corner.

Back in the dark house I climbed the stale-smelling stairs with a feeling of slackening tension. In the bedroom doorway I bent down to look for the sprawling body I should otherwise trip over, and the tension tightened again, suddenly, like a noose.

He must have got on his feet as I climbed the stairs. The moon had either set or become obscured by heavy cloud, and the room was almost completely dark, so that I saw him only as a crouching blur over the bed.

My stride forward lost surprise because I kicked the brass dipper, which rang like a bell. He spun round, and we collided like a couple of bulls and clinched, neither of us able to do much damage in the first few moments. His naked, sweaty torso was as slippery as a fish, and its formidable hardness was daunting.

Well, I suppose he wasn't the first pin-up to turn out rather a disappointment in performance. I doubt now whether the odds against me were ever much above fifty-fifty. He was a gunman without his gun, too—it was in my slacks pocket— and I suppose that made a difference to his morale.

Certainly he couldn't have had the relish for the fight that I had now. I was remembering Nona in the hospital bed, telling me the story of her ordeal in the sea that morning. I owed him a lot more than he owed me.

The door was still open, and the din we made must have been audible all over the house. But even if anybody did hear, this was a house, I imagined, where people asked few questions and saw and heard no more than suited them. After a minute we sprang apart and a neat job of tripping sent me spinning through the bathroom door to slam painfully into the tiled wall. He came charging in after me, and I met him with the last blow of the fight.

It was a good one. If the bathroom had been as big as the bedroom it might not have done him much harm, but it sent him sprawling off balance, and he collided with the wall at once, with the full impetus of his fall. In there it was quite dark, so I couldn't see what happened. But I heard.

I heard his head—his face, I believe—meet the wall like a cricket ball meeting the bat; then a slithering on the wet floor, and finally a second crash. That may have been his skull crashing on the tile floor, an ugly bursting sound.

None of it had disturbed Nona. I was calm now and moved methodically. From the bamboo table I took her handbag and passed the handles over her arm. Her stockings were in my pocket with the gun. At first, when I lifted her and disentangled her from the sheet that came with her, she seemed amazingly light; but down on the first-floor landing I had to set her down and take a breather. I felt for her heartbeat behind the hot softness of her breast, and found it the same as before, appallingly slow and heavy.

I didn't like pushing her like a sack into the black corner behind the foot of the stairs, but I had to go out and make a short reconnoiter before I took her onto the street. It was as well I did, too, because under the lamp at the corner I came face to face with a policeman.

He might have been Jaafar's smarter elder brother, handsome and lazy-eyed, broadshouldered in his grey shirt, shorts stiffly starched and pressed, black puttees coiled with perfect symmetry round his sturdy legs.

I said, "*Selamat malam*," with unconscious aplomb.

He returned my good night, his eyes discreetly masking any surprise or speculation at my appearance there after four in the morning. After a moment he asked in a soft, deep voice, "*Tuan chari taxi?*"

No, I wasn't looking for a taxi, I answered, and since I realized there must be some curiosity behind the reserved eyes I added, "*Saya jalan kaki sebab sudah terlalu minum.*"

Oh, walking because I'd drunk too much, was I? He looked as if he thought that would be all the more reason for using a taxi, so I squared my shoulders and took a deep breath to demonstrate the reviving qualities of a four A.M. walk.

He had halted with his legs wide apart, facing the opposite side of the street, and I had no clue as to which way he had come, so I couldn't deduce which way he was going and so set my course in the opposite direction. I realized that my scruffy appearance, the shirt and slacks that had dried in multiple wrinkles, went well enough with my story of a binge.

Then I remembered my wounded cheek and black eye. This fellow was going to remember my black eye.

Of course I could have told him the truth. If I'd had a couple of minutes to think it over, that's what I might have done. But now I'd started off with evasion and a lie, and there was a seriously injured man, possibly a dead man, in a house a few paces away. I gave a moment's thought to the extent and duration of the inquiries, the testimony in coroner's and criminal court, the impossibility of escaping from the police or public eye for days and perhaps weeks, and I rejected the idea —for myself, and for Nona too.

No, once this agreeable but inconvenient cop was out of the way it wouldn't take five minutes for me and Nona to be right out of the business. I grinned an easy good night and set off up the street.

He didn't come with me, so I hoped I'd guessed right and his beat took him in the opposite direction; but when I flicked a glance over my shoulder from the end of the block he was still standing where I'd left him. That was bad. I strode on in a crazy fury with the quiet, lonely constable, my fists shaking as if they itched to get at his calm face.

Forcing myself not to look back again before I reached the end of the second block, in case he was still watching me, I walked faster, picturing some of the things that could be happening to Nona, though I was scared by the possibility that none of them could be more dangerous than delay in getting a doctor's help for her. Hot and breathless, I reached the next corner and spun round.

He had disappeared.

In that time he couldn't have got out of sight in the opposite direction. He must have tucked himself in a doorway somewhere, for a forbidden cigarette, perhaps. Or he could have gone down the dead end.

I had left the street door open, I remembered now. The sight of an open door at four A.M. would itself be a suspicious detail to a patrolling policeman. Oh, God! I started back down the street, striding and sweating and cursing. The fear that I had made a false move when the situation had come within an inch of being saved grew stronger with every step.

The door was still open. Nona was still huddled in the dark corner behind the foot of the stairs, like a drunk or a corpse, but the house wasn't silent any more. Footsteps sounded on the stair above—not the soft, slippered footsteps of someone leaving a bedroom during the night, but the heavy, booted tread of somebody in from the street.

The policeman? The boss? I swept Nona up and got out as fast as I knew how. On the street I felt more conspicuous than an actor alone on a stage. The windows were all eyes. The silence was the concentration of hidden watchers holding their breath.

Just short of the corner where I'd turned back, the sound of footsteps startled me. There was a sort of boarded-up kiosk there, jutting out onto the pavement. I set Nona down in the shadowed angle where it met the wall, and by the time the two policemen came round the corner I had her wedged into the angle, upright on her feet, her uninjured arm up round my neck as I held her like a street-corner necker, my back to the street, my body masking hers.

They were talking as they rounded the corner, something about an officer they called PitzGerald (Malays find it difficult to pronounce an F.) My heart thudded against Nona's hot breasts as they drew level. PitzGerald talked a lot about discipline, one of them said, and then on Sports Day they'd all seen him being ordered about by his wife! The other began to reply, and then his voice and their footsteps stopped. My face was in Nona's hair, my taut body was pressed hard against her inert body. I wondered how her unconscious hand looked, hanging over my shoulder.

A single step. A tap on my elbow.

I turned, wondering how to tell the story, what I could safely leave out, how to counter PitzGerald's questions later on. A broad, incurious Malay face came closer in the shadow, a brown hand held out Nona's handbag. It must have fallen as I propped her in the corner.

I said, "*Terima kasih*," and disengaged one hand to take the bag. He made no reply to my thanks, and after a single glance of mingled discretion and contempt he moved away and the four footsteps resumed their patrol.

It was the last of the snags. The empty taxi appeared within three minutes; the Sikh driver ignored the time I took to get Nona in and get her out when we reached Sunderland Mansions. Zella's flat was in Derry House, sixty yards round the corner, but I hadn't risked taking the taxi any nearer.

After a second ring at her bell Zella said, "Who is it?" behind her door.

"It's Robert, Zella." I gasped like a runner bursting through the finishing tape.

She took a quick step back as she saw us. I was inside in a single stride, saying, "Shut the door, Zella, and for God's sake ring for a doctor you can trust."

"Darling!" She was standing rigid in a yellow brocade dressing gown, her hair tied in a sort of net, while I laid Nona on the silver corduroy cushions of the divan I would always remember. "Trust?"

"Yes, one who won't ask questions. Or keep the answers to himself, at least. Quickly, Zella."

She knelt beside the phone in the way I remembered and dialled a number. "Mick, it's Zella," she said after what seemed a ghastly long time. "Yes, Zella. Mick, you must come at once."

"Overdose of sleeping tablets," I prompted her.

"No, somebody staying with me, Mick. She's taken too many sleeping tablets. Far too many. Hurry, Mick."

I was thanking God for Zella. She hung up and came and stood by me, looking down at Nona. She said, "On the bed in the little room, Robert."

When I'd carried her in and laid her on the bed Zella turned down, I said, "Best if I don't see this doctor. Can you say—well, what you've said already, that she's somebody staying with you?"

There was a sort of awe as well as curiosity in her eyes. "Robert, who is she?"

"Nona Avery. But try not to tell him that. If he asks how many tablets she took you'd better say a whole bottle."

Her lovely eyes widened. "He may ask to see the bottle."

"Then say she must have thrown it down the chute."

I followed her as she went into her own bedroom for a nightdress. "Did she really, Robert?" she asked me, taking a honey-coloured nylon affair from a drawer. "Try to kill herself?"

"No, Zella. That's why I wanted a doctor who wouldn't talk."

"Wait there a minute." She left me in the sitting-room and went in to Nona with the nightdress. I poured myself some Scotch, but it didn't taste right. When she came back, with Nona's clothes in a bundle, I burst out, "It *is* true, isn't it, that when they're really bad like that, going to die, I mean, their breathing's noisy? I'm sure I've read that." I was fixing her with a wild, bullying stare.

"Darling, I don't know," she said. "But Mick's good."

"If he asks, say you saw her with a low, square bottle," I said, remembering the one I'd seen in the moonlight on the bamboo table. "Say you think it was the same stuff as that couple took in Aden Street—you know, that suicide in the papers yesterday."

"Yes, Robert. D'you know when she took it?"

I sighed and shook my head. "Try to stop him sending her to hospital," I said suddenly. I'd caught the rumbling, intestinal murmur of the ascending lift. "And don't tell him her name —make one up if you like."

The doorbell rang.

I went into Zella's room, shut the door, and switched off the light. The darkness was scented, smelling of security and sweetness and excitement.

"Zella, my dear child, what *is* this?" His voice sounded right —strong and confident.

I heard Zella say, "Mick, I can't tell you much because it's an unhappy story and it's not my story. She's in here."

And the worst hour of the night began.

2

It was more than an hour before I heard voices clearly again. By that time I was in poor shape. That room was one of the places where I'd been happy—one of the places where I'd been happiest, I suppose. It was odd to remember all that, while the first sickly glimmers of dawn showed through the windows.

The first words I heard from Zella's doctor when the door of the small bedroom opened again made me suddenly weak with relief.

"I'll look in later, midday perhaps, but you don't have to worry any more." The strong voice was easy and reassuring. "I don't mean the poor child isn't in an awful state—you must know she is. But this crazy fit is over, and I can't see her try-ing it again. You'll be good for her, Zella. Have some cosy girlish confidentials—that's what she needs as much as anything, I'd say. Oh, God, I'm tired!"

"Mick, I can't tell you . . ." Zella sighed in her incoherent way. "You were wonderful! Why not let me make you some breakfast? It's almost time."

He laughed and said no, and I heard them kiss.

I was in the small bedroom half a second after the flat door closed on him. Nona was staring round her with the sheet drawn up to her chin, like a frightened child unable to sleep in a strange room. Without noticing it, I went down on my knee by the bed.

"They put us to sleep, but we're awake again," I said.

She looked relieved, and that brought beauty back to her face. She said, "They tore me out of Harry O'Neill's car while he called in at his office. They—Robert, where am I? Who's that girl? I've seen her somewhere."

"You met her once. Her name's Zella Graham and she's an angel."

I knew Zella had come in as I said that, and I got up and took her hand and squeezed it. I had thought she was strictly for playtime, but this morning I knew her better. I didn't say anything, but I looked for a moment right into her eyes, and she ought to have remembered how to read mine. But she only said, "Go and have a bath, Robert. You're almost unapproachable! Nona's going to rest; doctor's orders. Coffee in ten minutes and you can tell me anything then that's good for me to know."

Under the shower I felt like singing, though I knew I was dog-tired and my head ached. I reminded myself to phone O'Neill, and as soon as I smelled bacon and coffee I went out and gave Zella the story, all of it, over the kitchen table.

"What beats me," I finished up, "is how Nona survived the

full sleeping-pill treatment. I suppose they underestimated somehow."

"Yes, they underestimated," Zella said dryly. "Only gave her enough to kill two."

I blinked with my mouth full of toast and bacon till she explained. "She hasn't been able to sleep for months, so she's been taking medicine—the same stuff as the couple took yesterday in Aden Street. When it didn't help any longer she doubled the dose her doctor had prescribed, and when that didn't work she doubled it again—and again. You should have seen Mick's face when she told him the doses she's been taking! He nearly had a miscarriage. But, of course, that saved her. She's got such a tolerance for the stuff now that half a bottle hadn't much more effect on her than half a bottle of Scotch on an old soak. All the same, without Mick she probably wouldn't have woken up again. By rights she should have been dead hours ago, but as it is she'll probably be up and around this afternoon."

The future had been given back to us, but it was as fog-bound as ever. Despite that, when my cup and plate were empty I leaned back in my chair, fed and drowsy and clean; I felt almost reborn in the heavy crimson silk dressing gown I'd worn more than once before.

Zella asked me then, "Robert, d'you really not know *who?*"

I told her, "His name may be Lyle. That's about as far as I've got."

"And that fat pussy Aragon knows it all?"

"No. But he says he knows all about Andrew."

"But this must be to do with Andrew."

"I suppose so."

She bent forward as I held the lighter to her cigarette. She was one woman who looked good without make-up. When she'd blown out a chaos of blue smoke she said, "Suppose Aragon knows because he's the one who— Well, suppose he got rid of Andrew somehow? There's murder in it now, so it may have started with murder."

I said, "Creditors sometimes murder moneylenders. Moneylenders don't murder creditors."

"Well—what if Andrew had made a will leaving everything to Aragon? Suppose he'd been forced to, somehow?"

"But what had Andrew to leave, so far as he knew? And why, in that case, would Aragon come forward and offer me the full story?"

"At a price he knew you'd never pay, darling."

"Did he know that?"

"Wouldn't he have known?" She examined the lacquer on her nails with dissatisfaction. "Anyway, since he's your only lead you'll have to work through him, or on him. How about kidnapping one of those eleven brats he's so wrapped up in? Wouldn't he think a little information a cheap ransom price?"

It was typically Zella, and I smiled. Logic carried too far was one of her tricks. Then I stopped smiling.

Was it an idea, perhaps? Was there anything Aragon wouldn't part with rather than lose young Marcos or Sophie? After that night wouldn't I be justified in seizing any tool, however temporarily immoral or lawless, to break a way out of the mystery that had entrapped us? For a short time innocent people would suffer—the mother, for one—but only as long as Aragon held out on me. And was I really too scrupulous and soft to attempt it, *now?* Now that I wasn't the only one in danger?

"Go to bed," Zella said then, and I realized that I had been yawning. "I'll change the sheets and then I'll put something on that eye."

Even in my reflection in the silver coffee pot I could spot

the black eye. It didn't hurt any more than the rest of me. I was a single dull ache from head to foot, and I knew then how I longed for sleep.

In Zella's bed I fell asleep like falling down a well, but I was awake before midday. I still felt pretty stale, and for two or three minutes the thought of the action that must be fought in the fog was like a weight holding me down; but I rolled out of bed with a deliberate tensing of muscle and stared grimly ahead.

Zella was unpacking stuff she had bought in the market. She had given her cook the day off, she said. Nona was asleep. I found Harry O'Neill's number and rang him, conscience-stricken that I'd forgotten to do it before I slept. He sounded a bit ragged when I got him finally at his office. As soon as he asked me where I was, where we were, I checked myself.

"We're safe," I said. "Honestly, I think it's better if you don't know."

"The police, Avery," he cut in. "Naturally, I reported to them and now they're looking for Nona and probably for you. Wouldn't it be better—"

I said no. "I'm looking after this myself."

"I was thinking of Nona," he said.

"I'm thinking of Nona. She doesn't want the police in this, and no more do I." I thought of the dead or injured male pin-up.

"Suppose you know what you're doing," O'Neill said wryly. "Is there any way Christina and I can help?"

"Only by being ready to help if we send you an SOS. It's damned good of you."

"Well, you know my number." I don't think he had a lot of confidence in my grip on the situation.

Zella was cooking. Nona was asleep. When I sank into the deep leather armchair to take a close, hard look at the immediate future I had to take up the white handbag that lay there. I held it absent-mindedly while I frowned and crouched like a dunce over an examination paper, idly opening and closing the ivory clasp. When I dropped it and it fell open, a folded letter skimmed across the floor. I had to reach under the gramophone for it, and as I slipped it back into the handbag I saw the word at the top of the folded and dog-eared sheet.

The word was only "Saturday," but it's a word in which the letter *a* occurs twice, and the only other times I'd seen *a* written like that, just like a printed *a* and standing out unmistakably from the headlong script of the word, was in the few short letters I'd had from Andrew after my two months at Sungei Sunyi.

I don't remember any hesitation or scruple. I unfolded it and read it at once, certain that it must be from Andrew.

Saturday

No, I can't see you, Nona. Ever again. You were the one who changed my mind about trusting people; because of you I gave up living strictly for myself and by myself. And then you were the one who changed my mind back again. For two years I'd thought I could trust, that I was trusted, and then I found out that you'd never meant any of it. I had been right all along. So there wouldn't be any point in our meeting again, or in my answering any more letters from you.

A.

The initial of the signature wasn't necessary, not even the characteristic *a*. The letter, every line of it, was Andrew. My throat went dry as I read it, I don't honestly know whether from excitement or from an unexorcized ten-year-old fear of the cousin I'd been unable to understand. He had come suddenly near as I read the letter; I could hear an echo of the old "Go away, young Robert. I don't want you here."

I had only begun to think about the letter and what it could tell me when a slight draught blew it from my hand up into my face. I looked up, and the small bedroom door was open and Nona stood there in Zella's honey-coloured nylon night-dress, looking at me.

### 3

I was on my feet, her bag in one hand and Andrew's letter in the other. My mouth was open to say something, God knows what, when I found myself hesitating. There was an unreal look about her, and her eyes weren't on me or the let-ter—a dreamy look.

Then I understood. She was walking in her sleep.

I dropped the letter and the bag and moved towards her as she came walking past me. With a gentle hand I took her arm, and she leaned against me and let me steer her back to-wards the bedroom. She said something, but I couldn't catch the words the first time. Then she said it again.

"I'm lost, Andrew. I'm lost. Take me home, Andrew."

It was the first time in my life I'd ever seen anyone dream-walking, and the eeriness of it had chilled me, but eavesdrop-ping on her dream talk with Andrew was an experience close to horror. All the haunted apprehension had gone out of her voice. In her dream she was back with what for her was real-ity, the presence of the man she loved, or had loved, and his strong reassurance.

At the bedside I turned her pillow and said, "There you are. Just lie down and you'll be all right." And she sank onto the bed as if infinitely comforted. I don't know whether she dreamed that my voice was Andrew's—I've no idea how sleep-walking works. But I watched her for a few minutes—pale and not really beautiful, her face as calm as ever I'd seen it.

For her it had been a good dream, for me a little nightmare. I hoped with all my heart that Andrew was dead, because I wanted her, and something told me she would never be mine as long as Andrew lived. If he still lived . . .

I went back and read his letter again. The outcast, self-pitying sentimentality of the phrases made me frown with impatience and distaste. I could imagine the pain it had given Nona. But what I needed most to know was when it had been written and where it had been sent from.

There wasn't much evidence of either—no envelope, no date or address. And though the sheet of good bond paper looked old and dog-eared, almost split at the creases, couldn't that perhaps have been the result of repeated unfoldings and readings within a short time? Couldn't it conceivably have been received any time between three years and three days ago?

Nona had known where he was at that time, whenever it was she had written to him, and she had suggested a meeting. But if that had been recently, why hadn't she gone straight to him anyway? Because, presumably, she had been uncertain of her reception if she had. Why had she wanted to see him? Surely not to warn him that I was hunting him—she could have written that in the letter to him. Or had it been that, but she longed so much to see him again that she had pleaded for a meeting to discuss something of urgency?

I knew that she and Andrew had parted at least eight months ago because she had begun working for the BBC in July of the previous year. This letter implied a break, some sort of showdown and separation, in the past—and not, it seemed to me, the recent past. Each time I read the miserable thing my suspicion grew that Nona might have received it since she had reached Singapore a few days before.

The paper was of good quality, thick and heavy—not the

paper you'd use for a letter to be sent by air mail. If, despite its frayed condition, it had been written recently, could I deduce that Andrew wasn't far away? No farther than Singapore Island, or the Federation of Malaya? It seemed likely enough.

My imagination, like my memory, is the visual, pictorial kind. And the picture in my mind then was of Andrew, of the youth I had known grown older and broader, but with the same vigorous black hair and the same Avery profile and the same vivid blue eyes. He stood in tropical sunshine, alone and aloof, and his bleached shorts revealed the lower end of a scar on his brown thigh, the scar of a burn at a campfire one night seventeen years ago. He was sweating under the same sun as breathed heat up through the louvres of Zella's green shutters, and he was thinking about me.

That was the picture in my mind as I folded Andrew's letter for the last time and replaced it in Nona's handbag. My imagination, running wild, tried to persuade me that he was alive and not far away.

The telephone bell rang, and Zella came in with an apron round her gold linen dress and knelt down to answer it as she always did.

"Yes." Her eyes turned towards me in a question I couldn't interpret. "Yes, he's just called on me. Just a moment." With her hand over the receiver she said, "For you. Should I have said you were here?"

I asked, "Who is it?"

"Could be that Aragon, I think."

It was. "Mr. Avery?" the furry voice purred. Yes, he was an old pussy; Zella's name for him was just right. "You weren't in at your hotel, and there is a lady who wants to speak to you urgently. I remembered seeing you with Miss Graham at lunch yesterday, so I thought of asking her. A lucky inspiration, wasn't it? Well, here is the urgent message."

A blank second, and then a sweet, breathy voice saying, "Uncle Robert? Are you there, Uncle Robert?"

"Yes, Sophie," I said.

She came through rather incoherently. "Uncle Robert, you didn't know today was my birthday and I didn't tell you because perhaps you might have thought I was—well, people sometimes think you are only thinking about presents when your birthday is coming close. But please don't think anything about a present, only please will you come to my party this afternoon?"

I said, "Well, now—"

"Oh, *please*. Daddy says men don't like iced cakes or ice cream, but you can have whisky or whatever you like. I do want you to come, because Angela had four men at her party and I've only got two."

I said, "How nice of you to ask me. Well—yes, I'd love to come. What time, Sophie?"

"Oh, you *are* nice, Uncle Robert! I wish you'd stay forever in Singapore. Can you come at half-past four?"

I said yes, and after a little more rather charming flattery she rang off. Zella had watched me all the time.

"A birthday party," I explained. "One of the little girls— quite a charmer in her way. I'm going."

Zella said, "I'm doing a *Coquille St. Jacques* for lunch. Will that be a good foundation for jelly and toffee apples?"

"Sophie says I can have whisky instead," I told her.

"Good for Sophie. I must put some make-up on that black eye before you go. Why not carry her off with you? We could give her a good time here while her father went mad and finally agreed to come up with the information about Andrew Avery as ransom money."

I'd even thought of that myself, reflecting that young Marcos was too young for the part. I'd never know what to do

if he cried, or how he ought to be fed. Sophie I could manage easily. She was more or less in love with me, and she'd
probably believe anything so long as I was nice to her. About
eighty per cent of my mind rejected the idea as criminal lunacy, but twenty per cent insisted on treating it seriously.
Kidnapping was something as far outside one's life and
thought as—well, as murder! There wasn't much exorcism in
that comparison. . . .

4

Sophie met me at the gate with the dog Trusty.

"Oh, Uncle Robert, I'm so glad! Now all my friends are
here."

"Except Uncle Andrew," I said.

She looked at me strangely. "Have you and Uncle Andrew
had a quarrel?"

"No, Sophie. I've lost him, that's all."

"He never talked about you. Once I asked him why he was
always alone, and he said, 'I'm the lonely sort, Sophie. Nobody cares about me.' So I asked didn't he have a family or
anything, and he said, 'Yes, but they're all white sheep,
Sophie, white as snow.' He liked saying things I didn't understand, I think."

"That was pretty mean of him, surely."

"No, I was sorry for him." She sighed, her beautiful eyes
troubled. "I do hope you find him. Will you tell him to come
and see us if you do? Please."

"Ah, good afternoon!" Her father came padding up to offer
a hand like a warm muffin. When the hand transferred itself
to my shoulder as we moved towards the house I felt a shrinking of nerve-ends. "My wife is anxious to meet you. Come
along."

Isabel Aragon was older than the photo in the long room, and stouter. There was a genuine simplicity and good-heartedness about her that was warmly attractive. She said, "It's good of you to come, Mr. Avery. Sophie's so fond of you."

"So is somebody else," purred Aragon, and I felt a tug at my knee. Young Marcos was down there, spruce in a white party suit, holding up tiny pink hands in welcome. I lifted him in my arms, and a smile of bliss transformed his face. His mother beamed. I felt slightly ridiculous, though in fact I was happy enough in this family atmosphere and not really acting a part. There were about a dozen children there, mostly girls of Sophie's age, with a couple of self-conscious boys and a young Eurasian who I gathered was a relative of Mrs. Aragon's. They were just sitting down to a large spread of juvenile party food on a terrace shaded by a blue-striped sun blind, and I heard Sophie saying urgently to one of the small boys, "No, not those sandwiches. They're Uncle Robert's. You wouldn't like them, anyway, because they're sour."

I was given these sandwiches, which proved to be Gentleman's Relish, a moment later, together with a pot of fine coffee. Young Marcos was taken from me, under protest, and consoled with a pink biscuit, and his father, after handing round plates of chocolate mousse and whipped cream, sank into a rattan chair at my side.

"I've something to tell you," I said. There was no need to lower my voice amid the chorus of child voices. "Last night, soon after I got your letter, somebody slugged me. When I came to, your letter wasn't in my pocket."

He turned slowly to stare at me and then, saying nothing, turned away to stare at his children. I wondered whether it was his death sentence that he had just heard from me, and I wondered whether he was wondering that too.

I waited for a reply, but he said nothing, so I reminded him,

"If this brings trouble for you, it's only what you've brought on yourself."

He turned then to ask, "How do you make that out, Mr. Avery?"

"There's somebody trying to stop me finding Andrew, or finding out what happened to him. You say you know it all, but you won't help."

"But I will help," he said, his eyes swerving lazily to meet mine. "Only not for nothing." He gave the dog Trusty a sponge cake, his eyes still dreaming.

"It's up to you," I said. "There's somebody trying to stop me finding out the truth, somebody dangerous. Which side are you on—mine or his?"

Even his blink was slow. The plump lids closed and opened slowly, stickily. "Yes, I know, Mr. Avery. You want my information for nothing."

I let my hate show. I stared hard down into his soft milk-chocolate-coloured eyes. "Aragon, is he alive or dead? You can tell me that much."

He offered me a plate of ginger cakes. "Oh, I could tell you that much. But how much good would the bare answer do you?"

"Is he alive or dead?" I repeated.

He met my gaze frankly. "Andrew Avery is dead. But the circumstances of his death—they are what you need to know, aren't they?" He caught Sophie's bright eyes and smiled fondly, as if what we were talking about were a boring business detail.

I said, experimenting boldly, "This morning I read a letter from Andrew Avery, written within the past ten days."

He only said, "That is impossible, and I fancy you know it."

I asked, "Why should I believe you?"

"Because I know," he said simply, shrugging a fat shoulder inside his shantung jacket and turning to speak in French to a small, timid girl over to his right. I felt outclassed. Moving away from him, I started a conversation with Sophie and a pretty Malay girl called Meriam, which went on until none of them could eat any more and Sophie began to open her gifts.

I got a kiss for the small bracelet Zella had bought on my behalf. Young Marcos came back and climbed on my knee as soon as he'd been washed clean of cream and chocolate stains. His father turned back to me, poured two whiskies, and started a conversation about England. I gathered he was getting out of Singapore before long on account of the British withdrawal and the inevitable absorption of the abandoned colony into Communist China's empire.

"Then you think that it's only overseas that the English are losing grip and responsibility?" I asked. "You think you'll find them different at home?"

"Clearly not," he answered lazily. "But the English still have some fat to live on. England can be pretty comfortable for a few more years, don't you think?"

I told him that the English, for the first time for centuries, were not concerned with the future.

"You mean the type of Englishman who feels responsibility for the future has had power taken from him."

I gulped my Scotch impatiently. An exchange of commonplaces about English politics there and then, while Rome burned, was more than I could take. The children were being rounded up and prepared for an excursion by private bus to the house of the young Eurasian, who was putting on a movie show for them. They went off, leaving only Aragon and young Marcos and the amah, who came to take the little boy from me as night began its swift swoop on the island.

"Let's go inside," Aragon said, taking up the tray of Scotch, ice, and soda, and we went into the long room where I had first met him. It was different, somehow, from the way I remembered it—though possibly only the difference between daylight and artificial light, I told myself at first.

Although he sidestepped my attempts to bring the conversation round to Andrew, I had a hunch that Marcos Aragon was leading up to something. When after half an hour the bead curtain at the end of the room parted I had a sudden idea that this was it, that someone of importance was on the point of appearing—Lyle, perhaps.

But it was only the amah, bringing little Marcos to say good night. I stared sombrely at the jewel-clean, guileless face that smiled at me. It was as out of place there and then as a nun in a night club.

I said when he'd been taken away, "The fellow who tried to get me last night—and the night before—isn't just having fun. He's made mistakes, but he isn't going to give up. He'll make another bid to get me, and now he's read your letter he'll be working out an exit for you. We're in the same boat. Shouldn't we pool resources?"

I didn't expect a useful response. As I spoke I'd been working it out that I'd have to do something to Marcos Aragon. He had the information, and I had to have it too. Without delay, tonight, I was going to have to make him talk at last.

He was good at stalling. He'd just poured me another double and found the bottle empty when he started to pour another for himself. With a grunt he held up the bottle, lumbered to his feet, and went out through the bead curtain, leaving me unanswered. Apparently the servants had gone out too.

I stared round the long room, wondering vaguely what was unfamiliar about it while I worried about Nona. Zella was on guard, but we were up against somebody smart and cruel.

Already, in the hour I'd been away from the flat, things could have gone desperately wrong.

My body was rigid with impotent fury. Aragon seemed so securely beyond my reach, pneumatically insulated behind his wall of fat and complacency, watching my predicament with detached mockery. When finally he came back with a bottle of Vat 69 I was on my feet.

"Look, Aragon, you've stalled long enough." I'd made the decision to act, to find the solution in action, and now; though *what* action was still obscurely unsure. I kept thinking of the child asleep upstairs. . . .

"Sit down, Mr. Avery," the soft voice purred, slightly breathless from his journey to the cellar. "Subject to certain guarantees, I have something to tell you, but let us discuss it without melodrama."

I found myself sitting down with a frown like a reproved schoolboy. I snapped, "Well?"—but he poured himself a very small Scotch with deliberation and didn't speak until he had sipped it.

"Your late cousin—" he began then, but I cut in impatiently.

"I don't quite believe that."

"Your late cousin," he repeated, ignoring my interruption, "told me something about his family. His word for you, I remember, was 'harmless.'"

That stung—and convinced, too.

"If your cousin had been alive and anxious to elude you, I really don't believe, Mr. Avery, that you'd have stood much chance of finding him."

I said nothing.

"Your aunt—his aunt—he was bitter about her. The last time I saw him—"

"That would be the time he came with Lyle?" I put in.

He blinked at that. Or at any rate his eyes closed and opened the way I suppose tortoises blink. I went on, "Did you imagine I hadn't got round to Lyle and his part in all this?"

He only said, "I haven't speculated a great deal concerning your quest, Mr. Avery. I didn't realize that you were looking for Mr. Lyle as well."

"Oh, yes." Something was disturbing me; something was intruding on my bid to bring this aimless talk to a crisis. "I told you, I'm going to split the whole thing open."

He had turned away, frowning, not listening. I said, "There's something burning."

"I was thinking the same," he said.

I thought again of the sleeping child, the strong weapon he would be if I could steal and hide him from his father. I was pretty desperate.

Marcos Aragon heaved himself to his feet and switched on a lamp shaded in yellow raffia by my chair. Beyond the window the garden was falling from twilight into darkness. The light from the lamp lit sparks in the perspiration on Aragon's forehead and jowls. A velvet penguin, one of young Marcos's toys, fixed an envious glance on my Scotch.

For a whole minute there was silence. I gulped my drink and struggled with a numbing sensation of missing clues, of things happening fast outside my range of reception. Then Aragon said, "You spoke of Lyle. What do you know of him?"

"Enough," I lied.

He'd fixed a tortoise stare on me, heavily glazed, and now his voice sounded absent and flat. "Oh, no. Mr. Lyle will be as hard to find as your cousin."

"You're saying he's dead?"

"I'm not saying anything, Mr. Avery."

He raised his head then, sniffing suspiciously, and I did the same. The smell of burning had grown stronger. Muttering and frowning, he heaved himself out of his chair and went out through the bead curtain. The dog was barking now behind a closed door somewhere.

Inside fifteen seconds he was back, tearing his way through the curtain, which threw two strands round his jowls. He said something breathlessly, and I jumped up from my chair to follow him back through the curtain.

A thin cloud of smoke was leaking through a half-open door towards the back of the house. There was a sound like wind in a cottage chimney and a faint crackling. Aragon's soft muffin hand gripped my biceps.

"*Marcos!*" He was coughing with the smoke in his throat and the emotion that shook his jowls. "His room's on fire!"

I went cold, either from horror at the thought of the child burning in his cot or from horror at the inescapable thing I was going to have to do. Aragon had already gone to pieces. He stood there as if he'd been hit over the head, staring at me stupidly, his great jelly lips struggling to say something.

When I went through the smoke to the doorway I found a curving staircase beyond it. Half of it was in flames.

"The other staircase," I shouted at Aragon.

He shook his head, and his lips and jowls swung. "No other way up," he gasped. "Marcos!"

"Then a ladder," I snapped. "And call the fire brigade, for God's sake."

Seconds were leaking away, and he stood there like an idiot. I had to make up my mind which was quickest, which offered the best chance. The ladder would take time, the telephone SOS would take time. I dashed back to the doorway to make a second assay of the chances of a baldheaded dash through the flames. Would the burning stairs bear my hundred and fifty pounds? They surely wouldn't bear Aragon's two hundred and fifty.

I took a deep breath and dived through the door. On the bottom step I paused a moment, staring through the smoke at the sparks and little flame-tongues up one side of the curving stairway, and suddenly there was the awful bursting pain at the back of my head and I went down in the smoke into engulfing blackness.

With my final flicker of agonizing consciousness I realized at last what had been different in the sitting-room beyond the bead curtain. *The photographs had gone.* The portrait of Isabel Aragon, the photos of the two elder boys and the two family groups, they'd all been removed from the two lighted recesses in the wall, and I knew now what was happening to me.

# FOUR

I had let my mind run on the possibility, how seriously I honestly don't know, of using the child Marcos as bait. I'd considered kidnapping him and demanding Aragon's information about Andrew as ransom.

But Aragon had got there first. He had used his child as bait, and I had walked into the trap, to be slugged and left to burn. For his third murder attempt on me Aragon had resolved to do the job himself, not to risk another fiasco at the bungling hands of bought or blackmailed thugs.

Only that was another fiasco.

It was the dog. I came back to consciousness with a bang, like a deep diver surfacing head and shoulders out of the ocean. My left arm was in agony, my head was a roaring, cavernous ache, and there was a savage tearing at my throat, or rather the clothes at my throat. It was the dog Trusty, working like a fiend to drag me back through the doorway. He had got me a couple of yards back, so that my head was outside the doorway and a draught from the front part of the house had revived my smoke-choked lungs.

But Aragon was there.

"*Trusty!*" The shout was mad with fury, and the big dog let me go and stared over my head in shock and bewilderment. His master, behind me and beyond my range of vision, was swearing in some language I didn't know. The dog lowered his head in dismay and fear until his trembling chin almost touched mine. And then the whine of the heavy club through the air and the brutal, cracking blow across the yellow skull.

Trusty fell, his strong legs kicking weakly.

I rolled over, but my effort to get up wasn't good enough. The club cracked down on my right shoulder twice, and the third time it glanced the side of my head. There wasn't a fourth.

I heard excited voices and footsteps. Consciousness flickered on and off, like a lighthouse beam, perhaps in rhythm with my heavy breathing. I was lifted up and taken out to a long chair on the terrace. There was a woman giving orders in Malay with a strong Australian accent, and several hurrying Chinese. Then a long, half-choking drink of Scotch.

I lay there, safe and bringing my bruised mind to painful focus on the next step. The why of it all I didn't waste time over. I knew my enemy and I need no longer scruple over the methods to be used in forcing Andrew's story out of him.

When the bell of the fire-engine sounded outside in a swift crescendo, I sat up shakily and looked round me. There seemed about twenty people in and around the house. A European woman in a white evening dress was bathing Trusty's injured head; some Eurasian youths in basketball kit had come in from a game nearby to make a noisy amateur assault on the fire; the amah stood at the door of the pavilion across the sweep of lawn, with young Marcos in her arms. The fire had never come near him; his father had seen to that, just as he'd seen to it that only expendable and insurable property would have gone up in flames round my corpse, not the prized and irreplaceable photos of his family. There was a shout as an Englishman in a sharkskin dinner jacket discovered an opened and almost half-full can of petrol only a few yards from the burning stairway. Aragon himself wasn't in sight.

Standing helped me. It made my head swim, but it required an effort, and that's what was needed to stiffen me. The Australian woman came and asked me about the dog.

"I fell on the stairs and he found me," I said. "His name's Trusty."

She was thin and nervous, with a look of illness about her, but all right. She said, "He's got a horrible head wound. We'll have to get him to the vet—after we've got you to hospital."

I told her I was all right.

"I saw the smoke and I made my husband stop the car," she told me. "I was in a fire once, my school was gutted when I was fifteen, and I couldn't bear to go by, wondering. We found Mr. Aragon pulling you out of the smoke. And then I saw the poor dog."

I turned my head and saw Aragon. He was staring at me, and perhaps his stare had drawn my eyes towards the dark shadow of the clump of nibong palms in which he stood. I could see he was afraid. The last time I'd seen him he had been afraid too, because he wasn't an active killer, and the emergency job he'd had to do on me had taken all the nerve he had. Perhaps he'd never murdered before; perhaps he'd always bought his murders ready-made.

And now it was worse—witnesses all around, a policeman arriving any minute, his word against mine, and ugly blows on my head and shoulders to support my story.

Or did he know me better than that? Was it only me, and not the police, that he feared? Did he know that I wanted to keep the police out of this almost as much as he did? First

Nona, and then I, had by-passed the police and to bring them in now would surely rouse a succession of suspicious inquiries.

It was something to know that his nerve was poor. I'd never been sure of my own, and the times when it had held up under heavy strain weren't so reassuring because I'd known how narrow the margin had been between holding and breaking. But I was steady enough now. Nerve and scruple were worrying me no more than the pain of my burned arm. Settling accounts with Aragon was an obsession that crowded out other preoccupations.

Somebody had come up with dressings for my arm, but the woman waved them away, saying the burned skin shouldn't be touched until something had been sprayed on at the hospital. Aragon watched me from the shadows. The fire brigade made a lot of noise and mess, but it was obvious that the fire hadn't a chance with them there. I asked the Australian woman for some aspirin.

She gave me three in a short whisky. Then I was ready for him.

As soon as he saw me step towards him he took a quick pace back. I was none too steady on my feet, but I broke into a stumbling stride. A great cloud of smoke and steam from the hoses came between us, and when I got through it he was falling back behind the wheel of his Buick.

I got my hand on one of the door handles and wrenched it open, but I didn't get in. The car shot forward as if snatched out of my hand, and I fell on my face in the driveway. The garden was swarming with people, but all eyes were focussed on the expiring blaze, and I don't believe anybody saw Aragon's escape and my stumbling pursuit. At the gate I fell again, tripped by a hose. I had lost hope of keeping Aragon's car in sight, but in fact he'd got no farther than fifteen yards. The fire engine had pulled up opposite a parked Humber

Pullman, and much of the space between them was blocked by shouting firemen with coils of hose. A second time I got my hand on the door before he finally succeeded in inching his way through the narrow gap.

There was nothing for it but to borrow the Humber and follow him. The ignition key was in position, and I guessed that the car belonged to the Australian woman and her husband. Before a minute had gone by I was within five yards of Aragon's tail light.

I stayed there for almost half an hour. By then I was quite lost. I don't know the island outside the main business and residential areas of the city, and Aragon had driven in a bewildering sequence of directions. I was thinking of what I could do, leaving the initiative with Aragon for the moment, not attempting to overtake or stop him. After the first few minutes he drove at normal speeds, carefully, like a man on his way to a routine appointment. I had no trouble at all keeping him in sight. What was he running away *to?* What sort of future could he see for himself?

The night was dark. Every time we passed through an avenue of vividly lit shophouses that marked a Chinese village, the darkness at the far end seemed to gulp us in like a drain. I was tired, driving carelessly. The petrol gauge showed an almost empty tank.

When Aragon braked sharply and pulled up beside a row of huts in darkness down a short, narrow track, I jerked out of a half-dream too late to avoid his rear fender. He was out of his car already, shouting.

"Ho Fung! Ho Fung!"

No light appeared in either of the two huts, but in the beam of my headlights a door opened an inch. Aragon lumbered towards it, shouting in Chinese. I know about twenty words of Chinese myself—of Kheh, to be precise—and Aragon was shouting two of them.

"Your knife! Your knife!"

There was a moment in which nothing happened, and then a short, thick-set Chinese in lavishly crumpled slacks and singlet slipped out through the door. I had seen him before. He was the man who had pushed me into the monsoon drain opposite Compton's. There was a short knife in his left hand.

I could smell the sea. I could hear it, too—close by.

I could have turned the car and got away, but I had to stay and settle with Aragon. I was tired and scared, but I couldn't turn back. There had to be a decision that night.

As soon as I saw thug Ho Fung moving swiftly out of the beam of the Humber's headlamps into the darkness, I slid out of the door on the opposite side. Away from the lights, I saw the dull gleam of water and a little wooden jetty beyond the huts and a couple of fishing boats moored or anchored there.

With a last breathless shout, Aragon retired into cover behind a dadap hedge. I set a course towards the near end of the huts over uneven ground booby-trapped with thorns and potholes. My hands were empty. It was almost as if I knew what was going to happen, because there was no conviction or zest about me now, even with my enemy in flight close ahead, even with the key to Andrew's disappearance so close at last.

When I entered a small grove of rambutans and tapioca at the back of the huts, a dog whined behind one of the shuttered windows, but the trembling sound was cut short and after that there was only a tense silence from the dark dwellings that smelled of jasmine, drainage, and *durian*. From the small hut or boathouse down by the jetty came the smells of dried fish and mud. Suddenly the Humber headlamps were extinguished.

I was thinking of the knife. From childhood, knives have been a horror for me, the weapon of violence that added nightmare to its intrinsic danger. The cold, silently slicing blade, the helpless, opening flesh, the leaking away of blood and life—it was my private hell.

There was one unforgettable hour of my life when I was a hero, and that was on the day I volunteered to give a pint of blood for an emergency transfusion after a terrorist ambush in South Selangor. It took everything I had, that absurdly trifling operation. When it's a question of blood-letting I'm not entirely sane, I suppose. Just the thought of the knife in the thug's hand, of the opening of my veins and the escape of the warm blood, had plunged me back into the secret nightmares of childhood. I was thinking more of the left-handed killer who hunted me with his knife than of the enemy I was closing in on.

I fell on my face into a mat of thorns, but as I got up again I saw Aragon's head and shoulders moving against the dull screen of the calm, dark water. He was down by the jetty, and I made my way down to him. I came down behind the small atap-thatched hut at the near end of the jetty, my hands groping for a weapon of some kind. I had a length of wood already, pulled out of the fence surrounding the gardens, but it was too light to lend confidence. My hand found a much heavier club leaning against the back of the hut, but as I took it up a loud rattling noise shattered the silence: it was attached to a length of chain, which fell clanking down a slope as I disturbed it.

Whether I heard the Chinese with the knife I don't know, but I became aware of him suddenly and spun round, both hands empty now and my heart half choking me with fear. Something gave way under my right foot, and I stumbled against him, fell into a pile of old baskets smelling of dried fish, sprang up again, but tripped up a second time and fell, cracking my head against the corner post of the hut and greying out.

He was standing astride me then, and I was on my back, pressing myself into the creaking confusion of baskets as the knife hung in silhouette against the starshine. The blade was spear-shaped but short, with a double edge, apparently, and the long left hand held it absolutely motionless, pointing down at my throat.

Now that I was looking up at the stars everything seemed lighter. The thug who stood astride my thighs, and particularly the knife in his hand, was vividly silhouetted. A moment later I understood. The moon was rising over the sea.

I had tensed myself helplessly for the swift stab, either a single expert one or savagely repeated plunges of the blade to ensure a quick death. Instead of that, the thug started talking.

It took me several moments to make out what it all meant. He talked in stiff, grating chains of monosyllables, and Aragon, somewhere behind me and out of sight, answered in slow, breathless sentences that lacked the crisp crackle of good Chinese. As often as not the thug cut him short, his harsh voice taking on a more urgent and vociferous edge. Then I caught a word I knew, several times repeated—the word for "hundred."

It was a dispute about the price of murder. The thug was letting me live a little longer while he bargained for a bigger fee. It went on for a minute or more. Once Aragon hissed something urgent, upon which the Chinese spat out a contemptuous word, reached down suddenly with his right hand to grab my hair, pulled up my head, and shook it violently from side to side before letting it go again. I had wit enough to slacken every muscle and fall like a corpse, sensing that Aragon had warned him that I might revive and open an offensive, and that this was the thug's reassurance that I was still quite out.

Aragon got only three more words out, stepping forward till I saw his feet close by my right ear, before the thug spat fiercely down at my throat and his left hand thrust the knife into Aragon's. I saw Marcos Aragon's fat fingers wriggle round the shaft uncertainly, and, in the silence that followed, a low cloud must have unscreened the moon because the light intensified till I could see the oily film of sweat on Aragon's hand. It was a monstrous version of his youngest son's hand, puffy and short-fingered, with dimples where there should have been knuckles, the third finger swelling round a gold ring set with a small ruby.

The wrangle went on in the echoing moonlight till Aragon gave an impatient exclamation and bent over me. My head and shoulders lay in the deep shadow of the hut, and I could keep my eyes slit-open safely while he blinked down at me, holding his breath, the hand stiffening round the knife shaft.

I was absolutely certain, somehow, that he wouldn't be able to do it. His shaky nerve was as unmistakable as if it had been a strong odour. Then he was so close I could smell him, the stale sweat mixed with a trace of scented talcum. His jowls hung over me, his jelly lips sagging open, his eyes in deep shadow under his oily brow. A still moment, with the knife raised unsteadily, and then the release of stale breath and a low, grudging word of submission.

But the offer wasn't the full sum the thug had demanded, or else, seeing his advantage, he was upping his price. A second time Aragon gripped the pointed knife and bent over me with a whispered curse of some kind. His meanness was fighting a tough battle with his squeamishness, and I backed his squeamishness to win. My head was clearing, and panic was lifting. The knife in Aragon's big baby hand was not the nightmare it had been in the taut Chinese fist.

By the time Aragon gave in and straightened up to hand back the knife, I was ready. A few milliseconds before the thug's left hand would have closed round the shaft, my hands seized his thin right ankle and I sprang to my feet, managing to keep the ankle firm in my left hand. He was easy to throw, and as he landed I kicked—a pretty vile sort of kick which had, I still hope, a permanent effect. The temporary effect was to tie him in a tight, heaving knot. I beat Aragon to the knife and, with the point of it pricking a hole in his sweat-sodden shantung shirt at heart-level, forced him back until he lay flat and gasping on the jetty in the moonlight.

"Now," I said, "I want it all."

He was shaking, and his fat lips were wet. I could feel the warmth of his fat as I bent over him. He didn't say anything. It was as if he hadn't heard me speak.

"I don't like knifing, either," I said, "but my guts are stronger than yours. I can do it if need be, and by God I'm going to, Aragon, if you don't give me all you know about my cousin Andrew."

He stared at me like a man driven mad with torture. I drew back the blade so that it wasn't touching him any more and moved my face nearer his.

"Those photos you hid out of reach of the fire—the people in the photos, young Stamford and David, and the little girls, and your wife and Marcos—you've seen them for the last time. Unless you give it all, Aragon, all I came East to find out."

A night bird on one of the trees in the gardens gave a low cry like a lookout. Aragon's lips didn't move; his eyes were fixed in their mad stare. A few yards away, the thug was writhing and retching; he didn't worry me any more, but I was unpleasantly aware of the possibility of reinforcements from the dark and silent huts.

I snarled at Aragon, "Can't you see I mean it, you bloody fool!" and to jolt him out of his idiot stare I drew a line around his fat throat with the knife's point. The line was red, I suppose, but looked black in the moonlight, and a large drop of black blood oozed from the end of it under his right ear.

"Now!" I snapped.

But all that happened was a sudden calm. The hot body stopped its trembling, the protruding eyes lost their wild focus, and the round head slumped slowly to one side. He had fainted.

In a fury I slapped his great soft cheek. The sound was sharp and violent in the moonlight, but it had no effect. There was a bucket on the jetty edge. I went down the crazy old steps and filled it with the gently rocking water. The whole lot, dashed over the puffy face, failed to revive him. Swearing in a fury, I seized the heavy shoulders and tried to shake him, but he was too heavy for me.

Then I suspected. The sensation of pushing my hand through his sodden shirt to flatten it against his puffy, hairless breast was a revolting one. Under my hand there was not the smallest vibration. Seconds dropped away into the past as I moved my palm across the soft flesh. I kept it there long after I knew there could be no other explanation, fighting off the admission that I was back where I'd started, that my enemy had escaped me and taken his secret with him.

I had killed a man, and for nothing. The tiny red scratch round his throat had been too much for his weak nerve and his fatty-degenerate heart.

I stood back and cursed the shapeless corpse with a bitter, exhausted fury. There was nothing to do but go back to Nona.

2

You get a glimpse of Sungei Sunyi five miles before you
come to it. Soon after you've crossed the twenty-four-hun-
dred-foot pass by Bukit Kuning there's a break, just for fifteen
yards, in the jungle that encloses the road—the result, I suppose, of a large-scale landslide—and you can see for ten miles
across the valley of the Riawan and up the valley of the tributary Sunyi. *Sungei Sunyi*—Lonely River.

I suppose I'm old enough to begin to take an interest in
myself when younger and the things that happened to me
then and the scenes of those happenings. It seemed now, as
Sam Chester pulled up to light his pipe and I looked across
the sunlit, crinkled jungle slopes towards Sungei Sunyi, that
something important was happening to me. The return to
Sungei Sunyi became an event—because it was my only link
with Andrew, for one thing, of course. But something else
besides. I don't like to hear people placing confidence in pre-
monitions, so I'm unwilling to entertain the idea that a pre-
monition touched me there near the summit of Bukit Kuning;
but for one reason or another I became tense and excited.

In the back of the comfortable Studebaker, Winnie was saying to Nona, "You just can't see the bungalow." She sounded,
with her serene, understanding voice, as if she were forgiving
the contours for sinking the bungalow a fraction below the
line of vision. "But you can see Eight Division."

Pale but putting on a good performance as an interested
tourist, Nona asked for the eighth division of the Sungei
Sunyi Rubber Estate to be identified. Winnie was good for
her. She had the same value as a conspicuously brave soldier
has for comrades whose morale is sinking under prolonged

strain. As soon as I'd got back to Zella's flat after Aragon had died so quietly at the prick of a knife-point, I had decided to accept the Chesters' offer of a lift to Sungei Sunyi and hospitality there. I'd rung the Raffles and found to my relief that they hadn't left and to my equal relief that they were leaving early in the morning. This was the second morning, after a night on a plantation near Rawang managed by a crony of Sam's.

The great sky was a burning blue, and the jungle lay like a coat of green astrakhan over the hills. The air was thick and lazy with heat. A noise like the vibration of a hundred thousand overstrung nerves surrounded us, the stridulation of the jungle crickets. Behind the blindfolding screens of leaves were hidden tiger and elephant, tapir and honey bear and leopard, crocodile and rhino, panther and seladang, python and cobra, gibbon and mouse-deer and jungle-fowl, hornbill and bulbul, and a hundred or a thousand other unseen creatures. The single ribbon of road through the square miles of jungle gave me, as always, a feeling of loneliness, even with Nona so near and the Chesters nagging each other affectionately.

During my months with the Army in Malaya I had grown to love and hate the jungle as sailors grow to love and hate the sea. I was shy about those feelings, as sailors are shy of their feelings for the sea. With the jungle only two yards away from me after five years of separation, a muted uneasiness and excitement came to life in me, something altogether beyond awareness of the half-million-to-one chance that stragglers from the defeated terrorist army might be within range.

Nona got out of the car and walked slowly to the roadside, her golden eyes wide and her hands raised a little, her yellow dress and gold hair dazzling in the sunglare. She looked almost as she had when she'd startled me by sleepwalking into Zella's sitting-room while I read the letter from Andrew I'd taken from her handbag. She walked right in, pushing aside the first screen of leaves and creepers, as if somebody in there were calling her and she were obeying unwillingly; then she was quite out of sight, as you can be in many parts of that jungle at a distance of a couple of yards.

A minute went by. An oriole flew across the road like a blazing comet. I was trying to remember whether I'd warned Nona to take Paludrine, reflecting that even in that one minute she could be bitten by an infected mosquito and go down with malaria. Then she screamed.

*"Robert!"*

It must have taken me another minute to find her. It sounds a lie, but this was *belukar*, the secondary jungle that replaces the more open primeval jungle after clearing, as tough to get through as a New Year midnight crowd in Times Square. She was no more than ten yards from the roadside, and she called my name repeatedly, but it took Sam Chester and me a full minute to find her.

She had pushed her way into a trap of thorns, not rotans but something just as murderous—long, pliant whiplashes of dark olive, armed with monstrous grey thorns hooked like scimitars. There was blood on her throat and arms. Her head was hooded in a hanging cluster of gigantic grey leaves like elephants' ears. It shocked me to see how little it took to tip her over the edge of panic, to realize how desperately a few moments' experience of the jungle had rattled her.

Shame quickly followed relief when I got to her. She said, "Yes, Robert, I'm a fool. It only takes a leaf and a thorn to scare me."

"They've scared me before now," I admitted, starting to disengage her dress from the thorns. She was trembling. Suddenly I found myself reacting strongly to her beauty and nearness, and I was trembling too. Even though Sam Chester had reached us by then and had started to free her right arm from a coil of thorns, I had to fight an overmastering impulse to seize her in my arms and tell her how it was with me and always would be now. There was a desperation about me too, because what had happened in that London theatre had put me on guard against hope. Hope was just a build-up for disaster.

As we emerged into the sunshine again she sighed and said, "It's worse in there than I ever imagined—so dark and cruel, like a dream."

Like her sort of dream, she meant, the dream that preyed on her lonely sleep which only a strong drug could give her.

"Ten minutes and we'll all be drinking a nice cup of tea, love," Winnie said, opening the car door for her.

## 3

I saw Winnie's hand go up and grasp the top of the sun-baked car door tightly, and then Chester said, "Ambush Corner. This is where they got that fellow last year."

A perfect ambush position—but then, that country was full of them—a bend, about sixty degrees, with a thirty-foot cliff overhanging the right side and a steep plunge falling below the left. Plenty of cover for the ambush party on the cliff-top, and a view along half a mile of the approach.

"Car dived down there, got wedged in the undergrowth and burnt out," Sam Chester went on, flicking a large thumb left. "Now, Winnie, it was all a year ago and the only incident up this way for two years; so stop tensing yourself up."

They were rounding the bend, and Winnie didn't answer until we were well past the cliff-foot. Then her hand fell back into her lap and she said, "I can't help it, Sam, it's no good. I just see it all happening every time we go by—the shots and the flames. They couldn't miss us."

"*They,*" her husband argued patiently, "aren't in these parts any more."

"What about that poor fellow over at Kalun?" she demanded. "They got him."

"Thirty miles away and four months ago," he pointed out. "You're safer along here than you'd be on most of the roads round Liverpool, as I've said before."

"Plenty of times, Sam, but that doesn't make it true."

"Oh, for God's sake, Winnie, don't let's—"

"And blaspheming doesn't make it true, either."

But now I recognized the road and exclaimed in sudden excitement, "Andrew's tunnel!" The recognition of the landmark across almost twenty years was oddly moving. As I turned back to stare up the deep stream bed which had been the entrance to the track leading to Andrew's cave and jungle hide-out, I saw again two oddly contrasted figures making their way along it, two children forced by their isolation into companionship despite differences in age and temperament. The warmth of Andrew's impulsive charm and the chill of his naked selfishness came echoing back in confusion, and he was formidably there.

Then I felt Nona's eyes on me and turned to meet her baffling glance. She must have felt Andrew's nearness too, I believe, but how it affected her I couldn't guess.

"Now you can remember, I expect," I heard Winnie say and looked up to see the bridge over the Sunyi and bits of the last mile of the road showing through the military parade of ten thousand rubber trees, with the white bungalow on its steep hillock at the end of it. I did remember, and again I was surprised at being so moved.

It was long and low, the bungalow my uncle had built, white-walled with a roof of curled scarlet tiles and a row of white pillars along the greater part of its façade, which were slightly dropsical, like the stems of the royal palms that formed a short avenue from the entrance gates. There was shade from a screen of fine albizzia trees, and a breeze coming down one of the steep jungle valleys to the east caused a metallic rustling in the clumps of fan palm below the long veranda.

As soon as I'd moved myself into the same small room I'd slept in before, and washed, the nice cups of tea were ready and Winnie called us out onto the veranda. There was a police Land Rover parked in the shade of a palm clump, and an officer with an RAF moustache and fierce green eyes was saying appreciatively, "We told Winnie to be sure and bring us back something nice from Singapore, Miss Nicolas, and Winnie never lets you down."

Nona looked better already. She had changed into a blue shantung dress, and Winnie had cleaned up the fine thorn wounds. I resented the easy way she took the police lieutenant's too obvious tribute, but explained it to myself as relief at being with somebody who didn't remind her all the time of Andrew, who wasn't a threat to the secret she defended so stubbornly.

Sam Chester introduced me to the policeman, whose name was Waring. He hardly took his green eyes off Nona as he shook hands, but five minutes later, when Winnie led her away to deal with a thorn gash on her cheek, which a smile had reopened to drip blood on the bosom of her dress, he turned to me with a little frown of recollection.

"I'm sorry, I never listen properly to names when I'm introduced," he apologized. "But didn't Chester say your name was Avery?"

I said yes.

"No relation, I suppose, to the fellow who was killed in the ambush down the road last year," he said.

Excitement shot through me like a thousand-volt shock. I heard myself asking, "Why, what was his name?"

He frowned again. "Angus, wasn't it? No, Andrew. Andrew Avery."

4

Just like that.

What had old Smithy said to his crony a day or two before his death? "It was under my nose all the time." Of course it had been. Andrew's name and the fact of his death in a terrorist ambush must have been on numbers of police records, but old Smith, with his criminal record over in Sarawak, hadn't wanted to approach the police direct. "If only I hadn't been a scared rabbit and told a stupid lie," he'd added, referring to his report to Uncle Max that the police records had yielded no clue. So in the end he'd come across the information in some dubious way—one that put Marcos Aragon on his trail, if my guess was right.

I said to Waring, "I'm his cousin. I came East to find out whether he was alive or dead."

Waring stroked the ends of his coppery moustache upwards. "But his wife was informed. I'm sure she was, though she didn't come to the funeral. You never heard from her?"

I said no. "None of his family knew his wife. We hadn't seen him for years."

"I see. Well, we merely informed his wife in Singapore and left the rest to the other fellow."

I asked which other fellow.

"The one who was in the ambush with him and got clear. Now, what was his name?"

On an impulse I suggested, "Lyle, was it?"

"That's right, Lyle," he said at once, but some variation in the pronunciation made me inquire, "Or Lyall?"

He nodded and spelled out the name. "Malcolm Lyall. You know him?"

I said, "I know nothing at all. It would help me a lot if we could go through the whole thing."

Winnie and Nona were coming back onto the veranda, and he glanced towards them doubtfully. "If I could come down to your office," I suggested, "see the report, perhaps."

"Come back with me when I leave," he offered, and turned away, drawn to Nona's beauty like a flower to the sun.

I listened anxiously for what he'd say to Nona, but I needn't have worried. Nona was pleasure, not business, and what had staggered me had only lightly interested him. He started talking about the dance at the club on Saturday night, the club's fine tennis courts, the swimming pool at Kuala Jeroh, and repeated his inquiry as to how long she would be staying at Sungei Sunyi. As soon as I was reassured that she wasn't in for a shock, I began drafting the cable to Uncle Max in my head and reflecting that Nona was definitely a widow now and I was a man with means to support a wife in comfort.

He was dead, then. I sat chewing a pâté sandwich and remembering the tall youth with the dazzling blue eyes and the romantic outlaw personality who had fascinated and bullied me in that house seventeen years before. Dead after all, his stormy life stormily ended in ambush and fire. I could hear his voice, tense and arrogant, calling across this veranda as he went off on some private ploy, "No, young Robert, I don't want you. You stay out of this"—and I could almost fancy the same voice calling the same words resentfully from the grave, warning me against intrusion. And the fascination survived in some odd way, because I felt an instinctive forlornness in being excluded once again. That must all sound dismally whimsical, but in those moments I most definitely felt an echo of my cousin's personality.

Could Nona feel it too? I wondered. Was that why, only a few minutes later, she sighed and closed her eyes briefly and then excused herself, her figure somehow lonely and driven as she turned back into the house? Was Andrew the closest link between us, as well as the force that kept us apart?

Seven minutes later I was passing for the second time that day beneath the jungle-smothered cliff-top on which Andrew's killers had lain in ambush. I said, staring up at the black skyline of leaves, "He hadn't much chance, driving into that."

Waring snapped a glance upwards. "Not much. He died easy, all the same. One round through his eye and another through his chest before the car caught fire. Lyall burnt himself badly trying to drag him out when the car was blazing down that slope there; but he'd been dead for a minute or more by then."

"Tougher for him than for Andrew," I said, as we left the bend behind us.

The Malay constable in the seat behind us relaxed the blunt brown hands that had alerted his Sten perfunctorily as we entered the ambush position, and Waring said, "I suppose so. Quite the windiest sensation I know, being ambushed."

I didn't mention it, but I knew all about it too. While we'd passed round the bend I'd heard and felt and smelled again every sensation of that rainy dusk on the Pahang jungle road a few miles from Jerantut, my platoon returning to camp in three trucks after a six-day patrol without a shot fired, filthy and dog-tired and chilled and as silent as if we were in contact with the enemy—and suddenly we were in contact with the enemy. Corporal Hardy dead and heavily slumped across my knees; our brave Dyak tracker Langgong wounded in the foot; two trucks colliding and one half overturning in the tangled bush of the roadside; Smith in action with the Bren in absolutely no time at all and probably saving the lives of half of us; the bomb that knocked young Hayes out and then didn't explode, even when Sergeant Parry threw it back up the cliff; the flash of tracer through the cold, darkening rain; fire then from the section that had got through the ambush and come back to engage the enemy we never once saw; and almost immediately the long blast on the whistle with which the terrorist commander broke off the engagement. And then the silence. It was one thing I was going to remember for always. . . .

I asked, "Is Lyall in Malaya?"

"No, but not far away. Over in Sumatra, not very far from Medan, I believe. We must have his address at the station."

A few minutes later we were at the station, a long wooden building on stone piles, with a veranda running all round it and apron fences of barbed wire isolating it from the small village. I'd spent a good deal of time in three or four very similar ones during my time in Malaya, and Waring's own office was entirely typical, with the usual collection of dreadful photographs of the terrorists believed to have been operating in the area at various times, some of them with a scarlet tick against them to signify that they had been killed or were known to have died, two of them even taken after death, and neither of them very neat deaths, either. Six dirty khaki uniform caps, Japanese style, with the red five-pointed Communist star above the peak, were set in a circle round a faded red flag. Pointing to one of the trophy caps, Waring said, "Belonged to one of the party who ambushed your cousin. One of those Japanese rifles, too." And he pointed to a junk-shop collection of weapons stacked in a corner.

"You mean Lyall got one of them?" I asked him.

"Winged one, anyway. He had a rifle and returned the ambush fire. I don't suppose he'd have got away with it, if—" He interrupted himself there and said, "But I'll give you the story as it happened.

"They were in your cousin's car, an old Morris Ten, on their way to see the then manager of Droga Besar Estate, thirty miles north of here. If you know this country you'll notice it wasn't the normal route for them to take, coming up from KL, but now that you tell me your cousin had lived at Sungei Sunyi as a boy, it's obvious that they made the detour to take a glance at his old home. Lyall is a South African, very nice fellow. He'd just inherited a small group of estates from an uncle of his, rubber plantations in North Borneo and larger mixed estates over in Sumatra. He'd never had expectations from his uncle and had never set foot in Asia, didn't know a rubber tree from a mistletoe bough. In Singapore he met your cousin and his wife, and they were soon friends. Lyall was looking round for a right-hand man, somebody with experience who could take full responsibility until he'd come by some experience for himself, and your cousin had recommended the manager at Droga Besar, fellow called Humphrey or Humphries. Well, they drove up from Singapore, spent the night at Ulu Maias Rest House, and made an early start. They ran into the ambush soon after ten hundred hours."

I said, "Pretty bad luck, in this area."

He frowned, resenting the implication that he had spent two years in a safe area. "In *that* neck of the woods, yes," he corrected me. "Sungei Sunyi is the one part of our parish that's been quiet through most of the Emergency. We've always thought they might be using that jungle south of Chester's place as some sort of rest or regrouping area; at any rate, they've staged only two incidents there in three years, and one of them accounted for your cousin."

"You were here at the time?"

"Yes—first on the scene after the action. The terrorists had cleared off by then, or they did as soon as they saw us arrive. There was that cap and that old rifle and a few leaves spattered with blood under the little sun shelter they'd made on the edge of the bluff by drawing together a few branches overhead. The troops from Droga came up with their trackers before noon, but they couldn't find the party's line of withdrawal before the afternoon rains started, so the follow-up came to nothing. Lyall was a pretty bad case of shock for a couple of hours, though he'd kept his head during the crisis, returning the ambush fire and getting himself badly burnt trying to rescue your cousin when the car burst into flames. I phoned the manager at Droga Besar—no, it wasn't Humphries, either, it was Hargreaves—and he came over and took charge. Four days later he drove Lyall down to Singapore to see your cousin's wife, and the last I heard he was still with him, over in Sumatra. Your cousin was buried at Ipoh. Naturally I imagined his wife would have let his family know."

I thought of Nona, of the shock of Lyall's news. Outside the window some of the constables were playing basketball, and beyond them the sun was beginning its swift fall towards the western skyline. "We'd none of us seen him for years," I said. "He went his own way."

Waring was surreptitiously reading a letter that lay open on his desk. "I mustn't keep you," I said. "You said you could find Lyall's address, though."

He found it after a search—a place called Kidumai, between twenty and thirty miles from Medan. "I might as well go across and see him," I said. It would be as well to have some sort of document signed by Lyall among those I took home to establish the fact of death. "I could fly to Medan from Penang, I suppose."

Waring nodded. "You'll like him." He got up from his chair and dismissed it all. "Well, I hope Miss Nicolas will be well enough to come down to the dance on Saturday. But I'll be seeing her before then, I expect."

I merely said, "How d'you send a cable from here?"

He fixed me up with a telephone and I drafted the message to Uncle Max: CONFIRMATION ANDREW'S DEATH APRIL LAST YEAR COLLECTING DOCUMENTS RETURNING SHORTLY ROBERT.

5

I switched off the news bulletin on Radio Singapore. There had been no mention of the discovery of the dead body of a coffee merchant named Marcos Aragon with a mysterious scratched wound round his throat. And there had been nothing in the day's newspaper, either.

Had the thug Ho Fung rowed the huge corpse out to sea and dumped it? But there was no word of a disappearance, either. I pictured, and not for the first time, the anxiety of the poor wife, the distress of Sophie and her sister. But now a new idea had crept up on me.

Had Aragon really been dead? Had the revolting layers of fat over his breast and round his heart insulated the vibration of the heartbeat from my shrinking hand? Had he merely lost consciousness and recovered it soon after I drove off cursing? Was he still hunting me? Until next day's newspaper carried a report of the body's being caught in a fisherman's net, the suspicion that I hadn't yet finished with Marcos Aragon disturbed me at intervals.

"Bad news on the wireless, Mr. Avery?" Winnie asked, coming in and studying my face with concern. She wore an enormous straw gardening hat and an unwise homemade dress patterned with larger-than-life-size birds of paradise.

"No-o," I answered her, but wondering whether no news really could be good news in this case. "I'll have to leave in the morning," I told her, "just for a couple of nights."

"Then you did hear something on the news," she said quickly, sinking into a chair with a trowel in one gloved hand and a frail seedling in the other. "If it's anything we can help over . . ."

I told her no. It puzzled me that I should be so unexultant, now that my mission East had come to a sudden end that was so entirely satisfactory, now that we'd all come into small fortunes, now that Nona was at any rate physically free of Andrew. I just wasn't responding.

"Only the car in the morning as far as Ipoh," I said. "I've booked the plane there up to Penang."

"To Penang?" Nona had come in as I spoke, and blinked.

"Only a couple of nights," I said. I wasn't able to meet her eyes because I knew things she didn't know I knew.

Sam Chester, back from the smokehouse, filled the bungalow with his deep, vibrating voice and protested when told of my leaving next morning. "Soon as you've gone, every nip I take Winnie'll call solitary drinking. Solitary Drinking, the Great Destroyer! She wouldn't like it any better if I went down to the club and got tight on social drinking!"

"How you harp on it, Sam!" Winnie sighed.

"And what about Robert?" Sam demanded. "Sitting there with his tongue out for the past hour, I suppose, and not a drop offered."

Winnie flushed because it wasn't far off the truth and she had forgotten. But she rallied with, "Robert's been told to make himself at home, and he knows where the stuff's kept. *Do* you drink in the middle of the day, Robert?" She made it sound like an inquiry into an abnormal craving.

I said I'd keep Sam company.

It was then that I saw the ancient figure behind Sam Chester, a small Malay, incredibly wrinkled and bent, leaning on a staff and wrapped in a black and green tartan sarong. And now I recalled seeing him as I'd strolled through the village early that morning, huddled in a sort of trance on the veranda of a small bamboo house.

"Tuan does not remember me, then?" an old voice sighed.

But now I did remember. "Ngari!"

He brought Andrew closer too. The old tracker—for he had seemed old to me when I had known him seventeen years before—had been our nurse-companion in the jungle and on the river in those days, and I recognized him now with emotion.

"But I knew you when you passed this morning," the old man said, hobbling close to look keenly up at my face. "It was the *mata-mata biru*."

The *mata-mata biru*, the Avery blue eyes, had identified me to him, even though I had been only just eleven the last time he'd seen me. "Ah, many white people have blue eyes," the old fellow declared, "but never so blue as yours, never so blue as the young tuan's and his father's."

The young tuan was obviously Andrew. I felt self-conscious as he went on staring into my eyes, dazzled by the blue he had remembered for so long. "And where is the young tuan now?" he went on, his bony fingers never still as they clasped the old staff. "Tell me the news of him."

He hadn't heard. When the ambush had happened neither

the manager nor the assistant at Sungei Sunyi—both drunks, according to Waring—had noticed that Avery was a name in the estate books, and villagers like Ngari would never have inquired or heard the name of the victim. When I told him, the old man was speechless with amazement.

The Chinese houseboy brought a tray of drinks, and Sam gave the old man a brandy that made his eyes sparkle. "Ah, what badness he had, that boy!" he exclaimed. "What badness!" But he said it indulgently, as a father might say with wry pride that his son was a young devil; only then he added, "Real badness as well. For surely there was a *saitan* in him."

Andrew came close as Ngari spoke, Andrew and his *saitan*, his devil, and I seemed to feel a sudden lowering of temperature.

"He was bad to you, though you were a good child," he said then, staring now into the glass he held. "He wanted to be a rajah, with us all kneeling to him. And sly he was, sly as a *pelandok,* and when he liked he could charm like a songbird. But he made himself lonely with his bad pride. Lonely, he was."

Oh, yes, he must have been that, with his conviction that everybody was always letting him down. And he had died in the belief that even his Aunt Julia, whose heart he'd broken, had let him down. But hadn't she done just that? I found myself asking then. Hadn't her devoted love deprived him all the same of the one cardinal necessity of a child after love, the discipline a child cannot teach itself and which even the sternest efforts in adult life can never fully make good. He had had a right to expect that from Julia, and in her selfish love she had never made the tough effort necessary.

I remembered the letter in Nona's handbag. Yes, he'd believed that she had let him down too.

6

Mohammed Khan's handsome smile confronted me as I strode gratefully out of the hammering sunglare of Alor Star Street into Number 15. Penang Island was frying under the grilling yellow sky, without its usual sea breeze to soften the hammer blows. Mohammed Khan's small shop smelled pleasantly of the twenty spices he sold for curry. As soon as I gave him my name he offered me a chair and a cigarette, and when I refused the latter sent a black-eyed boy running for a glass of very sweet orangeade.

I handed over a hundred and twenty-five dollars and said I was sorry he'd had to wait so long for it. Turning his head on one side in the little-girl fashion of Indians who are pleased and shy, he smiled and thanked me warmly. "I like to offer you my sympathy, sir," he added. "Mr. Andrew Avery very nice gentleman."

With a murmur of embarrassment I turned to the drink.

"That day he said to me, 'Sorry, Mohammed, nothing in the kitty till the end of the month. I won't forget you then.' But next day he is killed in the ambush."

I could see Andrew sprawling in this very chair, smoking Mohammed Khan's cigarettes and using his first name and telling him cynical lies. It had given me real gratification to pay over that hundred and twenty-five dollars—less than fifteen pounds, but a large sum to a small Pakistani shopkeeper. I asked, "And Mr. Lyall was with him that day?"

"Yes, but not in here. Mr. Lail stay in the car, but his name is in the paper afterwards when I read about the ambush, and my friend in Medan tells me Mr. Lail is nephew of old Mr. Van Dessen and lives now in his house at Kidumai. So I write to him and ask respectfully address of Mr. Andrew Avery's family, but not getting any reply unfortunately."

I reflected that if I had come to Penang before visiting Sungei Sunyi I should have had my first news of the ambush from Mohammed Khan. As it was, I had no more questions for him—except one.

"Do you know of any other debt my cousin wasn't able to settle?" I asked.

Yes, he did. Shyly he gave me the names of four other Punjabi traders and offered the black-eyed boy, his son, as guide to them in turn. In the next half hour I paid out a hundred, a hundred and twenty, thirty, and two hundred and fifty—checks cashed as a favour by small shopkeepers. Later I'd put advertisements in all Malayan papers and wait for the flood of demands to come in. It would be a pleasure to pay.

### 7

Lyall's house was a handsome old Dutch bungalow with a magnificent blue background of mountain and a foreground of young green ricefields. In the end I hadn't sent a telegram announcing my visit, having left it till too late at the airfield, so I was unexpected.

It was past eleven in the morning, after visa complications and a night in Medan, when I reached the place. Just the sort of beautiful Sumatran girl you'd expect to find in the backwoods house of a European bachelor came onto the veranda and told me that Tuan Lail had spent the night in Medan and wouldn't be back until sunset. In the thwarted pause that followed this announcement she invited me to lunch and a siesta in the house. I'd have said she was pretty free with any sort of hospitality.

I waited. The lunch was good. I love those Indonesian curries, with their prodigal variety of dishes, especially the delicate pale sauces that owe so much to coconut milk; the large, sweet prawns; and the delicious pink wafers they call *krupuk*, made—incredibly—from tapioca and shrimps. Afterwards I took my first siesta for more than a week in a large, bare guest room. The girl had laid out a green silk sarong for me and high wooden bathing clogs and a towel. When I asked her her name she answered, "Kuwadi," with a glance that was inviting as well as exciting. I wondered whether Lyall relied on her at all. . . .

He came in soon after five, when I'd drunk three cups of good coffee and eaten a couple of the little sweet things Kuwadi brought with it. I heard the car pull up and looked over the veranda rail to see a tall man getting out of a big American station wagon. He came up the steps, looking hot and tired, and when Kuwadi stepped silently forward on her pretty bare feet with the obvious message that he had a visitor, there was no mistaking the silent curse his lips formed. I backed swiftly to my chair, with a quick change-over from feeling welcome to feeling unwelcome.

He came towards me, blinking handsome dark brown eyes and dropping a bundle of mail into a chair on the way. I got up and said, "Sorry to crash in without warning. I'm Robert Avery."

He shook my hand doubtfully, blinking the almost black eyes again and saying, after a pause, "D'you mean, one of Andrew's family?"

"A cousin," I told him.

His good-looking face expressed what I took to be a rather remote and ill-at-ease sympathy—as well it might—until I explained that in England none of us had known of his death and I'd come East to find him.

He said, "I never realized he was that interesting to his relatives. Didn't he tell me they'd washed their hands of him?"

Despite his cool welcome, I felt attracted to him. He was a fine-looking man with a proud, square face, brilliant black hair, and strong brown limbs revealed by his short-sleeved shirt and brief shorts. But it was the eyes that impressed me. Ordinarily I scarcely notice men's eyes, only women's—in detail, I mean; but perhaps it was old Ngari's intent stare into my arresting blue Avery eyes and what he'd said about Andrew's eyes and his father's that had started up the interest. I'd been impressed by the black eyes of Mohammed Khan's son, and now I was noting the strength and personality of Malcolm Lyall's, which were almost as black.

I said, "We'd never even met him, most of us. I had, actually, when I was just a kid. You can't take much interest in somebody you don't know, somebody you'd only heard about. But it's a matter of a will now. We need to have proof of his death before any of the rest of us can inherit his aunt's money."

He said, "I thought he told me he had a rich aunt in England but she'd cut him out of her will."

"She did, but later on she changed her mind."

He had half sunk into a long cane chair when he frowned down at his grubby hands and creased shorts. "D'you mind if I take a shower and change?" he asked, getting up again. "You'll be staying the night, of course. Just call for anything you want."

He was soon back, in a cream shirt and blue slacks, his black hair damp from the shower. He lit a cigarette and said, "Yes, Andrew believed his aunt had cut him adrift for keeps. Around the time that I met him first, that was."

"When she was dying, ten months ago, she changed her mind. She hadn't heard from him for months, and her letters had been returned undelivered. She didn't know whether he was alive or dead, so she left all her money to him if he still lived, and to the rest of us, his cousins, if he were dead. So we had to discover whether he was alive or dead, and I came East to make inquiries. Three days ago I heard about the ambush at Sungei Sunyi, so I've come over to ask you to let me have a written statement, the sort of thing I can forward to my aunt's lawyers with the police statement and certificates."

"Of course," he said, pouring himself a brandy and ginger ale. Leaning back with the drink, he looked across at me and said, "I can see the family likeness. The eyes, I suppose, though Andrew's were even bluer. And the voice too, perhaps."

He held the glass in his left hand, and now I noticed his right. It was slightly misshapen, the fingers permanently half contracted into a clawlike gesture. That had been the reason for the unfamiliar feel of his handshake. Now I remembered how he had suffered burns in an effort to drag Andrew's body from the blazing car. I said, "I was in an ambush once, over in Pahang when I was soldiering in Malaya. It was bad enough then, with twenty-eight armed men with me. It must have been hell that time at Sungei Sunyi."

He simply said, "Yes, but worse somehow when it was all over. I wasn't much good for anything for a day or two."

That was a familiar reaction. Neither of us found anything to say then for a couple of minutes. Kuwadi appeared in the background, and he threw her what looked like a glance of irritation. She had changed into a diaphanous white *kebaya* and a rich gold batik sarong, and there was gold round her slim wrists and in her earlobes. She hovered a moment uncertainly, then switched on the two veranda lamps. At once he exclaimed in impatient Malay, without even turning in her direction. Silently she switched them out again and went softly away into the darkness.

"The minute the lights go up a million insects rush in," he explained to me. "She never learns."

I found it embarrassing, the treatment of a mistress as if she were a stupid sort of servant. Changing the subject, I asked, "How long was it you knew Andrew?" I had come to have an unquenchable curiosity about Andrew, and here was one of the very few sources of information.

"Just ten weeks," he told me. "When I came from South Africa there was nobody I knew in the whole continent of Asia, but a friend at home had given me an introduction to Andrew. We made friends, and he did a lot for me."

"You got on well with him, then?" I queried.

He gave a short, attractive smile. "Most of the time," he said. "He was a strong character, of course."

"A bit of a bastard, I understood."

The black brows rose above the dark eyes. "I wouldn't have said so. Whose word have you taken for that?"

"Nobody's. He was a bastard to me when I stayed with his father for six months."

"But weren't you children then?"

"Children can be bastards," I pointed out. "And a child of sixteen who's a bastard isn't likely to change much later on."

"Oh, he was a strong character, as I said," Lyall repeated. "Didn't suffer fools gladly, rather liked his own way, not always as tactful as he might have been."

"At war with the world because it didn't always give him his own way," I amended. But Lyall wouldn't accept that.

"I see you've got a down on him," he decided.

"That's what he'd probably have said himself—about me and about most people he had dealings with. About you, quite possibly, if he'd known you a little longer. That was his self-portrait, you know: a man who was always being let down, a man the world had a down on; a romantic outlaw, too strong a character for those he relied on, so that they let him down in the end."

"Had he never been let down, then?" Lyall evidently thought my view needed modification, and I liked him for his loyalty to the friend who had died at his side. Here, for a certainty, was somebody who had never let Andrew down.

"I suppose people got fed up with him in the end," I answered, a little troubled by a suspicion that I wasn't being entirely fair. "That's what happened with his Aunt Julia. He'd let *her* down so often that her heart broke and she tried to cut him out of her life and died a lonely death soon after."

"H'm. Well, I was his friend and I can only say he didn't seem like that to me. I found him—well, a better man than most." But I felt then, for the first time, that there was some reserve behind his words, a tinge of falsity in the pleasant voice. I suspected that I wasn't getting the whole story, and for the first time, too, I recognized a definite suspicion that I hadn't yet come to the end of my search for the truth about Andrew.

There was something more. There had to be. There were things I knew, things to which I hadn't assigned their proper significance, a detail or details which I hadn't recognized as suspicious but which disturbed my subconscious. And I was reassessing Lyall.

I never back my first impressions strongly. At times they're confirmed, of course, but there have been too many times when they haven't been. Now I was revising, or wondering whether I oughtn't to revise, my first impression of Malcolm Lyall.

Why was it his defence of Andrew now sounded unconvincing? Was it merely that in a conventional speak-no-ill-of-the-dead spirit he had overstated his esteem for him? Was it merely that he thought I'd gone a bit too far in denigrating

Andrew's character and in rebuttal had laid it on a bit thick in his turn, but was too essentially honest to be able to make it sound totally convincing? Or was there something more?

Now it was so dark on the veranda that everything had fallen into the sombre monotones of a charcoal drawing, with Lyall's cigarette end the only point of brilliance. Three miles across the ricefields we could see an occasional pair of headlights piercing the darkness along the straight main road. Fireflies traced their lighted wanderings through the darkness.

I said, "His wife doesn't seem to have found him a very satisfactory husband."

I saw him stiffen at that, and it was a moment before he answered me. "His wife? You know his wife?"

I said yes.

"Aren't marriages always pretty difficult for outsiders to judge?" It was a reasonable enough thing to say, but I felt it was a closely guarded reply.

"I suppose so. You know her too, of course."

He threw his cigarette over the veranda rail. It flew off like a swifter and more determined firefly. "I knew her."

I waited for more, but he added nothing to the bare admission. "I get the impression that he made a pretty grim mess of her life," I insisted.

"Not quite the wife for a man like him, perhaps," he said out of the darkness.

I cut in quickly. "She let him down, you mean? You accept his version?" I had a strong feeling that he was somehow on the defensive, or at any rate that he was ill at ease with this turn of our talk. I wondered how well he had known Nona.

"She was beautiful," he said inconsequentially in a day-dreaming tone.

"She is," I agreed.

"But—" He sighed. "Oh, well, I suppose there may have been faults on his side as well."

"Meaning that most of the faults, at any rate, must have been hers?"

His hands, the strong left one and the contracted right one, rose in a small gesture of protest. "Nona may have been utterly faultless, for all I know. You've evidently made up your mind that she was. Nona was—well, the wife of a friend of mine. Quite honestly, I'm not very happy to be discussing her."

I was puzzled. Now nothing rang quite true—or was I indulging in an amateur playwright's weakness for detecting dramatic stresses and riddles in quite normal behaviour? Accepting another pink gin, I was glad of the dark because I was confused and uneasy. This man Lyall seemed to be offering me a challenge every time he spoke, and I had an unaccountable feeling of being outclassed.

"Hello!" Lyall had leaned forward in his long chair. "Another visitor."

Up the side road to the bungalow the headlamps of a car were advancing, weaving left and right along the mud track, jogging up and down in the potholes and ruts gouged out by recent rains. I wasn't ungrateful at having an uneasy conversation interrupted.

The car reached the sweep of neater roadway that wove a circle, bordered by crimson and golden cannas, below the veranda, and drew up at the foot of the wooden steps. There was a pause, and then a door opened and a woman stepped out and came hurriedly up the steps, her high heels tapping the timbers urgently, her beautiful figure silhouetted against the pool of radiance formed by the headlamps.

Malcolm Lyall's sandalled feet swung down to the floor. We

recognized her in the same instant, but only he exclaimed aloud.

"Nona!"

8

She was pale and breathless, and her hair was in disorder. As Lyall clicked on the lights she halted like a small snared beast, and her right hand went up to her throat. She had seen me, but she stared at Lyall. She didn't say anything, just stared at him.

What I was feeling was pity—yes, the old ready reaction, keener than ever. I wanted to snap out the lights again and take her in my arms and tell her to leave it all to me. She had reached her load limit, anybody could see that. If she was driven much farther under that load she was going to crash.

We stood there, frozen still and silent, like a broken-down movie, until Lyall said, "You know Robert Avery, don't you?"

Her lovely eyes flashed me a glance, but I couldn't interpret it. Her light brown eyes, that had been locked to Lyall's dark brown ones, turned my way for a moment, and I wanted desperately to understand and respond, but I was baffled. Then she was facing Lyall again. She still hadn't spoken.

I was trying not to admit that it looked as if they knew each other well, those two. They were in on something that I was shut out of, that was my reading of their eloquent silence, and the exclusion made me mad.

*"Suka makan sekarang?"*

We all started as if a shot had been fired. The girl Kuwadi stood in the shadows behind us, asking Lyall in a cold, indifferent voice if he wanted to eat yet. Her bare feet had not disturbed our tense silence, and they were silent now as she moved forward, her perfect leaf-shaped eyes passing over Nona's face in serene scrutiny. I felt her warmth and her scent as she passed me.

Lyall spoke only one word. *"Pergi!"* Ordered crudely to get out, the girl gave him a long, cold look and left us like a bored empress. Nona's eyes followed her, and once again her glance was a complete mystery to me. As her eyes swept back to Lyall's face he turned abruptly away.

All this had taken only thirty seconds. The car which had brought Nona had barely disappeared through the high gates at the end of the drive. Malcolm Lyall's voice was still harsh as he spoke again.

"It used to be Martini and soda, or am I forgetting?" He was at the drink cabinet, turning over a glass, his back to us.

"I don't want anything," Nona said. She met my eyes for a moment, then turned away. I pushed a chair forward, and she sank into it, setting her big raffia handbag on the floor beside her.

"Well, it's nice to see you, Nona," Lyall said, deliberately drawling and looking at her over his shoulder. "I can't honestly say you're looking fine but— It's nice to see you."

She didn't know what to do with her hands. Even her stage training wasn't helping now. She seemed a thousand miles away from me, but in some disturbing way she seemed close to Lyall, as if they were understanding each other without a word spoken, as if I were an intruder.

But it wasn't an easy intimacy that I suspected between them. It was an uneasy one—on her part, anyway. Or was it only my presence that caused the uneasiness? As for me, I was holding on to my glass as if it were a lifeline, my mind crowded with ugly shadows.

Lyall came back and sat down. "Robert Avery's come over

to get some details about Andrew," he said. "He's just learned that he's come into a fortune—Andrew's money. Andrew's ill wind has blown him a lot of good."

His voice had changed. It was brittle and self-conscious. "He only heard about the ambush a day or two ago. Does that mean you never let Andrew's family know?"

She had found a little more assurance. "I didn't know any of them. Andrew said he was finished with them, and he never talked about them, ever."

"Robert had no use for him, anyway. He called him a bastard."

She didn't say anything.

"In fact, I seem to have been chief mourner," Lyall went on, his eyes challenging her. He was trying to provoke her into saying something, but she wouldn't speak. "Only mourner, maybe."

I got out of my chair. I said, "I'll take a shower, I think," and left them. Instead of going to my room, though, I went out into the garden and stood under a tall cassia tree that rained fragrance through the darkness. What I wanted to do was creep round the bungalow to listen under the veranda for what they would say now that they were alone; but I found I couldn't do that. I stood there for half an hour, resisting the ugly speculations that were forcing a way into my mind, feeling a tension mounting and straining, half maddened by a doubt that mattered to me vitally.

The dinner gong roused me with a start, and I went in slowly, wishing myself ten thousand miles away.

9

The night was hotter than in either Singapore or Sungei Sunyi, but it wasn't the thick, heavy heat of the darkness that kept me awake. We had all gone to bed at ten o'clock, but the luminous hands of my watch showed half-past midnight, and sleep was far away. It was cooler to stand by my window, feeling the slight stirring of air that came up through the louvres of the shutters with the wan reflected moonlight.

I had a feeling, which of course I can't explain or defend against scepticism, that the house was not sleeping either. I didn't believe Nona was sleeping, however much of her drug she might have taken, and perhaps not Lyall either. Was the girl Kuwadi with him tonight? I wondered. If not, perhaps she was awake, too.

The fronds of a palm in the garden rustled in a wayward night breeze like a giant crumpling sheet metal. A bird that had been roosting in the fronds squawked complainingly at being disturbed. Some winged creature, a night bird or a great night insect, whirred past the window. And inside the house someone was moving too. Somebody had just crept past my door.

My door opened soundlessly as my damp hand lifted the latch, and I put one eye to the inch-wide crack and stared down the corridor.

It was Nona. At first I thought it was Kuwadi, because she was wearing a sarong; but then I remembered that Nona had arrived with nothing but a handbag, like a fugitive or a refugee, so obviously she'd had to borrow a sarong for the night. She was moving away from me with a slow, gliding step, but at the end of the corridor she turned in a direct shaft of moonlight and a moment came back to me suddenly—the moment in Zella's sitting room when I'd looked up from the letter from Andrew to see her sleepwalking through her bedroom door.

I went after her, shocked again by the eeriness of the dream-walking. She had passed out of sight round a corner, and I followed swiftly on bare feet. At the corner, though, I halted sharply.

She was at the door of Malcolm Lyall's room. I knew it was his room, because he'd wished me a laconic good night from its doorway. She was at his door and lifting its latch softly— not sleepwalking, but opening Lyall's door, calling a whispered word into the darkness, and then stepping softly inside.

The door closed, and now nothing could stop me from tiptoeing towards it and pausing outside, holding my breath and listening. I heard low voices, hers and his, but it wasn't possible to distinguish words. I felt sick and somehow afraid.

On my way back to my room I passed a door which opened softly as I approached it. In a cream-coloured sarong, Kuwadi stood in the dusky moonlight, her eyes enormous, her glance deep. And slowly she smiled, or half smiled—meaning exactly what, I had no idea. Then she took a step back, and the door opened a little farther.

I turned away and plunged back into my room. Standing in the middle of the tiled floor, I let the shock tear through me, surrendering myself to it for a few moments, not thinking, only feeling. Slowly, then, several ugly thoughts came crawling out of cover, thoughts that had been lurking deep in my subconscious.

That ambush . . .

There had been one or two odd things about the ambush. It was odd to be ambushed on that road, to start with—the only ambush in more than two years, and the only incident, except for the wounding of a Tamil tapper suspected of giving information on terrorist supplies to the police at Kuala Jeroh, in almost three years. It was a quiet area, Sungei Sunyi, white on the operational maps, signifying free of terrorist aggression. But Andrew had been ambushed and killed there.

Then there was the question of a target. Terrorists were often cowards but not very often fools. They ambushed for two reasons: the first to capture arms and ammunition, the second to murder key figures in the war against Communist terrorism—police officers, rubber-estate managers, and such-like. And yet some terrorists were said to have laid an ambush in a district they were believed, on the contrary, to use as a rest or regrouping area. And to attack whom? Just two civilians they couldn't possibly have identified, in an old civilian car, with nothing in it for them beyond the possibility of capturing a couple of almost useless pistols or perhaps a rifle. It didn't make sense. What had the terrorists got out of that ambush? Nothing of any use to them at all. What could they have ever expected to get out of it? Hardly anything more.

Oh yes, pretty futile ambush attacks had been made from time to time—I knew of a couple myself, back in '52. But that brought in the timing, and the timing was odd as well. Both those pretty pointless ambushes I'd known of in Pahang had happened at the same hour, the sunset hour. And the explanation was surely simple enough.

The terrorists had mounted an ambush, and they'd been waiting through the broiling day for a worth-while target, or for a certain target they had reason to believe would be using that road or jungle path. Well, things had turned out differently and nothing worth their fire had passed through the ambush position. Finally, when night was not far off and a move back to base had to be made, they would sometimes, out of impatience and bloody-mindedness, shoot up just anything that moved into their line of fire—even a boy on a bicycle, in one of the five-o'clock ambushes I knew about.

But Andrew and Lyall had been shot up around ten in the morning. In itself that was a rather unusual hour for an ambush, unless the target was abnormally important. An ambush

before mid-morning left the security forces seven or eight
hours for a follow-up operation. If there were Iban Army
trackers from Sarawak around (and there had been half a
dozen at Kuala Jeroh at that time), then they'd have many
hours of light to search for tracks and follow them, another
reason why ambushes took place towards nightfall in the later
years of the Emergency, when the Borneo trackers had
proved their worth so splendidly. Of course, if the target was
sufficiently important or rewarding, an attack might be made
soon after sunrise, even; but Andrew and Lyall in Andrew's
old car must have been one of the most futile targets of the
Emergency. And the ambush party had been watching them
for thirty seconds or more in a good light before the car entered the target area—little possibility of a mistake in identification.

Another thing: three Iban trackers had been on the scene
within half an hour and they'd failed to find the ambush
party's approach or withdrawal routes. Now that, to anyone
who had worked with those fine boys from Borneo, just didn't
ring true. Certainly, trackers varied in their skill; some of the
youngest and those from the spoiled down-river areas were
pretty moderate, and admittedly there were places where not
even an Iban could find tracks—Piccadilly, for instance, or
the hard, beaten paths through the jungle which were the
roads made by elephant herds when there had been no rain to
soften their surfaces. But at the top of that cliff there had been
an average patch of dense secondary jungle, and even I, after
a year on jungle patrols with Tracker Langgong, would have
guaranteed to find some sort of tracks there, though, unlike
Langgong, I'd probably have lost them the first bit of difficult
tracking terrain I came to.

So what did it all add up to? This: I didn't believe in that
ambush any more. I didn't believe any real terrorists had ever

waited on top of that cliff and opened fire on Andrew's car.

So what *had* happened?

I believed, now, that this had happened: just short of that bend Lyall had asked Andrew to stop the car for some reason. He'd got out then, with a gun of some kind, and from a certain distance he'd turned and shot Andrew twice, once through the heart, once through the eye. And it was something he'd planned ahead. He had the props ready to mount a fake ambush. He'd got up the cliff and planted a terrorist cap, the old Japanese rifle, and the spent rounds from his own rifle and a few splashes of blood (his own or Andrew's, never mind whose) on conspicuous leaves, trampled around a bit, and finally tied a few branches and creeper together to form a shaded lookout position, as he could easily have found out was a frequent terrorist custom—though there perhaps he'd overdone it, because from below the top of the bluff had looked as if there was plenty of normal shade.

Then—standing on the running board, pushing down the hand throttle, kicking in the clutch, and running the old car to the road edge and letting her go over the drop, following to start a fire if one didn't break out naturally, which was a possibility. And then the wait for the first of those who'd heard the distant outbreak of firing, the run down to the flaming wreck to be found making a gallant attempt to save the friend he hadn't realized was already dead. And there he'd done a really thorough job, getting more than he'd bargained for, a maimed hand for the rest of his life.

That was how it had happened. It must be. And the motive?

The motive had just been thrown at me, hard.

Lyall was a killer; he'd killed Andrew to possess Andrew's wife, the old savage story. And Andrew's wife?

I shied away from that, passionately.

# FIVE

I was out on the veranda by six, a few minutes before the sun rose in fierce magnificence over the blue-black straits. Kuwadi didn't appear, but a young houseboy brought me coffee and offered me eggs, which I declined. When Lyall's step sounded along the corridor I had to signal almost every muscle in my body to relax the sudden tension that gripped them at his first footfall.

He looked spruce and at ease in a short-sleeved khaki shirt and slacks, and since I'd heard the tapping of a typewriter from the direction of his room I was ready for the single sheet of script, signed in green ink, which he handed me. As I took it my hand brushed his permanently crooked fingers and a momentary spasm of nausea disturbed me, now that I knew how he'd injured those fingers, the real story. . . .

"I'm afraid I made no arrangement to be picked up," I said after I'd thanked him and folded the typescript. "How do I get a taxi here?"

"You don't want a taxi," he said, only his words, not his voice, expressing hospitality. "You can take the car. I've got a jeep as well here. Any time you like."

I thanked him and said I was ready whenever the driver was. He roared "Sutan!" in answer to that and frowned until a small, thin youth in a black *songkok* and an orange Hawaiian shirt came up the veranda steps, looking round him defensively. Brusquely Lyall ordered him to drive me to Medan. "Well, there's a pile of work waiting for me, I suppose," he said to me then, holding out his distorted hand. "Always the same when you take a couple of days off, isn't it?"

I had to take the twisted hand, but I didn't meet the dark mahogany eyes. By tomorrow I'd be denouncing him to Waring, who'd said, "You'll like him."

"Good journey," he said in answer to my confused murmur of thanks and good-bye. "Car'll be here in a couple of minutes." And he went off, to my relief. Almost at once a blue station wagon appeared round the far end of the bungalow and pulled up at the foot of the veranda steps.

Absent-mindedly I'd unfolded the paper Lyall had given me, and absent-mindedly I found myself reading the opening paragraph:

> On the morning of March 30 last year Mr. Andrew Avery and I drove from Ulu Maias rest house, at which we'd spent the night, towards Droga to meet Mr. Ian Hargreaves, then manager of Droga Besar Estate, who had been recommended to me as a suitable general manager for the estates I had recently inherited in North Borneo and Sumatra. Mr. Avery proposed a detour via Kuala Jeroh, telling me that Sungei Sunyi, a few miles from Jeroh, had been his childhood home for three years. . . .

The chauffeur Sutan interrupted me there, reporting from the top of the veranda steps, "*Sudah sedia, Tuan.*"

I refolded the paper, took up my bag, followed him down to the car, and got in beside him. We had moved forward two or three yards when a cry sounded from the bungalow.

"Robert! Robert!"

Nona was running down the veranda steps. If the bungalow had been in flames she would have run out just like that.
Her face was shockingly white, her pale lips desperately
parted, and her lower teeth gleaming through. Even after the
car had stopped she went on calling, "Robert!" as if I
still might not have heard.

"I'm coming too," she said breathlessly when she reached
the car, and her hand pulled clumsily at the door. I let her in,
and she collapsed on the seat behind me with a deep sigh and
closed her eyes. Sutan drove on.

The car carried us south through village markets and green
landscapes of rice and occasional plantations of rubber and to-
bacco. I sat there like two men who didn't know each other,
one of them shrinking from a woman who wasn't so much
better than a murderess, the guilty lover of her husband's
murderer at least; the other agonized with love and pity for
the same woman. There was nothing I could trust myself to
say, so I said nothing.

By the time we reached the airfield I had decided that there
couldn't be anything in my first panicky suspicion that she
and Lyall had plotted Andrew's death together. That was
something that just couldn't be believed. The other suspicion
was the one that explained the whole riddle of her and her behaviour ever since I'd first met her.

She and Lyall had fallen hard for each other, and Andrew
stood in the way. Lyall, the young South African new to the
violence launched on Malaya by the Communist terrorists,
hearing about the occasional ambushes in which the terrorists
still sneak-killed their enemies, had been presented with an
easy method of getting his rival out of the way. The long
drive over lonely jungle roads to meet Hargreaves offered a

hundred opportunities for a murder that, given reasonable luck, would never be suspected.

And it never would have been suspected, either, if the shock of seeing Nona creep into his bedroom that night hadn't released my subconscious observations on one or two slightly abnormal features of the ambush.

Nona knew. After it had happened Lyall had gone down to Singapore to his friend's widow. What happened then? Did he tell her or did she suspect, at once or gradually? She knew, sooner or later, at any rate, and it was that shock that had turned her into the horror-haunted creature who had made such a devastating entry into my life. She still loved Lyall crazily, but her horror of his crime had parted her from him, even though the parting was slowly killing her.

So my determination to find out what had happened to Andrew had come as another desperate shock to her. In an effort to warn Lyall or head me off she had flown East herself, ill and terrified, and now—was she exhausted with relief that I was ready to return to England without having suspected a thing, or was she being eaten alive with anxiety lest I should still uncover the monstrous secret. Which?

I gave Sutan a fifty-rupiah note, gesturing to Nona to stop fumbling in her raffia bag, and he carried my valise to the counter, where I was able to get her a return ticket. She hadn't thought that far ahead—or had she possibly thought of staying?

"Thank you" were the only words she spoke to me until we were in the air over the Strait of Malacca, a vast expanse of gooseflesh blue with a small island surrounded by a dirty, iridescent stain of drift-oil. She said then, "Robert, I want to talk to you sometime—but not now. You've been wonderful."

It was my turn to be silent then, simply because I couldn't

think of a word to say. I had been thinking some more, and my thoughts were sombre and ugly.

"You've been wonderful," she said again, her head turned away, her hands lying open helplessly. She said it as if I were an understanding sort of brother or uncle, and it maddened me. Very soon now she wasn't going to think of me as any sort of wonderful, not when I'd talked to Waring. . . .

Up there in the silent sky I worked it all out, every detail, finally fitted almost the last scrap of evidence into place. By the time we touched down on Malayan soil—and the temperature inside the plane rose stiflingly in the minute before the door was thrown open—I had it all. As soon as I'd sent Uncle Max a second cable (IGNORE MY LAST STOP WRITING) I took Nona into the bar and ordered two double brandies despite her protest.

When hers was in front of her I raised my eyes miserably to her pale face and said, "So that we understand each other, Nona. I told you I'd know it all before I finished. The contact lenses fooled me yesterday, but in the past hour I've worked it all out."

She stared at me like a madwoman, tried to say something, and fainted.

2

Her recovery was surprisingly swift. I suppose it was suspense that had been killing her: now that the worst had happened she found the reality easier to face than the shadow. She drank her brandy, and I began explaining.

"Up to the time we left the ground in Medan I thought Lyall had been your lover and killed Andrew to get him out of your way. That would have explained a lot, but not all. I began thinking about Aragon, and I just couldn't fit him in. . . ."

I gave her the story, which was now falling into a neat synopsis in my mind.

"Aragon had attempted murder, and not only once, to stop me finding out what had happened to Andrew. But if Andrew was dead, and murdered, why would Marcos Aragon fight so hard to keep the truth from me?—unless he was the murderer, and pretty obviously he couldn't be. He was a moneylender, of course, and a shady sort of moneylender, but Lyall was well off, Lyall had come into a large property three months before Andrew died in the ambush; so Aragon couldn't have had a moneylender's hold over Lyall. Andrew, though, was a born moneylender's client. Nothing likelier than that Andrew had got in deep with Aragon, and of course shady moneylenders, like blackmailers, wish their clients a long life with desperate sincerity. So could Aragon have believed that Andrew was alive and that I was somehow a threat to Andrew's life?"

She wasn't looking at me. She wasn't looking at anything, though her eyes were on the second glass of brandy she held. Her expression was lonely and resigned, much as it had been that day at her corner table in Stagford House.

"That idea threw a searchlight beam across the whole mystery. If Andrew was alive, and Aragon had wanted to keep him alive, what could have been the motive? Nothing but money, obviously. And certainly, for one thing, Andrew might well have owed Aragon a lot of money and, for another, Aragon had known all about Andrew's rich aunt and his expectations, or one-time expectations. He had evidently known about her death and her will, as well.

"Only if Andrew had been alive, but failed to come forward to claim his inheritance, what could have restrained him? Something pretty powerful, obviously. If he had—well, if he'd been wanted by the police for a serious crime, then maybe he couldn't have risked revealing himself. He'd have been hiding, either in some remote hide-out or behind an assumed name and identity.

"I'm not putting this well, but up there in the sky half a dozen ideas were pushing through my brain at once. For a time I wondered if it was just that Aragon had been black-mailing Lyall, having found out somehow that he'd murdered Andrew in the fake ambush. Lyall's well off, I reasoned, and he could be milked for years by a discreet and patient black-mailer, as I could well believe Aragon had been. But that couldn't be the answer—I saw that as soon as I came up against the failure of Aragon and Lyall to ensure that I and my family knew all about the ambush. Aragon had tried all ways, murder included, to *stop* me from finding it out, and I believed he'd murdered the man Smith who was our investigator in Singapore as soon as Smith turned up news of the ambush. No, that was out.

"And then the whole thing clicked into focus, like an inspiration. One moment I was groping in thick darkness; the next, my finger had found the switch and snapped on a search-light; it was as sudden and complete as that. I just assumed, for the sake of argument, that Andrew *was* alive, that he had become a fugitive from justice and lived somewhere under an assumed name, that he had been blackmailed by Aragon and that, despite his inability to claim the fortune that was his, he still controlled enough money to be able to pay Aragon large, regular sums. That of course suggested a successful crime for gain, even a murder for gain. Andrew had known somebody with money and found a safe way of murdering him and getting his hands on a good deal of the money. But who would Andrew know with a lot of money, Andrew, a man who went round the country stealing small sums from Asian shop-keepers? Well, he'd known Malcolm Lyall."

I drank a lot of brandy, still sorting out final details in my mind like a dramatist working out details of a plot.

"There's a pretty girl in Hollywood, forget her name for the moment, who's played the fetching red Indian squaw in horse operas. When she started in colour, her blue eyes struck the wrong note, so an oculist fitted her out with corneal contact lenses of a dark hazel colour. Suddenly I remembered her. In the few weeks after Andrew had murdered Lyall in that phony ambush he must have taken a quick trip to Australia or America, maybe, and fixed himself up with some dark brown contact lenses. The conspicuous Avery blue eyes were the most noticeable thing about him, and Lyall's had been brown, I suppose. Not that he needed to look more like Lyall, only less like himself. He could be pretty sure of never meeting anybody who'd known Lyall more than very slightly, but there were numbers of people in South-East Asia who knew Andrew, who might even show up one day in Medan on one of his rare—I imagine they're rare—ventures into the world outside Kiduai. He'd got hold of Lyall's passport. Perhaps it was forgetting the passport till almost too late and then having to tear it from one of the corpse's pockets while the car blazed that burned his hand so badly—but even that paid a dividend, because for weeks he wouldn't have been able to sign his name and when he could nobody was going to expect a firm replica of Malcolm Lyall's old signature. Anyway, he had Lyall's passport and all his private papers, and we can be sure he'd pumped the fellow dry those last weeks—of course, you must have seen him at it."

She looked up at me then. "You think I knew," she said.

And I was sure then that I didn't. "No. Not until afterwards."

She put her hands over her eyes and said, "I knew he was working out a scheme to get money out of Malcolm. He was an easy victim, Malcolm. All he really cared about was whisky. He must have been tight for quite half the two months he spent in Singapore. Andrew met him the day he arrived from Cape Town, and he was with us night and day; he had the spare room in our flat in Orange Grove Road, and we were almost the only people he met. I suppose towards the end Andrew was taking care he didn't get known to anybody. He was happy just drinking at home and talking to me. He liked me. He hadn't the least interest in his estates, though he was glad to be well off. He never saw his plantations, chiefly because there was endless delay in getting his Indonesian visa —or perhaps Andrew fixed the delay. He kept postponing a visit to Borneo, even. That could wait, he said. When the manager at Kiduai wrote saying that some discussions were urgent, Malcolm told him to use his discretion. When the man proposed coming to Singapore, Malcolm wrote back not to worry, he'd be over in a week or two, which annoyed the man. He wrote and said he was coming to Singapore anyway, and Malcolm was so fed up at that he fired him—or there again, it might have been Andrew's suggestion to fire him. I was surprised when Andrew strongly recommended a man called Hargreaves to take his place, talking about him as if he knew him. Actually, we'd never met him; his name had come up at the Tanglin a week or so before, when somebody said Hargreaves knew more about rubber-estate management than almost any other man in Malaya. He's general manager at Kiduai now."

I nodded. "I see. Hargreaves was little more in the first place than an excuse to drive Lyall into the ambush position. Andrew would have known plenty about ambushes, and from his time as security officer in Johore he'd probably have one or two trophies of anti-terrorist action—that bandit cap and the old rifle, they'd probably have been knocking around in the boot of his car for years."

"Yes," she confirmed.

"So he was able to do a pretty good mock-up of an ambush, though there were one or two small points that puzzled me subconsciously. Afterwards he cracked up rather, because he's not a born murderer and the thing had been a nightmare to him. I suppose he was in pretty grim shape when he showed up in Singapore."

Her pale hands tightened over her eyes. "I'd thought for three days he was dead, and then he came in the night, wearing Malcolm's sombrero, and his arm in a sling and his eyes so changed I didn't know him for a minute. He'd flown up to Tokyo and got those contact lenses a month *before* the ambush. He was wearing them by the time the police came on the scene there."

I said, "But he wouldn't have been wearing them when he turned up unexpectedly at Aragon's house a week later, or young Sophie would've noticed and remembered. She remembered his arm in a sling and she remembered overhearing her father making a bad joke as Andrew left by taxi late at night, telling Andrew to look after Lyall and Lyall to look after Andrew. And—good God!" I clapped a hand to my forehead. "She told me *everything* that day outside Hong Kong and Shanghai Bank! It was the week after her young brother's birthday that Andrew had been at Aragon's house for the last time and the kid's birthday is March the thirty-first! No wonder Andrew got mad when she told him she'd announced to the whole class that her Uncle Andrew Avery had turned up unexpectedly—the schoolmarm or one of the kids could have remembered a headline about Andrew Avery getting killed in an ambush the week before!"

After a moment's pause, I said, "I wonder how Marcos Aragon found out about the ambush and got his hooks on Andrew."

Nona looked up again and said, "I've always believed Aragon put him up to it. You just said Andrew wasn't a born murderer. I believe he was an unwilling one. I believe Aragon was behind it all, even perhaps engineering his first meeting with Malcolm. I think Andrew was in so deep and Aragon had such a hold that Malcolm was a doomed man before he set foot in Malaya."

Maybe. I looked at it and I thought maybe, and when I looked at it again I thought probably. For all his heavy fat, Aragon had been vigorously active in evil. He'd been on to Smith like a flash and once he realized that Andrew's family had never had news of the ambush he worked fast to keep it from them.

Why? To prevent from happening the very thing which had happened yesterday—to prevent a meeting between any member of Andrew's family and "Malcolm Lyall." At first that wouldn't have mattered, but the moment the news of Aunt Julia's will reached Aragon he'd become nervous, and quite rightly. Andrew's death would have to be properly established and his alternative heirs would be making close inquiries. They had a lot to gain, and Aragon had a lot to lose.

I asked Nona the question. "Exactly what did Aragon get out of it?"

She said, "I believe Aragon wanted to have the North Borneo plantations made over to him completely, but he couldn't get Andrew to play. As far as I know, Aragon was made a director of both the North Borneo group and the Sumatra group and drew five thousand pounds a year or more. Of course, Andrew never visited the Borneo estates because there are plenty of people over there who know him quite well." She added inconsequentially, "He hates it in Indonesia, but he daren't leave." Then she caught back her words, remembering what must lie before her husband now. Her eyes slanted away from mine, a millisecond before mine lowered.

She wasn't a riddle to me any more. Everything she'd done, from start to finish, the lies she'd told, the evasions, the desperate appeal to me that day at Stagford House not to come looking for Andrew, the way she'd suffered Aragon's murderous attacks in silence rather than show me the way to Andrew's hideout and cover-identity—everything was explained. Andrew was a murderer, but he was her husband and she loved him unforgettably. So what else could she have done?

I wanted to know what had happened that night in Singapore, when Andrew had come back from the dead and Nona learned what he had done. Clumsily I said, "Of course you couldn't have gone with him then. So what did you do?"

She blinked. "Do?"

"I mean, you couldn't go straight off with him, or you'd have spoiled his scheme, Mrs. Avery going off with 'Mr. Lyall.' So what did you do? Wait and marry him again under the other name?"

Her face went cold. "You think I would live with him, after that?"

No, I hadn't really thought so, but I'd wanted to hear her say it. It had been worth shocking and hurting her to get that unmistakable response. She was staring at me with chill aversion, and the cold stare warmed me. Though in the past two hours I'd had to surrender another all-important dream, I could take some comfort in the reassurance that Andrew's crime had placed her forever out of his reach.

And there might be hope yet. She wasn't a widow, as I'd

believed for two inspiring days, but surely she would be soon. If they got Andrew now, surely he could never escape a death sentence. If they got him . . .

Was there an extradition agreement between Malaya and Indonesia? I didn't know. And if there were, couldn't Andrew make an escape while it was being set in motion to arrest him? Was there any way in which he could be—well, kidnapped or enticed into venturing onto Malayan soil? My wish-fulfilment dreams swirled along like a river in spate, all of them centred on a day, however distant, when Nona could be my wife.

She broke the silence with a slow question. "Then you never recognized him? Not even half-consciously?"

I shook my head. "I was ten when I saw him last, and he was just sixteen. If I could have really seen his eyes, maybe. Or if he hadn't ordered his girl to switch off the lights as soon as he knew who I was, and changed from shorts into slacks before I saw him in a good light. He thought of the long scar on his thigh that I'd given him, you see, like the one on my thigh he'd given me, and he went off to change into slacks." I told her the story of the scars.

"I might have suspected, I suppose, from the way he defended himself to me, the fine fellow he made out Andrew to have been. He had hated my bringing up one or two of his failings; he came back with the loyal sort of defence you'd have expected from a lifelong friend. That was so like Andrew, I ought to have suspected."

She had risen to her feet, not quite steadily, and now she excused herself for a few minutes while I bargained with a Sikh taximan for the fare to Sungei Sunyi. We couldn't get on a plane to Ipoh, and I wanted Nona back with Winnie without any delay. I had to talk urgently to Waring as well.

As the taxi took us through the airport gates she turned to

me and said, "I'd better tell you, Robert. There's a telegram on its way to Andrew from me. Telling him. Warning him."

## 3

As soon as we reached Sungei Sunyi that evening, Nona went to her room with Winnie and I didn't see her for twenty-four hours. In the morning I had an interview with Waring.

"If you can get hold of him," I told him, "you can get a conviction on his eyes alone, the coloured contact lenses and testimony from anybody in South Africa who'd known Lyall. You won't want me as a witness, or Nona either."

I said that last with a little anxiety, because as soon as my interview with Waring was over I intended to ring BOAC for two reservations to London, the first two they could offer. But Waring didn't demur. After all, there was other evidence—the duplicate photograph of Lyall at the passport office in Cape Town, for instance, or any of Andrew's debtors up and down the country; they would offer prompt identification in response to an advertisement. (Letters from some of them, in response to my original advertisement, had surely been among those stolen by Bah Feng at the Sultan Mustafa and passed on to Aragon.)

No, the only problem was to get him into court, but Waring seemed to think there might be a way, despite my warning him that Andrew knew by now that I had worked out the whole story. "Indonesia's a difficult country to get into," he said, "and it's just about as difficult to get out of. If you get out illegally the obvious exits are to Malaya, or perhaps North Borneo, either of which would suit us well enough. And what would you say he stood—an inch over six foot, anyway. Pretty conspicuous, that." He sounded confident.

I went and booked the flight back to London. There were two seats for four days later, and I took them. Driving back to Sungei Sunyi, I felt relaxed and tired. It was all out of my hands now.

As I turned the bend beneath the fake ambush position, I thought of Andrew and his loneliness. Could he find life worth living, with the unbanishable memory of those minutes at this roadside, even though he had a large income and a lovely if scornful plaything in place of the wife who'd left him in horror? Could he sleep? What could he look forward to?

But I saw that, however lonely and empty his life might be, he'd have invented a comforting fable to account for his isolation. It was all something that had been done to him, never something he had done to himself. Yes, he'd sleep all right: the murder was no more than an illegal act performed under compulsion—the guilt of it belonged to Marcos Aragon, just as the idea had been his. Nona had let him down, as all the rest had, deserting him when most he'd needed understanding and help through an ordeal of risk and danger.

Me he'd see, I supposed, as a vindictive weakling with hands itching to seize the money that was his by rights. I wondered what might have happened to me if I'd stumbled on the truth that night in his house, and let it show. . . .

Now I was passing the tunnel entrance to the track leading to Andrew's jungle hide-out, the scene of so much delight and terror in my eleventh year. I wondered whether I could find my way there now, through the four or five miles of tough going to the cave and the two pools to which Andrew retired for short periods of solitary make-believe when the world wouldn't give him all his own way. My homing instinct was sound—as sound as an Iban tracker's, my old CO once declared—but the jungle was a blindfolding deceiver, and nobody born outside it could hope to be at home there for years.

At the bungalow Winnie told me Nona had asked for me, but now she was sleeping. She looked up at me speculatively and I wondered how much she had got out of Nona. Well, Nona needed somebody to talk to, and perhaps now she would at last.

I told Sam Chester the whole of it over a couple of whiskies. When I'd finished he stared across the valley of rubber to the jungle-masked slopes beyond and his deep voice made the unexpected comment, "Tell me, Robert, what *is* it about this bastard that makes you so sentimental about him?"

"Sentimental?" I resented it.

"You make it sound a sort of tragedy—for him, I mean."

I said defensively, "He's somebody I used to know. A relative."

"He's a cold-blooded murderer."

"I'm not so sure about the cold-blooded, if I know what it means."

"Doesn't it mean that he planned it all beforehand, worked it out, lived with the fellow he was going to kill, ate and drank and chatted with him while he fixed the details of the killing? And if that's not cold-blooded I'll join the Salvation Army!"

"He was driven into it, blackmailed."

"Do you *know* that?"

"Nona believes it."

"You can be sure she sentimentalizes him too. Calls it loyalty, I suppose."

"D'you think the worse of her for that?"

"She's a woman," was all he said to that. His very straight eyes were glaring. "Easy to see he'd get off if you were on the jury."

"I've given Waring all the facts," I pointed out.

"And if they ever get their hands on him and he has to pay for his crime, you'll have times when you're going to feel like Judas Iscariot. And Nona, she'll make a tragedy hero of him, and a fine time you'll have of it, you two! That bastard'll always be *there*, and neither of you'll know how to kick him out."

I wondered. Sam was speaking only half in earnest, I think, and I'd begun by scouting his theory completely. But he had something there, I couldn't help suspecting after a moment's reflection—and before the hour was out I knew it.

Winnie came in, very large in a feverishly spotted dress of ginger-red and violet. "Now stop making a public house of my veranda with Sam and go in and see Nona," she said briskly. Her eyes, though, when I passed her on the way into the house, were very gentle and quietly speculative behind their brilliant lenses.

Nona had been watching the door, I think. I wondered if she knew that this had been Andrew's room—but how could she have known? I felt him near as I went up to the bedside, and wondered whether it was because this was where I had spent so many hours with him or whether it was some sort of confirmation of old Sam's words, the fact that Andrew was uppermost in both our minds. . . .

I smiled down at her and took a chair, not saying anything. She was wearing a flamingo nightdress, and it looked as if Winnie had been brushing her hair. She was less pale, and her faint scent and the nearness were exciting.

I waited.

"I wanted to explain yesterday," she said after a while, not looking at me. I could see that her hands were clasped between her breasts under the single sheet. "Not that I can explain, really. I behaved as if you were an enemy. Three times you were almost killed, and if you had been it would have been because of me, because I hadn't told you what I knew."

It was true. It was a true thing I'd never faced.

"I didn't tell you because—because somehow you can't treat people the way they deserve. Andrew—" And her voice fell as she spoke his name, as if he might be listening at the venetian blinds beyond her bed. "Andrew deserves the same from me as he deserves from anybody else, and maybe more. There were things you don't know. But it was impossible, Robert. I couldn't go to the police, I couldn't even tell you, not even when you were in such danger. And Andrew is bad and you are good." She turned her eyes on me. "How can I expect you to understand?" She sighed.

Andrew's bed had been on the opposite side of the room. I could see him now, sprawling across it and half opening his blue eyes and saying, "Get out, young Robert. Don't keep coming in here"—and my abashed and lonely retreat.

Her eyes had turned away again, right away. "I don't know. Men are the sentimental ones, and women are the realists, real men and real women, I mean. Men are romantic and women are practical. That's what they say. But when I found out about Andrew, bit by bit, worse and worse, I kept on behaving as if I were still in love with him."

A new excitement tingled through me, but I put myself on guard against it. I'd hoped enough in the past few months, and the verdict, when it was shouted brutally from a thousand throats in the theatre that night, had put me on guard against hoping for a long time.

"Somehow you can't treat people the way they deserve," Nona said again. "Or I can't. Andrew deserved nothing from me, and you've been wonderful; but somehow I was always for him. Why?"

"Isn't that simple?" I said. "You love him and you don't love me."

She looked at me and said, "No, Robert. No."

Then something like thunder and lightning went through me and she was in my arms and her fingers were in my hair and her mouth against mine. She was half sobbing and shivering in my arms, and I was staring into a sudden future that dazzled like a searchlight.

Only— It was as if Sam Chester's words were coming true already. This had been Andrew's room and this had been Andrew's wife. He was near, somehow. He was there with us, and I could tell after a while that Nona felt it too. She kept turning to the window, to the closed jalousies painted a soft lilac pink, to the darkness beyond that led over jungle and the Straits of Malacca to the coastal plain of Sumatra, where Andrew would know by now that I had set the police on him and he would have to fight for his life.

We both grew silent, as if we were listening.

### 4

I was awake, or half awake, when the thin, shivering horn sounded in the coolie lines half a mile away to rouse the women to cook the early-morning rice—about four or four-thirty, I suppose. Then I went to sleep again.

It was after five, still dark, when Sam Chester came roaring into the room, clicking on the light and shaking my shoulder roughly through the mosquito net.

"Robert, get up, man. Hell and all out here. Nona's gone!"

Dazed with shock, I made a frenzied, fumbling job of pulling some clothes on while Chester's deep boom echoed painfully in the small room.

"The car's gone too. One of the Home Guard sentries down

in the village saw it coasting down the hill around two o'clock."

I blinked crazily at him. "She took your car?"

"No, you fool. He took her—that bastard of a husband, I suppose. Get moving, man! Can't you wake up?"

The fat amah, Ah Yin, came to the door then with a large bowl of coffee, which I drank while Sam filled in the story. The Home Guardsman had been astonished to see the car coasting slowly down the slope through the village with its headlights not switched on. As it passed him he saw a man at the wheel and a woman at his side. Just beyond the village the motor had started up and he saw the reflection of the head-lamps across the river. He had not done anything about it, knowing that the Chesters had two guests at the house, a man and a woman, and deciding obscurely that some kind of amor-ous adventure must be the explanation; but as soon as the bun-galow staff got up to prepare for a rubber-plantation manager's early working day, he had called to inquire about the explana-tion.

"Land Rover's ready," Sam said as soon as I had some shoes on. "We've got to get after him. There should have been a sentry somewhere by the bridge, and he'll know which road he took."

As I swung into the Land Rover seat beside him I said, "So he *was* there last night. Right outside the window, and we both knew, if only we'd trusted our intuitions."

Sam drove us down the hill at a speed that created a cold dawn breeze and whipped tears into my eyes. Some villagers shrouded to the nose in sarongs blinked one by one as the headlight beams swept across them. Trailing spider webs, beaded with dew, whirled madly in our slipstream. We went the first mile in silence.

"If Umbi didn't fill her up last night, there can't have been much in the tank," Sam boomed suddenly. And before he could say another word we'd cut the corner where seventeen years ago my uncle had almost run down two tiger cubs, and there was the car in the middle of the road.

Beside it, in a thin film of mud from the early night rain, a pattern of tracks told a story—large, nailed boot tracks and small soft ones. The small ones had run headlong to the side of the road and into the jungle, the striding large ones in pursuit. When Sam turned the headlights that way, I saw at once the two tiny pennants of flamingo gauze, torn by fishhook thorns from her nightdress; the torn and crushed leaves, one of them bloodstained, where the fugitive had hurled herself against the jungle barrier; the two long, stubborn grooves in the slippery wet soil where she had been dragged back by her pursuer.

I was sweating, but cold too, at the thought of Nona seeking escape in the jungle, the dark midnight jungle that had so terrified her even at midday with friends only a few yards away. The larger prints then strode back down the road alone, and I fancied that they were a little deeper and heavier—I knew, anyway, that Nona had been carried helpless in her husband's arms.

I knew, too, where they had gone. I didn't need to read the tracks any more.

I told Chester, "It's worse now, Sam. He's taken her into the jungle. There's a place four miles in that used to be his hide-out when he was sixteen and I stayed here. There's a cave. He's taken her there."

"He's mad," was all Sam said.

"Maybe, but what else could he do? No gas in the car, and the nearest place along the road ahead more than two miles—and that a police station, anyway, and the police after him."

"He could have left Nona and made a getaway himself," Sam argued, turning the Land Rover in the narrow roadway.

"No," I said. "If a getaway was all he'd wanted he'd have kept out of Malaya."

"What does the bastard want, then?"

"To play God. Jehovah. We've offended and betrayed him, Nona and I, and he can't allow us to get away with it. I know him, Sam. It's the way he is."

Sam said something that would have curled Winnie's hair. The ribbon of sky above the road showed grey now against the black of the jungle walls. As we came near the tunnel entrance of the old path to Andrew's hide-out I put a hand on his arm, and he pulled up.

Yes, they'd gone in there. Of course they had. I gave only a single glance at the heavy, slipping footprints in the bank of the small stream that marked the entrance to the old route to the cave. I drew a deep, sighing breath that was tinged with the alcoholic odour of decaying leaves, with cold and mould and the fragrance of an unseen jungle flower. Sam waited in the Land Rover.

As soon as I'd made up my mind I got in beside him again and said, "Take me to the bungalow, Sam, and wait while I collect some brandy and food and a gun and put on some more suitable clothes. Then drop me here and I'll start an emergency follow-up. After that you can collect Waring and a couple of trackers from the Army at Droga, if you can. They can do the professional manhunt."

He drove me in silence up the hill to the bungalow and yelled for Winnie as he cut the engine. By the time I'd changed into a pair of green canvas jungle boots and a suit of jungle green that had been cut for Sam and hung in folds around me, Winnie and the amah had fried half a dozen ham rashers and half a dozen eggs, and thick slices of buttered toast steamed in two racks by a huge pot of coffee. I ate and drank the lot in silence. When I got up, still chewing, Winnie handed me a smallish Bergen rucksack, open so that I could see what she'd packed in it.

She'd done well. Two Fair Isle sweaters, a whole bottle of Hennessy (that must have caused her a qualm), three plastic bags full of food, a small first-aid kit . . . There was more, but I didn't wait to inspect it. Sam handed me a *parang*, a pistol, and about twenty rounds, which I took without examining them.

I said, "Before the main body sets out have a word with old Ngari. He could lead you to the place blindfold if his legs would only carry him, poor old bastard. But maybe he knows a youngster who could guide them. Anyway, talk to him first."

Then I was ready. At the top of the steps Winnie swept forward with her hands up and hugged and kissed me. There were tears in her nice eyes. "Bring her back, Robert," she said. "I love you both."

I kissed her and jumped in beside Sam, who had the Land Rover moving before my backside touched the seat. The sun, huge and smoky red, climbed over the green jungle horizon as we shot through the bungalow gates.

I was ready to leap out before the Land Rover came to a standstill opposite the entrance to Andrew's old jungle trail, but Sam held me back with a huge red hand and glared into my eyes.

"When you find that bastard," he said, "shoot him. Don't stop to agonize and sentimentalize about him. Shoot as soon as you sight him. If you don't he'll swallow you in one gulp."

I said, "Good-bye, Sam, and thanks." Then I put my head down and pushed into the stuffy, dark coldness of the dawn jungle. Three strides and I could look back and see no more of him than if he'd been parked in Regent Street.

A fine tendril hooked with almost invisible thorns tore

across my lips, and I tasted blood. The patterned rubber sole of my jungle boot slipped nearly a yard down the damp clay of the stream bank, and my face fell in a miniature pocket of black swamp shaded by the heavy grey-green leaves like elephant ears. I heard the Land Rover's engine-roar receding in a swift decrescendo and finally vanishing. When I was on my feet again I saw another filament of flamingo thread caught in the rough bark of a dying tree.

From far ahead, muffled by a hundred million leaves, came the wild, exultant voices of the wahwahs. The long-armed gibbons cry their bubbling chorus in the treetops as the sun rises, and for me this had always been one of the deepest thrills the wild could give. Even now a quiver of response ran through my nerve system.

What I felt most, though, was loneliness.

I longed, with fierce nostalgia, for my platoon and Tracker Langgong—for Sergeant Parry's quiet imperturbability; young Wilson with the baby monkey that always went on patrol with him; poor old Corporal Hardy, the stocky Dorset gamekeeper who'd been so swiftly at home in the jungle and had died at my side in the Jerantut ambush; Fatty Lines and the bawdy north-country songs he sang at every sing-song back at base; tough Ginger Bramley, who could cut a path nearly twice as fast as anybody except the trackers; and the young tracker Nangau, whose amazing sense of smell had twice given us the chance of terrorist kills, once when he smelled cooking through more than a thousand yards of jungle, and once when he'd detected that a man had urinated inside the hour within a hundred yards of a spot where the patrol gathered for a ten minute fall-out. I longed for them.

Now there were tiny pricks of sunlight high above, like stars in an almost black sky. Around me the light was an unhealthy greeny-grey, and it was still rather cold, though before

I'd got fifty yards in I was soaked in sweat and so was Sam's jungle-green battle dress. Every step was a fight against the creepers and thorns that caught me like traps, against the slippery earth the sun could never reach to dry—against the air, too, the air that was too damp and thick for panting lungs.

At first there was little difficulty in picking out traces of the overgrown trail, but in fifteen minutes I was lost.

## 5

To be lost in the jungle is as bad as being adrift in a small boat in the middle of an ocean—worse, maybe. If you've never been lost in a jungle you just have no idea of how lost you can be. Your body is as lost then as your brain is during unconsciousness.

Of course, it wasn't the first time for me. But the other times I hadn't been alone. There had been some of my platoon with me and always one of the trackers, and with an Iban tracker you can't be lost for long. You can't be really lost.

Alone, you can get scared. Particularly, perhaps, if you have a strong sense of direction, as I have. To find that built-in compass suddenly out of action is an eerie sensation, and I had it now.

I don't know how many people are like me, but when I'm alone and in any great difficulty I talk—not so much to myself as to people who aren't there, but I wish were. Now I stopped myself in the act of raising the long-bladed *parang* and said aloud, "Langgong, help me now." And I pictured Langgong on the veranda of his longhouse built above one of Borneo's great rivers, and I saw his naked strong limbs with the handsome dark blue tattooing, and I saw his pretty bare-breasted wife and the toddler whose birth he had announced to me in a letter written for him by a government clerk down in Kapit, and I tried to remember everything I'd learned from him. After a moment I turned back along my own tracks to find the last signs of the trail I had noted. If I'd gone forward I might never have found my way back.

"Langgong, help me now." And at once my eyes seemed to move to a new focus, and I was seeing small things one at a time instead of a huge, daunting confusion. I had left a trail like a rhino's, and Andrew's, when I got back onto it again, was as obvious now. It looked as if he'd taken no pains at all to conceal his tracks, though he must have known that I would be after him. Or was that, maybe, just what he wanted now?— a last chapter of death and destruction in the jungle, now that his own escape was impossible. . . .

Or was he, I suddenly wondered, lying in ambush somewhere ahead? A familiar sensation came back to me then, the old tenseness of advancing along a path that was possibly ambushed, the feeling as of long nerve-ends coiling ahead, the painful sharpness of ear and eye, the difficulty of normal breathing.

And all the time there was the fear for Nona.

For a year she had carried a load of anxiety and fear that had almost crushed her. Breaking point had been close for a long time. I was choked and sick with hatred for Andrew and swore like a madman as I fell on the slippery ground and fell again twice in my efforts to get upright again.

Already I looked as though I'd completed a deep river crossing; sweat and raindrops brushed off the choking vegetation soaked me. I was swearing softly, continuously, and filthily, as I do when I'm alone and things go badly wrong. The pack on my back caught in every creeper, and I cursed it a hundred times. I stopped only to drink a little from one of the furry grey-green plants Langgong had taught me to seek whenever I needed sweet water in the jungle, but my progress was a slow struggle, possibly no more than half a mile an hour. And the worst was ahead.

There was the shelf ahead, where the ground-level rose a hundred and fifty feet in a steep wilderness of boulders—huge boulders, most of them, the biggest as big as a grand hotel, and the whole slope unsteady, like a patch of scree in the Cairngorms enlarged a hundred times. You came upon it suddenly.

Here it was.

I was afraid I'd lose Andrew's tracks there, and I did. It was the sort of place that always set Langgong's face in a grave frown because he feared he was going to let his platoon down. Several times he'd been beaten by one of these tilted wildernesses, and I knew that this one might beat me. I had no idea how far it stretched to right and left of the track, but I feared it might be a mile wide or wider. It took an age to get up the slope of tilted, unsteady boulders, and the risk of a twisted or broken ankle was not negligible. The rock was wet and as slippery as the clayey jungle floor, and each boulder was liable to roll underfoot. A few thorned creepers crept between the wastes of stone, but mostly it was bare.

The sun by now was high in the clear sky. Tropical suns do not linger in the twilight zones just above and just below the horizon. They bounce up or plunge down whenever they approach horizon level. The climb up the open slope drenched me in a new flood of perspiration and dried out my throat. At the top the jungle again, pitch dark at first to my sunburned eyes.

I wasted a good deal of time casting along the jungle edge, looking for the point at which Andrew had gone in, or else for signs of the old trail. After perhaps an hour I decided to give it up and just make for the cave, because that, I knew, was the place Andrew was headed for anyway.

The Malayan jungle is densely populated with beasts, birds,

and reptiles, but you see few of them ever. Once I flushed a
small jungle cock, a brilliant creature the size of a bantam, and
there was a snake I didn't know asleep along a low branch
above my head when I paused for a breather soon after.
I heard hornbills above me several times and the noisy skelter-
ing of unseen monkeys. The crickets set up their maddening
din as soon as the sun was well up, and there was always
a murmur of dripping from a million leaves.

For three hours I was lost—not totally lost, as it turned out,
because when finally I reached the torrent I felt sure that I
must be just upstream of the point at which you had to make
the first of two crossings to avoid impassable cliff faces and
that the cave was no more than two hundred and fifty yards
downstream. I was right.

When I knew I must be within a hundred yards of the cave
I came upon a path. It wasn't our old path, naturally; that
would have been grown over completely years ago. But it
didn't look to me like a game trail, either. Down on my
haunches beside it, I made out one or two impressions among
the drifted dead leaves that could have been unfresh human
tracks, and there was a single broken-off twig at human shoul-
der-height. Certainly Andrew hadn't come this way, but in the
past week or month a man or men had used the trail, I suspected.

The jungle slope at this point was so steep that there were
bald patches of limestone cliff in places. One cliff was much
bigger than the rest and rounded like a great bow window
three hundred feet high and half as broad. The precipitous
drop was in two steps, a short one of twenty-five feet, ending
in an uneven rock ledge, with the long drop below it.
Andrew's cave opened onto the ledge.

Down the north side of the cliff fell the River Avery—as
Andrew had called it, unable to find any other name either

from the estate maps or from old Ngari—in two falls. The first dropped the twenty-five feet to form a small pool that spilled over the lip of the ledge in a majestic white fall that could be heard, even through the thick, muffling jungle, for almost a mile.

The only approach to the ledge, except for rock-climbers, was the one I made. There was no need to step softly because the roar of the torrent masked any normal sounds of approach; but the thought of Andrew in ambush was still with me vividly. I longed for a plunge into the cool, deep pool, but there could be none of that.

Finally I came to the conclusion that Andrew hadn't yet reached the cave. I had circled the approach in a stealthy reconnaissance and satisfied myself that I had crossed no new track. Relaxing with a sigh that eased every weary muscle, I slipped through the spray-cool passage behind the column of falling water and moved openly onto the rock shelf that led up to the cave.

At the cave mouth I went stiff again. Beside my right foot lay a short length of wood, obviously cut for a fire. And round a spur of rock, in the miniature cave the size of a taxicab, were the remains of a fire, of many fires, with a *kuali* for frying propped alongside, and an old cloth, one or two old bones of fish and animal, a chip from a white china plate, and a couple of durian husks.

It was a familiar picture. I knew then what I should find in the cave. I went in warily, the safety catch off my gun just in case.

6

After a thorough examination of the site I calculated that the terrorists had not been in camp for five, six, or seven days. Langgong could have told me to a day. Examining one of the newest lengths of firewood, he could have told, by the degree of discolouration and dryness of the cut surface, in conjunction with the type of the wood, how many days had passed since it had been cut. There were outer skins of the kernel found at the root of certain jungle bamboos that are sweet and nutty, and from them he might have been able to confirm his opinion. Footsteps in a patch of old mud beside the little stream that wandered through the cave would have told him a great deal more than they told me, too.

It was a small camp, with roughly made bamboo bunks for sixteen men—one of the rest or training camps suspected by the security forces to have been set up in this area, which had been deliberately kept free of terrorist action to safeguard them. The condition of the camp testified to low morale, and several bottles of Chinese medicines on a shelf of bamboo suggested that the place may have been a hospital for part of its time. More than twenty tattered books in Chinese suggested training courses of some kind. In the small recess in the roof where Andrew had kept his air gun I found about twenty Mills bombs and a British Army box of .303 ammunition. Some of the rounds had been filed down to make ugly dum-dum bullets. There was a small clothing store, none of it new, some not even clean. The blankets on the ramshackle bunks were filthy.

This was the old stuff, and strangely the discovery gave me some sort of assurance. The jungle seemed less lonely, and I was a soldier again, back on the battlefield. Leaving the cave, I went to the pool, took off my pack, and set it on a rock slab and put my gun and *parang* on it. Then I walked straight into the pool and into the hissing curtain of the little waterfall. After a minute my body had cooled and most of the sweat had been rinsed out of Sam's jungle green battle suit. I stood there, thinking of Nona.

I had to hope she hadn't escaped from Andrew, because alone in the jungle she would probably die a lingering death. I recalled with horror the dead terrorist we had found on a patrol once, a young Chinese who had died of a wound alone, possibly abandoned by his comrades. He couldn't have been dead for more than a few hours, for his body had not putrefied, but before and after death the leeches had been gorging on him in thousands, choking his ears and nostrils with their bloated bodies, while ants had devoured his eyes and most of the skin around them. An animal had bitten off his right hand. . . .

Had Andrew lost his way, or had he merely taken longer than I because of his having to drag or carry or force Nona through the jungle? Or was he deliberately lying up at a distance, knowing I would make for the cave, alone or in company, to deal with me? The last, I thought. He would want to know first whether I was alone.

A tiny brown squirrel on a lone tree above the falls had spotted me and sat staring and chattering at the unusual sight. Looking down at my sodden body—I had gone all the morning with my jacket and even my flybuttons undone, as we always had on patrol to get the benefit of such weak breezes as could find their way into the more open stretches of jungle— I saw that leeches had started to feed, as usual. I had never got over my repulsion for those obscene creatures, and I shivered convulsively at this renewal of the acquaintance.

I had no lighter and no cigarettes, so I couldn't touch a glowing cigarette end to each one. There might be salt in the provisions Winnie had packed for me, and that too, applied to one leech after another, would cause them to convulse and drop to the ground. I averted my eyes from them and left it all until later. They didn't hurt as they fed;

the total unawareness of them was one of the sinister things about them.

So as not to leave a trail of water, which the sun wouldn't dry for perhaps twenty minutes, I collected my pack and revolver and waded upstream along a tiny tributary between the boulders for thirty yards, then found the way to an old hide-out at the forest edge, perched a hundred feet above the falls. I was like a statue stuck in its niche there, in the limestone alcove screened by a cataract of hanging ferns.

I had drunk thirstily from the falls, opening my mouth to the cool sweetness that fell thirty feet with a sting like soda water. Now I took a long swig of the Hennessy and ate a sort of cold Spanish omelette from the pack, blessing old Winnie with every bite.

"Bring her back, Robert," she'd whispered, kissing me. "I love you both."

The heat was now insufferably clammy. It astonished me how soon my clothes dried, even though the atmosphere seemed as damp as a Turkish bath's. I waited for Andrew in the same leafy hide-out to which I had withdrawn more than once seventeen years before, when his unpredictable temper had suddenly turned against me. "Oh, get out, young Robert! I don't want you here."

It was something like four hours before I saw him.

I had dozed for a while and been wakened by the ants, which had got inside my clothes and, when they couldn't find their way out, panicked and stung. Nothing had changed as I slept except the slant of the shadow across the rock floor in front of the cave mouth. My throat was so dry there was pain there.

With the sluggish, bad-tempered feeling a siesta always leaves with me, I went down to the falls again, though only after I'd taken a long look round. Under the cool water-curtain I enjoyed a luxurious shiver, finally opening my mouth, closing my eyes, and turning my face upward into the vertical torrent. For a half-minute I stood like that, and when I lowered my head and opened my eyes, gasping, Andrew was coming out of the cave mouth.

If he'd been looking my way, or even if he'd been looking to his front, he couldn't have missed me. The white curtain of the falls hid less than half of me, my back. But he turned left as he came out, and his eyes were turned left already.

A single pace back in the knee-deep water, and I was completely concealed from the direction of the cave; but between strands of falling water, where the fall thinned in the middle, I could watch him.

There was a lot of blood on his face and a gun in his hand. His khaki tunic and slacks were torn and mud-stained, and he wore ordinary brown shoes. He was pretty nervous, dodging immediately behind the great fang of limestone that rose to the left of the cave mouth and staring in a slow semi-circle round him. He looked dangerous.

If I'd had Sam's gun with me I could have taken Sam's advice. "Shoot him as soon as you sight him," Sam had told me. But the gun was in my hide-out upstream.

Then Nona must be in the cave. I pictured her, close to death with fear of Andrew, fear of the jungle, of the dark cave, and of the great bats hanging upside down above her head. I pictured her, torn by great thorns, exhausted by her struggles with Andrew, leeches feeding on her soft honey skin. . . .

My hands tightened into fists, and I hated myself. Leaving my gun behind in the hide-out had been a sort of court-martial offence, stupid, dangerous, and dishonourable. It might even cost me my life, or Nona hers. Daytime sleep had always been bad for me; even after a night ambush in my Army days in Malaya I'd always hated to take a siesta, knowing the demoralizing hangover effect it would surely have on me.

I watched Andrew through the water curtain.

Like me, he had two enemies to watch out for. He must know that I'd be after him, possibly supported by the local police and even an Army patrol; and he'd have found his cave now a hide-out for jungle terrorists. His lips moved. He was talking to himself, or just cursing.

Suddenly he raised his head, as if a warning had been whispered in his ear. He stared across the rock floor straight at me, straight at the white falls that hid me, still and strained, his lips no longer moving. There was a formidably animal look about him, and he made a fine target for a shot from my direction, though screened by the high tongue of limestone from all others.

A mosquito bite put an end to his alert. His lips twisted in a curse and his hand rose to slap the back of his neck. Then he was gone, passing beyond the shallow little cave that was the terrorist kitchen.

I was turning away to get back to my hide-out and Sam's gun when my eye caught a flash of movement in the cave mouth.

The shock was like a physical blow. Nona ran limping out of the cave, after giving a hunted animal's wild look round her. She was almost completely naked; only a few sodden strands of her flamingo nightdress hung from her waist. Her hair was disordered and damp, and she must have been in the pool at the back of the cave, for there was little blood on her and her bare feet left wet prints as she ran across the hot rock ledge.

It took me a second to realize what she was doing. She wasn't just escaping. She was escaping in a final, despairing gesture, over the cliff.

I stepped through the falls, shouting as soon as I was past the water-screen.

"*Nona!*"

She halted on the brink of the drop, as if my shout had lassooed her, staring at me as if she didn't know me. Andrew came striding round the rock buttress beyond the cave mouth. He saw Nona first and started towards her, but then he saw me and backed swiftly into the cave.

My eyes on the cave mouth, I ran and seized Nona's arm and swept her along the cliff-edge towards the jungle that was now a sanctuary. Andrew, with a rifle (one of the terrorist cache, I supposed, and loaded with dum-dum bullets), was out of the cave while we were still on the bare rock ledge, just before we'd reached the spray-filled rock tunnel behind the falls, but his one shot went wide. A second after we'd plunged into the green shadow of the jungle beyond, he hadn't a chance.

Silent and panting exhaustedly, Nona clung to me. But we had to get farther in. I swung her up in my arms and pushed ahead; but that was hardly more than a futile gesture.

You just can't get through the jungle that way. After three paces a creeper was threatening to strangle her, thorned branches were tearing out her hair, and we were effectively halted. Clumsily I switched to a fireman's lift, and that way managed to make a little headway. I was taking the opposition then, and my body protected her from most of the tearing, strangling undergrowth.

There's no point in making a long story of my return with Nona to the hide-out where I'd left my gun and the rucksack Winnie had packed for me. It *was* a long story—half an hour for the climb that was less than a quarter of a mile. But it was the old, monotonous story of a man struggling through the jungle barrier, one of the things reasonable men would never attempt, something that was never *meant* to be attempted—and without a *parang*, at that, to cut a way.

We spoke very little. During the first ten minutes we often heard Andrew trying to track us. If he'd been half the tracker I was he couldn't have failed to find us; but he'd never been Langgong's friend.

Then he lost us completely and we didn't hear him any more rasping out his curses and taunts. The first thing Nona said to me was, "He's mad, Robert. He's mad."

Her voice was weak and shivering. I kissed her and swore, "He'll never get you, Nona. By tomorrow this will all be over."

She only said, "He'll kill you, Robert. He knows he's got to die, but he's always been lonely and now he doesn't want to die alone. He's going to take us with him."

I kissed her again, hoisted her across my back, and struggled on. And so we reached my old hide-out. I gave her a swig from the Hennessy bottle, showed her the food, and drew out a sweater. The sun had almost gone, and the night would be damp and cold.

"Stay here, Nona," I said slowly, whispering close to her face between kisses. "*Stay.* I'll be back."

She clung and tried to keep me there when she saw me take up the gun and check the loading. I had to push her back, struggling with her warm, naked body that was covered with a thousand cruel thorn wounds.

The sun must have set just then over the unseen horizon of leaves, and all the light went sick and grey. I was only a few paces from the hide-out when I checked suddenly as a thin chestnut-coloured snake crossed the track ahead of me in a swift, liquid movement. It crossed from left to right; that was why I checked.

The Homeric warriors retreated in dismay whenever omen

birds crossed their war-path from left to right. Langgong and all the up-river Ibans of Borneo preserve the tradition. I have seen him insist on a retreat if an omen bird cried to the left of the line of advance on a jungle patrol; I've seen him gravely concerned if a heavy iguana scuttled across our path from left to right.

I couldn't help seeing the chestnut snake as an ill omen. I'm shy about admitting my slow half-conversion to Langgong's belief, the belief of millions of the best warriors and hunters of antiquity, so I won't recount the several incidents which caused me to suspend much of my unbelief. I'll just confess that the chestnut snake upset me.

Two minutes later what I was half expecting happened.

All the afternoon, blood had been welling through the eyelet holes of my jungle boots, showing that leeches had got in and were busy sucking me. Now there was a sharp pain by my right ankle, suggesting that a scrap of wood or rock had got inside the boot and sock to rub on one of the bleeding leechbites. Impatiently I sat down on two square yards of limestone outcrop and took off the boot, removed the tiny stone and three leeches, put a scrap of my handkerchief over the bloody mess, and drew on the boot again.

When I reached in the dusk for the gun I'd placed at my side, it wasn't there.


# 7

Before I was on my feet two hands reached out from behind me and clamped over my mouth—dirty hands, smelling of sweat and nicotine and soya sauce. Above the deep whush of the waterfall and the shrill whining of the mosquitoes around my ears, I heard breathing now. Something poked bruisingly into my ribs. My eyes, turning wildly right and left, saw two green-uniformed figures with pale grey profiles and caps with five-pointed red stars.

One, with the gun, was a man, young and powerful, though not tall. The other was a woman, her eyes more aslant than the man's, the other side of her face as she turned to meet my stare stained gentian violet against the skin disease that had contracted it into a maze of tiny wrinkles. The man had a rifle; the girl had a carbine and a bomb hanging from her belt.

I wasn't far from the track I'd found that morning, the track that marked the approach to the cave used as a terrorist unit's headquarters. This pair had been on their way to spend the night there, I suppose, when they'd spotted me. They had me badly scared.

I pointed to my biscuit-coloured nylon hat, the only thing I wore that wasn't identical with military jungle green. "Not soldier," I said. "Not police."

As if that could have helped.

The man said, "You go in front," slowly, as if recalling some English lessons with difficulty. "We shoot you if you try run away."

I believed him and I didn't try. Walking down the track to the cave through the deepening dusk, I pictured Nona in the hide-out, waiting—alone, as darkness came and the jungle night that was so much more alive than the jungle day. One of the big nightjars had awakened already and cried *teeda-boo* tragically from an unseen branch. The beasts of prey and the beasts that were their prey would be yawning and waking in this hour.

None of them would be a danger to Nona. There is nothing in the jungle that is a danger to man except, very rarely, a *seladang*, the ill-tempered and powerful wild buffalo. But there were other dangers—the tormenting fancies civilized man has about the jungle, the belief that it is a region of peril so that to penetrate its darkness is an act of daring. Imagination would torture her in the jungle darkness, and she would wait for me in agony.

Swearing monotonously, I followed the track until we were close to the expanse of open rock between the cave and the cliff-edge. They stopped me there, and the man startled me with an imitation of the nightjar's call—not a lifelike imitation. Out of the dusk round the cave's mouth a thin, bedraggled figure stepped forward, making a circular gesture with both hands. The muzzle nudged the small of my back, and the voice behind me said, "Go on."

Two terrorists were eating inside the cave, presumably from some cache of food they'd dug out, because there was no odour of cooking and it looked like cold rice with a little dried fish. Far back in the cave there was a candle burning on a ledge, and underneath it Andrew sat sprawled, mopping blood from his forehead.

They pushed me across the uneven floor to join him.

8

It must have been an hour, or possibly two hours, past midnight that Andrew began to talk. Until then he ignored me, just as he had so often in the old days, though now he didn't even say, "Shut up, young Robert. I don't want you here." He ignored me altogether, mopping a long cut in his brow with the remains of his singlet, which he'd soaked in the pool beyond us. After a few minutes he'd turned away from me, lain down, and slept or appeared to sleep.

I tried to sleep too. Whatever lay ahead, it was worth conserving what strength and smartness I had left. Perhaps I could have slept if it hadn't been for the mosquitoes. I remembered now that they seldom touched Andrew, but they were round me in a whining cloud, digging their torturing needles into flesh already itching to madness from earlier bites.

It never occurred to me that I could have attempted to strangle him as he lay sleeping at my side. If it had, I don't believe I'd have given the idea a moment's consideration. Now that I hadn't to fear him any more, or fear what he could do to Nona, I was almost back in my old bewildered relationship with him. That I should be sleeping again with him in his cave filled me with a complex of repulsion, pity, and fascinated apprehension that was an echo across seventeen years.

He started talking sometime well after midnight, suddenly throwing out a taunt as if in the middle of a conversation. "Well, young Robert, you were just too smart, weren't you?"

I wondered a moment, coming out of a doze, whether he might be talking in his sleep. He'd been muttering words I couldn't catch, an hour or so earlier. But he moved closer and said it again.

His voice shook me out of my tired, neutral reverie. I didn't say anything.

"It's quite safe to talk," he said then. "There's a sentry outside the cave, but he can't hear us because of the falls. The others are asleep. He may be, too."

But as he spoke a figure appeared in the cave mouth, and it was joined a few seconds later by another. Both carried rifles. They looked in, shining a flashlight in our direction, then turned away.

"Before they brought you in," he said after a moment, "they were arguing what to do with me. Had to wait for their platoon commander to get here first was the decision. When you were brought in I wondered if the fellow who got you was the platoon commander, but evidently not."

"There's only one thing they can do with us," I said, though I'd half resolved not to say a word to him.

"Only one," he agreed. "You've fixed things magnificently, young Robert."

I said, "You can even fool yourself at a time like this."

So much so, in fact, that he didn't even see what I was getting at. For him responsibility was something for other people to carry, just as loyalty was something for other people to show towards him; he didn't have to be loyal to anybody.

He only asked, "Can you see your watch?"

"It hasn't a luminous dial," I told him.

"Must be two or later, surely," he said, and added after a short pause, "You're leaving it pretty late, aren't you?"

"How d'you mean?" I asked, but I was afraid I knew.

Yes, of course he'd remembered. "You know the way out, young Robert. When are you moving?"

Obviously it still rankled, the fact that he'd never been able to find the tunnel. I had discovered it on one of our camps there with old Ngari, and when I boasted about it and he couldn't find it himself he had resorted to a scene of petty torture to extort the secret. I'd been tough enough and stubborn enough to keep it to myself.

I had suspected that, for all he was six years older than I was, he hadn't the nerve to climb the slippery dark walls at the back of the cave and disturb the crowd of warm, lousy bats that hung upside down around the entrance to the tunnel, no more than twenty inches high and a little broader at that point. Anyway, he'd never found it.

"You were going to make a getaway without a word to me," he said, lowering his voice. "Was that it, young Robert?"

I fought the feeling of disloyalty his tone was intended to evoke—quite successfully, but there was a moment in which it had to be resisted. Yes, I had decided to make the attempt alone, grateful that the terrorists would make a quick job of executing him, without the humiliation of a trial in Ipoh or

Kuala Lumpur; without the repulsive necessity, maybe, for me to do the job myself in the dark jungle.

"Leaving these bastards to do your dirty, murderous business for you," Andrew went on, with a fine edge of scorn to his voice.

"You'd prefer one of Her Majesty's hangmen?" I was stung into asking.

We were sparring and taunting like a pair of children, a grotesque exchange of crosstalk, with death rushing close in the darkness.

Shadows moved in the shadow, and he was on his feet. "Right. Let's go."

I didn't move and I didn't speak.

The heavy, hissing roar of the falls filled the cave, and now there was another pervading sibilation on a higher, softer note, the echo of a tropical rainstorm. I thought again of Nona. . . .

"I said, let's go."

When I didn't answer him again he bent over me. "You're not getting out alone, young Robert. You always like to think you can ignore me, but don't you see, I've got nothing to lose now. I'll wake the bloody lot of them if you try it solo."

I got on my feet with a bitter taste of disgust in my mouth. "It wasn't so easy when I was a shrimp of ten. Now, it may not be much better than the eye of a needle."

By now there were a dozen or more terrorists in the cave. One of them was badly sick or wounded, and he couldn't sleep. He moaned like a damned soul in hell and he'd called pitifully once or twice to the others; but, apart from one harsh ejaculation that sounded like a curse, there'd been no reply.

Andrew got behind me and with a sigh of defeat I made my way along the cave wall, feeling for the small hollow, always filled with water, that formed the first foothold for the climb up the wall. It was much lower than I'd expected, of course, like a miniature holy water stoup, and instead of having to strain to reach it with my right foot, I found the thing no higher than my knee. I started the climb without a word to Andrew.

Up on the platform that was slippery with bat guano, I groped for the opening. I'd expected all the bats to be out in the middle of the night, but there were plenty hanging there, and the feel of them round my head was unpleasant. They were big bats, as big as cats almost, and they mewed softly and bad-temperedly at being disturbed. Andrew slipped in the guano and swore.

I said, "You have to get in feet first, because there's a steep drop to start with."

He was quick. As I braced myself to grip the sides and drop my legs in I found my way blocked. He was half in already.

I said, "The water here is nothing. Never more than a few inches deep," and climbed in after him. At once the place seemed far smaller and more airless than I'd remembered. With Andrew's bulk in front of me, too, I felt more than ever like one of those model ships trapped in a bottle, doomed never to sail free of its glass harbour.

I'd known it would be easy for the first hundred yards, easy though slow—much slower now than in those long-ago days when I'd discovered the tunnel and come face to face with a porcupine on my first recce. But far ahead lay the short waist of the tunnel, an ordeal even in my eleventh year; and again, just short of the exit, the corkscrew ascent in which I'd fought for what seemed hours before I'd discovered, in a frenzy of panic, the heel-and-elbow lift that could hoist me out.

It was completely dark in there. A hundred-per-cent darkness is rarely experienced, and I wonder how many are free of some trace of fear when it closes round them. Not that it was merely the darkness that scared me now. There was the fear of getting stuck in the narrows ahead and the fear that the terrorist sentry would flash his torch again into the corner where we'd lain and track us to the tunnel entrance. They surely hadn't found it yet themselves, or they'd hardly have put sentries on the cave entrance only. But if they tracked us to the tunnel they could merely throw one of their Mills bombs down it after us.

Before they slept the terrorists had moved the bombs and the rest of their little arsenal from the shelf on which, in the old days, Ngari had set his smoking kerosene lamp and Andrew his air-gun, and I kicked myself for not having grabbed a bomb when I'd discovered them. I hadn't been searched by the terrorists and might have escaped them with some sort of weapon in hand.

As we wriggled forward, the burned skin of my arm in agony from the repeated grazing on the fretted limestone, the air changed. The stink of the bats faded, and a stale, unwholesome fungus smell took its place, a tomb smell. The temperature rose, too, or seemed to rise. Very faintly I heard the sick terrorist's groan and call for help back in the cave, but none of the others roused and, after holding my breath for fifteen seconds, I crawled on, getting a kick in the face from one of Andrew's ruined brogues when I caught up with him. We were crawling face first now, slightly uphill and without real difficulty, though very slowly.

Once when something halted Andrew in a stretch where the ceiling was higher, I overran him and found my bruised hands grasping the calves of his legs. It gave me a moment of malicious satisfaction to find that he was trembling violently. The next moment he started spasmodically, and I heard movements in the tunnel beyond him.

"The old porcupine!" I exclaimed. Him or his son or grandson, anyway.

Deep blurred echoes of my voice rumbled through the tunnel, giving me a start in my turn. Andrew began moving forward again, though more cautiously. The porcupine's smell was sharp and wild, and it wasn't difficult to imagine a larger, fiercer beast in the tunnel with us.

As soon as I felt the rock walls grow smooth and damp, I remembered that the tunnel's "waist" lay close ahead, and almost at once I found Andrew halted just beyond me. I wasn't sorry now that he had slipped in first. When I'd been waiting to be sure he slept before I could make my way out alone, the thought of getting stuck in the subterranean darkness had chilled my spine. Now he'd be the one to get stuck if the passage was as narrow as I feared.

I jerked his ankle and said, "Turn over. The ceiling isn't smooth, and you should be able to pull yourself along with your hands."

I had to say it three times before he could hear me properly. I was already on my back by then and had to wait while he turned himself. It was a long job. It seemed stiflingly hot by now, and there was the feeling that the air wouldn't last long.

There was a picture of it all in my mind's eye. The mind's eye cannot accept darkness and projects its own pictures. Now I was seeing it all, lit by a dark, blood-red light: the smooth rock which no physical eye had ever seen, the exudations of slimy alkali that stained it; the pitted ceiling, possibly still stained with blood from my small ten-year-old fingers; the two men bathed in foul sweat, straining to force a way through the narrows, two men with identical scars on their right thighs.

Then I was trying to work out whether Andrew or I was the larger. Unless a man is noticeably taller or shorter than myself, or lighter or heavier, I'm seldom aware of any difference. Andrew I thought of as bigger generally, but now I wondered whether that might not be partly derived from those other days in Malaya, when his much greater size and maturity had so awed me. I couldn't decide whether the narrows were going to be more difficult for him or for me.

Escaping through the tunnel was an enterprise demanding a high degree of mental and physical concentration, and I was in pretty poor mental and physical shape. The return to the jungle had exhausted me, and I was short of sleep. My head had ached ever since that first blow, as I dialled a number on the Sultan Mustafa phone what seemed a few weeks rather than a few days ago. The burns up my arm from Aragon's attempt to roast me alive were agony, torn by thorns, bitten by ants and mosquitoes, and now torn again by the limestone's sharp teeth in the earlier stretches of the tunnel. I was so thirsty that lustful dream pictures of tankards of ice-cold beer kept swaying in front of my mind's eye, and I couldn't get rid of a dread that, with my exhaustion and the airlessness, I might fall asleep and never wake up.

Andrew took an age to get through the waist. He wasn't so very far from panic, I believe, and tried too hard, attempting a direct passage by force when serpentine insinuation was the only possible technique. But he got through finally, and when I made my own way through, more easily than I'd expected, he was so far ahead that I couldn't hear him at all.

I didn't catch up with him, in fact, until I reached the final stretch, not much more than a hundred yards short of the exit. And there he stuck.

By the time I reached him he was whimpering in panic, kicking with his one free foot and now and then shouting words I couldn't catch. It took some time for him to react to my tug at his ankle, and when he stopped his noise he took ages to hear what I was trying to tell him. His body blocked the rising, twisting passage almost as tightly as a cork in a bottle and blurred sound between us. And his first attempts to follow my instructions were too clumsy, too crudely headlong to get him more than a few inches.

Now I was furious that he had got in front. Sweating and leaning my forehead on the clammy rock, I persuaded myself that of course Andrew was far broader and heavier than I, that he was blocking an escape route I could have bolted through like a silk handkerchief through a wedding ring. Soon I was shouting at him, touching off an explosion of echoes, regardless of whether they might travel the whole way back to the cave.

"Twist yourself, you bloody fool! It's a corkscrew!"

I suppose it took him an hour, with me pushing at his legs and twisting them when he got stuck and kept trying to fight the rock with muscle instead of eeling his way up the spiral. The great rock tooth that protruded into the passage at one stage was less of an ordeal than I'd expected, but once past it he was in the final turn of the corkscrew, where it widened suddenly but lowered at the same time. This was what I'd dreaded most of all. Straining my memory, I'd been unable to place the vertical clearance at more than ten inches, with less in places where the floor or ceiling bulged.

When Andrew stuck there, really stuck, hadn't made three inches of progress in half an hour, I began to let go hope. I knew that now he could see the exit, that ahead of him lay nothing except the little deep pool of rusty water and then the easy, wide slope up to the creeper-muffled exit that was shaped like a Gothic window tilted to the right. He would be making his maximum effort now, breathing fresh air already, his eyes seeing again, even if dawn had not yet broken. But after the long suspense of waiting, his foot kicked into my face and I felt him trying to edge his way back again. He'd given up.

And that was impossible. His panic began to infect me. There wasn't enough air behind us; we'd never get back through the waist feet first, and there was no place on the way where we could pass each other and I could make my own attempt to get through. Instinctively I had gripped Andrew's ankles and started to push, trying to halt his retreat.

He let out a howl then. There we could hear each other better, because the widening of the passage had just begun, leaving a little free space alongside his flattened body. Feeling him stiffen violently, I had an idea.

"Hold yourself rigid, Andrew, and I'll push."

I'd remembered the slimy, rust-coloured slope on which his hands must have been trying hopelessly to seize a hold, the rock constriction above and below his knees that deprived them of leverage.

"Get back, young Robert!"

"We *can't* get back! Do what I say; stiffen up, and I'll heave you forward."

But he only struggled another inch back towards me. That maddened me, and I seized his feet, and we fought in that blind, constricted fashion, he straining to force himself back down the spiral, I heaving like a maniac to thrust him forward.

For a minute our efforts cancelled each other and we stayed motionless. Then I had to give a couple of inches; but that brought my left foot against the great rock tooth that hung like an uvula down the centre of the tunnel. At once this re-inforcement proved its power. Very slowly Andrew was being forced back up the spiral now.

Drenched in sweat and shuddering with the effort, I pushed him forward, millimetre by millimetre, inch by inch, and then it was a foot, more, a yard, and he was shuddering too, and just as my strength gave out and my straining heart felt as though it must drown in its own blood I felt Andrew abandon his resistance, and almost at once the ankles were torn from my hands and the space ahead became empty and cool; disturbed air came curling down the spiral towards me.

I heard a foot splash in the pool of rusty water, and then hands tearing at the creepers. I saw weak, greenish light ahead, and by the time I'd hoisted myself into the narrows Andrew was crouching in the Gothic opening. With an exultant gulp of the sweeter air, I heaved myself forward and upward, reaching the final squeeze of the narrows in one long, eeling motion, so that the little pool was within reach of my outstretched fingers.

There I stuck, though.

Roof and ceiling had closed in to clamp me in a grip that would allow only short, shallow gasps of air. My lungs could not even quarter-open, and my rib-case felt bent already and on the point of cracking. Now I realized that, though Andrew was taller and broader, I had the deeper chest. There was nobody to heave at my feet and thrust my powerless body the last inches forward; but Andrew was just beyond me, and a heave at my hands, which sought ineffectually for holds on the wet, sticky rock, would have me out in no time, surely.

But Andrew's hands weren't stretched down to haul me out. They were closed over a small grey bomb, and he was smiling.

## 9

He was smiling in the sick, green light, and my sluggish brain took a moment to adjust itself to a reality outside the tunnel and the all-devouring concentration on escape. Normally, with me, danger clears the brain and refocuses the moment to a new and vivid intensity; but not then. I was like a man waking with a dark blue hangover to face a crisis.

"Smart, but never quite smart enough," Andrew said. "That's you, young Robert, isn't it?"

His black Japanese hair was caked with sweat and blood from the long wound over his right eye. His torn khaki shirt was soaked with the rusty red alkali from the tunnel floor. There was something wrong with his eyes. . . .

Yes, he'd been smarter than I had. He'd pocketed one of the little bombs from the terrorists' armoury as soon as he'd reached the cave and found them, and he'd kept it effectively hidden when they caught him. I'd thought of that too late.

"You don't have much luck with bombs, do you?" he said, his voice the exact echo of itself seventeen years back when he'd tried to extort the secret of the tunnel from me. I realized that he'd never really grown up much beyond those days. "That one in London last month—a dud, they said."

Yes, he'd have loved the scene in the theatre that night. Even in that moment it made me sick that he knew.

He seemed to be waiting for me to say something, but there was absolutely nothing to say. I thought of Nona, for the first time in hours, cursed the evil chance that had taken her to that party in Hampstead to meet me. That had been the worst of all the evil things that had happened to her.

Andrew sighed—possibly the sort of sigh that follows the admission that all good things must come to an end. With the precise movement of a weapons instructor demonstrating to recruits, he raised the bomb a little and drew out the pin.

I began to count.

If it was a modern Mills bomb I had four seconds now to live. If it was one of the old ones, still encountered in terrorist armouries, or one of the Jap imitations, I might have seven seconds.

*One . . .*

Andrew said, "Too bad about this. There was no need. If only you hadn't—"

*Two . . .*

"—always had a down on me."

*Three . . .*

He was moving. He said, "So long, young Robert!" his face now rather young and awed, and then he dropped the bomb.

*Four . . .*

Andrew was gone, and the disturbed creepers over the tunnel mouth discharged a shower of heavy raindrops. The bomb rolled gently and slowly down the slope towards me, jigging from side to side like a rolling rugger ball. It was rusty, and I lived on the hope that, like *Time Bomb*, it might be a dud.

*Five . . .*

It was either a dud or one of the old ones with a seven second fuse. Or had I been counting too fast? A second was longer than ninety-nine out of a hundred people imagined. The bomb had been rolling straight for my face, and it took an effort to keep my eyes open and watch it. It made a soft rumbling noise on the smooth wet rock. Now it slowed down and veered slightly to the right and fell *plop* into the little heart-shaped pool of rust-red water. It sank out of sight, and the thick water was level and calm again in an instant.

*Six . . .*

Something stronger than me, something that seemed outside me, jerked my body forward—just two or three inches forward, compressing my ribs like the Nuremberg Iron Maiden and filling my mouth with a gush of bitter fluid, but enough to plunge my left hand into the pool and seize the bomb. In my head there was a throbbing roar like dive bombers attacking. My contorted hand could not throw the thing back down the spiral, though there was a clear space a foot wide alongside me. I could only drop it again and pray for it to roll down the gently sloping corkscrew beyond and behind me. Only there wasn't time. . . .

*Seven* . . .

It began to roll, drunkenly, from side to side. Was it a dud, or had I counted too fast? I couldn't see it now, but I felt it roll into me, a little above my knee. I couldn't be sure whether it stayed there or only touched and rolled away again.

The explosion was in my brain. Suddenly my pinned-down body convulsed in a seal-like motion forward. I believed I made some progress, and I threw my rigid body into a second effort. The bomb exploded in the same moment.

In a whirl of shock my right leg was on fire and I was spinning through space, miles and miles of black space, like some star being born out of the womb of nothingness. I spun through a dark cloud of semi-consciousness, feeling Andrew close, his face looking old and tragic close to mine, and then I was feeling heavy water drops on my face and dark green creepers were subsiding into motionlessness again. For half a second I saw the back of Andrew's ruined brogue and his sodden trouser leg above it, and then the blood from my wounded head flooded my eyes and he was gone.

10

I shall never know whether I could have got out without the bomb-blast down the spiral behind me to give the final impetus to my final heave forward. I suspect not, because the violence with which I shot out and struck my head on the rock wall showed how powerful the propulsive force had been.

And I won't ever know whether Andrew really did bend over me, looking old and haggard, as the echoes of the explosion died along the tunnel, nor why he assumed so readily that I was dead. But he hadn't much stomach for murder, once the deed had been done; that had been proved after the death of Lyall. It could be that he experienced some compunction at the sight of me lying bloody and "dead," and he couldn't bring himself to touch me. It would have been in character.

Aching and giddy, I climbed out through the Gothic arch and into the dark shadow of the jungle. The sun was up. My watch showed six-thirty. A splinter of shrapnel or rock was embedded in my right calf, and the whole leg was more than half numb. My head ached as never before.

I'd just started to make my way towards the hide-out in which I'd left Nona, when rifle fire sounded down by the cave —two or three exchanges. A peacock rose in panic in front of me, screeching. Then a single shot, closely followed by a double blast on a pocket whistle, and finally, silence.

Pushing on towards the hide-out, constantly having to make detours along the line of least resistance, for want of a *parang* to cut a path, I gradually formed the conviction that I wouldn't find Nona there any more. It was a conviction that grew and persisted so strongly that when I reached the little rock niche and found it empty there was no shock. I called, "Nona!" softly, stupidly, and saw how water had collected on the niche floor. Had she been flooded out by the midnight storm?

The rucksack was still there, which surely meant that the terrorists couldn't have found her. They'd have taken the remaining sweater, food, brandy, and first-aid kit. Only half consciously I was eating, drinking, and fixing a bandage round my forehead—the last in the hope of stopping blood from flooding my eyes, as it had several times already.

I found her tracks easily enough in the small expanse of new mud outside. She had left alone. Her tracks were easy at first, but it worried me that, however much they wandered, they led steadily downhill, steadily nearer to the cave. Once I found a thin clump of grasses that were still rising, very slowly, after being trodden underfoot. Langgong could have told more exactly, but I knew she had passed this way between fifteen and forty minutes earlier. She was close.

But only a minute later I halted at the edge of a patch of swamp. Nona's right sandal, a Javanese sandal of yellow leather with a crossed thong for the instep, lay there, upside down. One of the thongs had rotted through, and there had been no way of repairing it and keeping the thing on her foot. And here surely she must have been badly scared, because I could see clearly that she had run right into the black, bad-smelling swamp from which she'd have shrunk in fear and disgust if not driven into it.

I stood there, cursing silently, scared and sick.

Then I saw what had panicked her. One of the terrorists lay at the swamp edge, dead or dying. The tangle of creepers and scrub into which he had fallen kept him suspended a foot from the ground, and the matted sling creaked and swayed a little with his feeble struggles to rise.

I went over to him. When I saw the blood and ants in his mouth and the nameless mess below his waist I knew that the only way to help him would be to kick him unconscious for his last few minutes; but I was too squeamish for that. He was a youngster, and though his eyes were open he didn't see me.

There was an old cloth bandolier across his chest, twisted and bloodstained, but no ammunition in it. I looked around for his rifle, but it wasn't there. I turned away.

Had Nona seen him shot? Or even—his wound made it possible—bayoneted? I hoped she had seen no more than I had. And hadn't the firing and the dying bandit meant that the patrol, with Sam and Waring, had at last made contact? A sense of sharp acceleration possessed me, and I tore my way round the edge of the swamp and found her tracks again, and the other sandal. She was completely barefoot now.

And not three minutes later I saw her. She was leaning back against a blooming penaga tree, her eyes closed, her hands loose and desolate. She wore the torn Fair Isle sweater of Sam's, from the rucksack, which came as far down on her as a one-piece swimsuit.

Andrew, a rifle at the half ready, stood opposite her, his dark face twisting as he talked.

11

The thermometer was rising fast. I looked down at my empty hands and cursed. Andrew had stolen another march on me, finding the dying terrorist and disarming him a few minutes before I discovered him.

Against the background of the roar from the falls, I fancied I heard repeated sounds, indefinite but warning me that the jungle was no longer empty. Now it was a perilous place, with armed friend and armed enemy moving stealthily through it. I wondered what troops or policemen had come in with Sam, how experienced they were. A trigger-happy rifleman could be as dangerous as a terrorist in ambush.

I stepped back into deep shadow and looked impotently round me. There was a sharp stone rising from a patch of the luminous moss we'd sometimes worn in our hats on night patrols for the man behind to follow. It took some time to dig out with my fingers, and it was too big, anyway; but it was all I could find. I moved obliquely down towards the stream with its black cliff on one side and its white sandbank on the other to make an approach behind Andrew.

Every step I took shook a shower of raindrops on me, but I

was drenched already. I was sweating, too, the hot sweat pouring down my face and arms and legs. The jungle floor here was uneven and so slippery that I fell at every third or fourth step. When I came in sight of Andrew again, he was raising the rifle and Nona had thrown up her hands to cover her eyes.

I couldn't afford to wait to get into dead-sure range. Swiftly I dodged to and fro until I found, at the stream edge, an angle that wasn't blocked by branches or creepers, and hurled the sharp-cornered rock at his back.

I'd begun to run forward before it hit him. It didn't catch the small of his back, as I'd intended. It got his left shoulder, and the range had been so great that there wasn't much velocity left by that time. Instead of throwing him on his face, it knocked him down momentarily on one knee, and then he was up again. By the time I'd hoped to be collecting myself for a spring onto his prostrate body, he was facing me and levelling the rifle.

Attempting to pull up sharp, my heels slipped in the wet clay, and I sprawled helplessly on my back while Nona cried out my name and Andrew smiled.

"Right, young Robert," he said slowly. "On your feet and up with your hands."

I had to do it. I managed to edge a couple of yards nearer Nona before he snapped, "Keep still now!" and moved forward. When he stopped he was no more than four yards from me.

"Correction, Nona," he said. "Robert didn't die at sunrise this morning. He's going to die now."

She was looking at me, her face so blank and calm that I wondered whether she was aware of what was going on. I couldn't think of anything to say to her.

Andrew's face was twitching under the black stubble. He looked handsome and horribly mad, and there was something uncanny about his eyes. He smiled again and said, "Well, young Robert, in the review of *Time Bomb* I saw they said you had an unhealthy appetite for the wilder kind of melodrama. You'll possibly be the first melodrama merchant to die in character."

I needed to move a yard nearer Nona. It was a risk, because he might shoot at my first movement; but he was enjoying his line of talk, and I prepared for the move.

"It's neater this way," he went on, turning the muzzle towards Nona this time. "And more traditional. Adulteresses and their lovers were condemned to die together in old Malaya, in these jungles."

Taking a deep breath, I moved a pace to my left.

"I said keep still, young Robert!" he rapped out, eyes blazing in the reflection of sunlight from the sandbank. "Just for that—"

He closed one eye and raised the rifle swiftly.

My two hands seized the thick, serpentine branch two feet above my head, and my feet left the ground. As I leaped to meet the branch, it dipped to meet me, and my ankles crossed above it for a moment. A shot split the silence and went I don't know where. Andrew's head and shoulders were buried in a dense mass of sodden leaves, the end of the branch.

He charged out just as I swung forward and dropped. My right foot caught him in the belly, and he scissored and fell. That time I didn't do a thing wrong. My feet didn't slip as I landed, and I had his rifle in my hand before I'd straightened up. He was still not on his feet when the bullet tore through his ribs and burned through his heart.

I turned my back on him and went to Nona. She had turned away to stare across the stream to the black-shadowed rock, standing rigid, her small, bleeding feet planted on the edge of the white sand.

"It's finished," I said and put my arms round her.

Very quietly she asked, "Is he—" She couldn't say the word. She wasn't thinking of me. It was still Andrew.

I said, "Wait, Nona. Stay there." And I went back to Andrew. It wasn't time for relief yet. He was trying dreadfully to get to his feet, his face gone old and tragic as I'd seen it after the bomb exploded. A desperate awe that wasn't quite pity took hold of me, and I found myself lifting the hair that had fallen blindingly over his eyes. I saw then what was so odd about them; when he'd got the wound on his forehead the brown contact lens over his right eye had been smashed or dislodged, and it was one of his own blue Avery eyes that my gesture revealed. With his blue eye and his brown eye he looked from me to Nona down by the stream, and then slowly they filled with tears.

Tears of self pity, it may be, as he took his last look at the two who, like the rest of the world, had let him down and thwarted his destiny. I don't know. Then he turned away and fought hard for a few seconds and died.

He died, and some sort of link snapped in that moment. I looked down at him only with a bitter resentment that he had made me do what had to be done, and I didn't linger a second longer. Down at the edge of the sandbank I took Nona's arm and said, "Yes. It's finished." And I added as I led her away, "Everything starts from now."

She said, "The last words I spoke to him were, 'If you've really killed Robert you can't frighten me with a gun.' Then you came."

The morning jungle seemed beautiful, despite my exhaustion and wounds, full of the freshness and relief of exorcism. I was dizzy with it all, and Andrew had already begun his fall back into unimportance—for us both, I dared to hope.

Sam's booming shout startled us both before we'd gone very

far. I answered, and we started forward down a game track with new energy. But Nona halted suddenly with a little gasp. She was staring down at the track, shrinking against me.

Beside the track, in a neat green spiral, slept a slender snake. I thought for a moment it must be Hantu Ijau, Andrew's snake of seventeen years ago. It could have been, I suppose.

It woke while we watched it, and the neat coil unwound. My breath came out in a slow sigh as it crossed the track in front of us with flickering speed—*from right to left*. It pleased me in that moment to remember Langgong and all the other faithful Iban trackers, and the classical warriors and the hunters of Asia for three or four millennia, and to fancy them all assuring us that now everything was going to be well.

"It's a good little snake, that one," I told Nona. Later I would explain.

I don't know if she heard me, because she had spotted Sam and two Malay soldiers on a limestone outcrop over to our right, and she raised a cry. We turned towards them, like the sole survivors of a fatal disaster, dazed and numb, but moving into a future we thought we had lost.